ARKHAM HORROR

It is the height of the Roaring Twenties – a fresh enthusiasm for the arts, science, and exploration of the past have opened doors to a wider world, and beyond…

And yet, a dark shadow grows over the town of Arkham. Alien entities known as Ancient Ones lurk in the emptiness beyond space and time, writhing at the thresholds between worlds.

Occult rituals must be stopped and alien creatures destroyed before the Ancient Ones make our world their ruined dominion.

Only a handful of brave souls with inquisitive minds and the will to act stand against the horrors threatening to tear this world apart.

Will they prevail?

Also available in Arkham Horror

Wrath of N'kai by Josh Reynolds
The Last Ritual by S A Sidor
Mask of Silver by Rosemary Jones
Litany of Dreams by Ari Marmell
The Devourer Below edited by Charlotte Llewelyn-Wells
Cult of the Spider Queen by S A Sidor
The Deadly Grimoire by Rosemary Jones

Dark Origins: The Collected Novellas Vol 1
Grim Investigations: The Collected Novellas Vol 2

ARKHAM HORROR™

In the COILS *of the* LABYRINTH

DAVID ANNANDALE

First published by Aconyte Books in 2022

ISBN 978 1 83908 169 9

Ebook ISBN 978 1 83908 170 5

Cover art by John Coulthart

Distributed in North America by Simon & Schuster Inc, New York, USA

Printed in the United States of America

9 8 7 6 5 4 3 2 1

ACONYTE BOOKS

An imprint of Asmodee Entertainment Ltd

Mercury House, Shipstones Business Centre

North Gate, Nottingham NG7 7FN, UK

aconytebooks.com // twitter.com/aconytebooks

For Margaux, who is the
beautiful in my life.

O Rose thou art sick.
The invisible worm,
That flies through the night
In the howling storm:

Has found out thy bed
Of crimson joy:
And his dark secret love
Does thy life destroy.

WILLIAM BLAKE, "THE SICK ROSE"

PROLOGUE

Galloway, Scotland, 1925.
The village of Durstal

October ended, and the last of the trucks drove out from the Stroud Estate. They came along the narrow road that ran down the hillside to the village, their cargo shrouded by ropes and canvas. Their loads were as heavy as all the others, Tom Spalding thought. He stood outside his inn and watched the convoy turn onto what passed for Durstal's main road, rumble past the Ash Inn, and head off into the woods, leaving the village behind. He wondered if he should feel relief that they were going. He wanted to. He couldn't remember when he had last felt real, honest, bone-deep relief.

All he felt was the chill in the air, the cold promise of an evening drizzle.

"Do you think things will be better?" Ben Laurie asked. Skeletally thin, his shoulders and back rounded with age, the old man was still half a head taller than Tom.

Tom looked at the old man with some surprise. Direct questions like that weren't the done thing in Durstal. "Hard to say," Tom said, noncommittal and honest at the same time. He stroked his graying goatee thoughtfully. He didn't know. He couldn't guess. But oh, how he wished he could have said *yes* to Ben and meant it.

Ben nodded in understanding. "Fair enough," he said, and shifted the conversation to safer terrain. "Easier to call the weather."

Tom snorted. "I can tell you what tonight's is, right enough. Tonight's is miserable."

Ben nodded again.

The rumble of the trucks faded to silence, and they turned back to the door of the Ash Inn. Before they could go in, Harriet Duncan came hurrying up from the direction of St Andrew's Church. "Is the vicar in there?" she asked, broad face flushed deep crimson with the effort of her run.

Tom shook his head. "He's not at the church?"

"No, and we're coming up to Evensong."

"I think he went up to have a look around the Stroud land," Ben said quietly.

Tom frowned. "Why? I thought no one had been there in weeks except the work crews."

Ben shrugged. "Maybe Donovan came back to close up. Or maybe the vicar just thought he might."

"But why go?" Tom insisted.

The other two said nothing.

Tom grimaced. He could imagine a few answers. Peter Wilson wanting to see if the Strouds were really gone, or heading up for a last chance to satisfy his curiosity while the gates were open. Tom would not have gone, but he understood the impulse. Everyone in the valley lived in the shadow of the Stroud Estate, and the need to do *something* could be hard to resist.

Do what about what?

Always best not to ask that question. Answers might come.

And maybe the most likely thing was that Peter had gone up carrying the same hope that Ben had given voice to, that Tom wished he could feel, only Peter had had the courage to put the hope to the test. Maybe he had gone up to the Stroud Estate to see that, after the weeks and weeks of blasting and the noise of construction, convoy after convoy carrying massive loads, there was now nothing to worry about there. Of course, no one had ever come right out and said they should be worried about the estate. But even so, even so, if whatever might have been there had left, if it was all just ordinary ground up there, that would be something, wouldn't it? Something worth looking into, if you had the nerve.

"What should we do?" Harriet asked. She looked worried. Being even older than Ben, she'd had that much longer to live with all the unspoken fears of Durstal. That made a person fragile, in the long run. And she had taken a maternal interest in Peter since his arrival five years earlier.

If Tom could spare her something, he should.

"We'll look for him," he said.

"Oh, thank you!" said Harriet.

Tom opened the door of the inn. "You come in and have a warm," he said. "I'll fetch my jacket, and Ben and I will be off."

Harriet went in willingly enough. Ben looked grim, but willing too, ready to take on the responsibility Tom had accepted for the two of them.

The two men climbed up the road to the estate. The iron

gates were shut and padlocked. The estate would not have them. Tom didn't want to insist. He looked at Ben, who gave him an unhappy shrug.

"I don't think he's in there," Ben said. "But even if he is, we're not going to be able to find him."

"No," Tom agreed. They had come up here because they had to start somewhere, and he had hoped they'd meet Peter coming down the hillside.

No, *hoped* was the wrong word. He'd *wished* that would happen.

"Where now?" Ben asked.

"If he's in the village, he's fine, and he'll turn up," Tom began.

"While we catch our death of colds tromping up and down like fools."

"Maybe." Tom wished again, this time for such an outcome. It would make a story to laugh about afterwards. But if the vicar wasn't in the village… "I think we should try the clifftops," he said.

Ben nodded unhappily.

Midway back to the village, a path branched off from the dirt road and wound back up, making a wide detour around the wall of the Stroud Estate to finally come to the top of the rise, and onto the open moor that ended at the sheer drop down to the sea. A mist began rolling in well before they reached the moor, and by the time they did, visibility had dropped to a few dozen yards and was growing rapidly worse.

"We'll never find him in this," said Ben. "We could be right on top of him and not see him."

"We can at least try. I'll sleep easier knowing I did."

Ben grunted. "There speaks a man expecting the worst."

Tom didn't answer. He started calling for the vicar. Ben joined in. They walked forward carefully, conscious that they were drawing closer to the cliff edge. They called Peter's name, waited for an answer, then called again. The fog gathered around them, turning the landscape into gray, fading dream. The sound of the waves crashing against the base of the cliffs grew louder, a cold and relentless answer, a slow rhythm of mockery.

They heard the vicar just before they spotted him. His cry of "Tom!" sounded mournful. A few steps later, Tom could just make out Peter's shape in the fog, moving back and forth erratically, much too close to the drop.

"Vicar!" Ben shouted. "Stop where you are! We'll come to you."

Peter did not respond. He kept moving, jerkily and too quickly. They hurried forward and caught up to him with less than ten feet between him and the edge.

The call of the waves boomed.

The vicar walked with a harsh, determined gait at odds with his direction. He took ten steps, jerked to the right, went five, jerked back toward the sea for another five, then back, and then another shift. He looked like a puppet being yanked by a capricious showman. Sweat drenched his ashen face. He stared at Tom with pleading, despairing eyes.

"What are you doing?" Tom asked. "Stay still." He took hold of Peter's arm. The vicar kept walking, and he pulled away with a strength that took Tom by surprise. He felt as if he had been trying to restrain a moving vehicle. "Help me," Tom said to Ben, who grabbed the vicar's other arm.

Peter pulled free from them both without seeming to try. "I can't stop," he said. Tears ran down his cheeks.

The fog pressed in closer. If it got much worse, Tom realized, they would have to stay where they were. It would be too dangerous to try to find their way back to the slope leading to the village.

"Go get help," he said to Ben. "Come back with lanterns and torches so we can see you."

Ben nodded and set off as fast as he could. For the moment, they could still tell in which directions safety and danger lay.

Peter had moved off again. Tom caught up and tried once more to hold him. No use. And Peter's twisting path kept bringing him closer by degrees to the drop.

"What is happening?" Tom asked.

Peter tried to speak. His throat seemed to close, and he started choking. The vicar shook his head.

"I'll stay with you," Tom promised. "You'll be all right."

Face agonized, Peter shook his head.

He walked faster. Tom struggled to keep up. The zigs, zags and twists of Peter's path made him dizzy. Cold fingers touched the back of his neck. Then, even as the fear spread through his limbs, Tom felt himself begin to slip into Peter's rhythm. He found it easier to match his pace. He could anticipate when each sudden shift in direction would come. His feet knew the path they had to take. He didn't have to think. He could just let go, and join in the dance with the vicar.

Just let go. Let go. Follow the path.

Let go.

No.

Tom came to himself with a start. They were only a yard away from the cliff's edge. He leapt away from Peter. He threw himself down so he could not take another step. Below, the waves thundered in judgement. The fog came down, devouring the world, and after taking only a few more steps, Peter became a vanishing silhouette.

"Please stop," Tom begged the unseen puppet master.

"Oh, Tom," Peter said, with such terrible grief in two words.

The silhouette vanished.

The waves roared.

"Peter?" said Tom.

Only the waves answered.

Tom stayed down. He clutched at the ground. He would not move, no, he would not, not until the fog lifted and he knew his body would obey him.

He shivered in the whiteness that turned to grey and then to black as the light failed, and he knew all those trucks had not removed the fear from the Stroud Estate.

Instead, they were spreading it.

Part I

CHAPTER ONE

The exhaustion had turned into a python. The image came to Miranda Ventham as she struggled to the end of her morning class. It took all she had to keep upright at the front of the lecture hall. She forced herself not to lean on the lectern, worried she would collapse against it. Heavy as lead, the python wrapped around her and squeezed hard. She couldn't project her voice anymore. She couldn't stop rasping. She managed to hold her cough in check, but only barely. It scrabbled at her chest and throat, demanding to be let out.

She released the students ten minutes early. A few of them had some questions for her, and she supposed that she answered them, but she had no memory of what she said by the time she found herself back in her office on the second floor of Miskatonic University's humanities building. Miranda sat in her wooden swivel chair, head slumped down on her arms.

Somehow, she managed to get through her afternoon class. She remembered even less of it. The students were a sea of blurry faces in the classroom; their questions, when they came, distant signals from a storm-tossed ship.

Miranda ended that class early too, and then returned to her office again to engage in the pretense of marking. She didn't get through a single essay before she put her head down again and fell asleep.

"Miranda?"

She jerked awake and upright, blinking, trying to shrug off the python. It responded by squeezing even harder. Agatha Crane stood in the doorway, frowning with concern.

"Hey," Miranda said. "Sorry."

"You look terrible," said Agatha.

"If I look half as bad as I feel, then I must be a fright."

"You're definitely getting there."

Miranda grimaced. "Thanks."

"Wednesday," said Agatha. "That means you had your freshmen today, didn't you?"

"Two sets of them. Trying to get them interested in Byron."

"That's your field. I hope they were suitably appreciative."

"Ha. Hilarious." Miranda shook her head, trying to clear the worst of the cobwebs. "To be honest, it was a struggle getting through my upper level Romantics class yesterday, too, and at least those students are engaged."

"Byron too?"

"Yeah. Some overlapping prep this week. Small mercies." She chuckled weakly. "We were doing 'On This Day I Complete My Thirty-Sixth Year.'" She recited the last two lines. "'Then look around, and choose thy Ground, / And take thy rest.' I thought I was going to do just that."

"At least you weren't teaching Keats. That would have been a bit close to the bone."

Miranda gave Agatha a hard look, and saw that she wasn't joking. "You're serious."

"I am. Have you seen your doctor?"

"Overwork, he said. Making this cold drag on longer than it should."

"Is that what he said?"

"It was."

Agatha grunted, her expression skeptical. It was a look Miranda was used to seeing on her friend's face. The parapsychologist was in her late sixties, more than twenty years older than Miranda, and she wore her years like an armor of hard-won wisdom. Her wavy white hair framed features that were sharp as a chisel, though not unkind. Agatha was one of those people who seemed to grow stronger with the passing years, as if time were the forge for her tempered steel. Technically, she had retired three years earlier. All that meant was that she no longer taught, and devoted herself entirely to her research. She still came to the university every day.

Miranda had always admired Agatha's strength. Today, she envied it. Miranda was forty-two. She didn't often think of herself as middle-aged, though the signs were there. The crows' feet were starting to gather around her eyes, and the first sprinkling of gray was appearing in her black, upswept hair. But she didn't feel that different from how she had in her thirties, and in her thirties she had felt as she did in her twenties. Hadn't she?

She felt forty-two today, though. Hell, she felt sixty-two.

"Just how long have you had that cough?" Agatha asked.

Miranda tried to think. “This is March?” she said.

“Last I checked, yes.”

Miranda counted back, became confused, gave up. “I’m not sure,” she admitted.

“You need to see a specialist.”

Miranda took a few ragged breaths before answering. She looked around her office, as if something might offer her support, as if the books, overflowing on their shelves and stacked around the edge of her desk in a nearly unbroken wall, should offer her physical comfort. “You think that’s what it is, then?” she said to Agatha. She couldn’t quite make herself speak the word *tuberculosis*.

“Don’t you think that’s what it is?”

Miranda closed her eyes for a moment. “I don’t know,” she said. *Liar.* She heaved herself out of her chair. “I just want to go home.”

“Then let’s go home,” Agatha said, and helped her on with her coat.

Under an overcast March sky, they walked north-east from the university and into Rivertown. The clouds brooded with thoughts of sleet, and it felt much later than five-thirty. They stuck to the main thoroughfares of Rivertown, making their way past warehouses blackened with soot and age.

Never scenic, hardly pleasant, the walk had been a bit more interesting for the past few months. In the northern reaches of Rivertown, where the expanses of the graveyard held sway, renewal bloomed for the first time in Miranda’s memory. Decrepit seventeenth century buildings lined the graveyard, and a number of the most decayed had been torn down. Miranda and Agatha had watched the project develop over the course of the winter, going from demolition of the old structures, to the digging of the deep foundations, to the rise of the new walls.

Today, they paused at the iron gates for Miranda to catch her breath.

"It looks like they're finished," said Agatha.

A discrete bronze plaque on the left-hand gate pillar identified the building beyond as the Stroud Institute. Out of the center of the main block, four stories high, a central tower shouldered up, adding one more set of windows. They looked down like vaulted eyes on the grounds. The Institute could almost have been mistaken for a neo-gothic apartment building. Long, gabled wings stretched out from the main block to the east and west. The constructions had not disturbed the thick oaks of the grounds. There had been some landscaping done around the new drive, with trimmed hedges lining the approach and a circular fountain in front of the entrance. The water hadn't been turned on yet, and the stone griffins surrounding the basin looked angrier than Miranda thought. She wondered if the play of water might soften the impression they made. Light, a dull orange, shone from the windows of the tower. Darkness pressed up against the panes everywhere else.

"It opens tomorrow, according to the *Advertiser*," Agatha said. "Our new tuberculosis clinic."

"New." Miranda touched the brickwork of the gate pillar. "Not even open yet," she said, "and it already looks old."

The bricks were dark, pitted, and weathered. They were cold to the touch and felt damp, as if it had just rained. Miranda's fingers ran over a patch of moss.

"It looks like it's always been here, doesn't it?" said Agatha. She sighed. "I had hoped it wouldn't. It would have been nice to see something that actually looked shiny and novel in this town."

"The contractors were from out of town, though, right?" Miranda asked hopefully.

Agatha nodded. "I've been keeping track."

"Really?"

"When something changes in Arkham, I like to know why, and who's behind the change."

"Our guardian," Miranda said, only half joking.

"I try," Agatha said, not joking at all. "Anyway, the contractors and the construction firm are out-of-towners. As far as I know, there's been no local involvement with the project."

So things hadn't altered from what Miranda had first heard. "That's something, at least," she said. New people in Arkham, creating a new thing, even if it did look old, even if the stonework whispered that it predated the town. She shouldn't be surprised by that. Age in Arkham spread through its architecture like a contagion.

Miranda started coughing, and she couldn't stop for a full minute. The fit left her bending over, clutching the pillar for support. She took her handkerchief away from her mouth and saw blood.

She straightened slowly, staring at the plaque. It didn't state the purpose of the Stroud Institute. It didn't have to. The sanatorium's wings, designed to accommodate many for a long time, made its intentions clear.

Miranda glanced at Agatha. She shook her head at her

friend's worried stare. "I know," she said. "Wracking cough outside a TB sanatorium. I know. A bit heavy-handed, though, don't you think." She grimaced. "I really don't want this to be a sign." Her voice shook.

"I understand," Agatha said softly. "But if it is, you'd be wrong to ignore it."

Miranda nodded. She started walking again, taking her time. "Yes," she said. "You're right. I'll make an appointment in the morning."

They carried on out of Rivertown and into French Hill. They lived in neighboring buildings, former mansions that had been converted into apartments. Miranda said her goodbyes to Agatha, pulled opened the heavy entrance doors and let herself in to the foyer. The cool breath of the March evening followed her inside and gave her one last shivery touch on the back of her neck as the doors swung closed. Miranda crossed the checkerboard marble pattern on the floor and took the stairs to her suite on the second level. A few minutes later, she had the lights on in her living room, and she was curled up on her couch, blanket around her shoulders, a warming snifter of Armagnac in her hands.

She still felt cold. The cough shook her.

Floor-to-ceiling bookshelves took up most of the wall space in the room. Books squeezed in tightly, defying her to add to their number. She would and she did, and the newer arrivals lay horizontally on top of the rows. One day, she would have to purge and reorganize. Not today, though. Not tonight.

Her windows looked south, down the slope of French Hill, and over a prospect of the graveyard in Rivertown. As night fell, the graveyard became a darker patch surrounded by the lights of Arkham, the silhouettes of the tombstones sinking out of sight into a rising tide of black. In the right mood, she enjoyed the gothic flavor of the view. It didn't appeal to her tonight though, not with her body feeling like a jumble of pain and heavy weights.

From where she sat, she saw only the gables of the buildings across the street, poking up through the bottom of the window panes. Above them, the blank sky shaded darker, the passing minutes turning gray into black.

Miranda's eyes wandered from the window to the walls on either side, the one space in the living room free of bookcases, and where she had mounted some framed prints. To the left of the window, Caspar David Friedrich's *The Abbey in the Oakwood* hung above JMW Turner's *The Fifth Plague of Egypt*. Miranda's favorite painting, Théodore Géricault's *The Raft of the Medusa,* dominated the right-hand section of the wall.

The painting haunted her. It had since she had first seen the colossal original in the Louvre thirty years earlier, when her parents had taken the family to France during her father's research leave. He had taught at Miskatonic too, though she had followed her own path into the English department instead of history.

She stared at the print now, eyes traveling up and down the pyramidal composition of human misery on the raft. The father, grieving over the body of his dead son at the bottom of the frame, had no interest in the frantic activity at the top, where desperate survivors waved rags at the vanishing small sail on the horizon.

Miranda never tired of the ambiguity of the sail. Coming or going? A sign of hope or the mark of despair? No way to know, no way to determine which flavor of human agony Géricault had captured. Most days, Miranda reveled in the perfect undecidability.

Some days, like now, she felt certain the ship would disappear in the next second, even as she needed it to draw closer.

She coughed again. She wiped away another few drops of blood.

Go to bed, she told herself. She would. In a few minutes. When she had the strength to get up.

She sank into a dull stupor. Her attention wandered from the *Medusa* to the window, drifting between pain and dullness. She could have slept, but the cough wouldn't let her. When it came, it shook her entire body with its hoarse, barking strength. Her ribs ached. It hurt to breathe. She felt worse than she had all day, and worse than yesterday.

She would call a specialist tomorrow. She should have sooner. For too long, she had held on to the comforting delusion that this was just a cold, just a bug hanging around longer than normal.

Go to bed.

But if she did, that meant surrendering to the torture of a sleepless night. It meant becoming a thrashing prisoner of the bed and the endless hours before dawn.

She needed rest, though.

Go to bed. Try to sleep, at least.

Her mantel clock chimed eleven before she managed to struggle up from the mire of her stupor and shuffle to the bedroom. The ordeal of changing into her nightgown took the last of her energy. She collapsed into the bed, barely able to pull the covers up to her neck.

She coughed, moaned in pain, and closed her eyes.

So tired. So weak. Maybe sleep would come before the next coughing fit.

It did not.

Hours later, something came for her. It reached out from the night's great dark. She didn't know if she slept or woke, if she felt the touch of a dream or something more frightening. She couldn't move her granite-heavy limbs, but as the vertigo hit, she seemed to be spinning, faster and faster. In a moment, she would fly off the bed.

At the same time, she sank deeper and deeper into the mattress. Stuffing turned into quicksand, pulling her down.

Spinning, sinking, the depths beneath her infinite and hungry.

She tried to scream. She had no voice. She had no breath. Her mouth opened wide in panicked silence.

Spinning, sinking, now drowning.

Down, down, around and around, endlessly, down and down the serpent's coil.

CHAPTER TWO

Miranda sat in the examination room and thought about being in bed. She had to work hard not to topple out of the chair. Exhaustion reached all the way to her bones, and she felt numb with the expectation of bad news. It had taken all of her energy and then some to get from her home to the office of her doctor, Henryk Kravaal. He sat at his desk, going over her test results.

Why she had to come all the way here for the bad news, she had no idea. Miranda already knew what Kravaal was going to tell her. She could read the signs. She had canceled all her classes for the past two weeks because she knew what she had and she wasn't going to spread it to anyone else. Why did she have to put herself through the trip and sit here, teetering? A phone call would have been fine.

Just get it over with and let me go home.

Except home wouldn't be an option for long, would it? And home didn't feel much like home during the night. The dreams kept coming, the variations of the same theme over and over.

"How are you sleeping?" Doctor Kravaal asked, as if reading her mind.

"Not well. Three or four hours a night, tops."

A stern shake of the head. "That isn't enough."

"I know, believe me. What about the tests?"

He turned in his chair to face her. His lined, narrow face, made longer by his gray goatee, arranged into an expression of professional sympathy. "Well," he said, "it's tuberculosis. I guess that's not a surprise."

"Anything else would have been." Exhaustion turned fear into numbness. "What happens now?"

"Now we arrange for your admission into a clinic. You're too sick to be at home, and you're not going to get better without care."

"You mean I would die."

Kravaal opened then clasped his hands. "Nothing is certain. There's so much we don't know about TB. But would things get worse on your own? They definitely would."

"And with care? How are my chances?"

"I'm not in the business of odds and percentages," Kravaal said smoothly. "If I were, I'd be a bookie, not a doctor. You are strong and otherwise healthy, though."

"I sure don't feel it."

"But you are. We've caught this at a stage where I'd think your prognosis, with care, should be a positive one."

That was good news, wasn't it? She supposed so. She felt like she was beyond reacting to anything, good or bad.

"In some ways, your timing is good," Kravaal went on. "If you're going to have TB, better now than a few months ago. You have a couple of options for a sanatorium."

"St Mary's Hospital or the Stroud Institute," said Miranda.

Kravaal arched an eyebrow. "You do your research."

"I walk past the Institute every day after work. It's open now?"

"It is."

"Which would you recommend?"

Kravaal leaned back in his chair and folded his arms. "St Mary's is a known quantity," he said. "Their record for recovery is as good as any other hospital's in the state."

And as bad, Miranda thought.

"It's too early to say anything definite about the Stroud Institute," he said, "but I've heard some promising things about its director."

"But which would you recommend?" Miranda insisted.

Kravaal gave her a knowing look. "For most of my patients, I would lean toward St Mary's," he said.

"Am I most?"

"You aren't. I have an idea that you would not do well under a strict rest cure, and probably make life difficult for other patients and the staff at the same time."

"You make me sound horrible."

"I mean you have a restless mind."

"That's part of my job."

"I know," said Kravaal. "But it isn't a good fit at St Mary's, and I gather they have a different approach at the Stroud Institute."

"Is that a recommendation, then?"

"No. I'm just giving you the information. It's up to you to decide where you want to go. There are some open beds at the moment in both clinics. You make a decision, and I'll get the process started."

•••

A week later, on Friday, under an April sun whose warmth felt thin and brittle, a taxi dropped Miranda and Agatha off at the doors of the Stroud Institute. Agatha helped Miranda out of the cab and held her as she looked up the wide stairs leading to the entrance. Miranda counted the steps. Six. They looked like a hundred. She shoved her hands into the pockets of her trench coat and shivered. The Institute towered over her, as imposing now as it had been at night. No orange eyes glowered in the tower in the day, but now all the windows wore blank, expressionless gazes. The stonework of the building was the color of granite and old sorrows.

"It really doesn't look new, does it?" Miranda said. The building seemed as ancient as she felt.

"Just like the gates," Agatha agreed.

The cabbie put Miranda's suitcase on the ground and drove off. The car passed the fountain, which sent a prismatic spray waving back and forth across the width of the basin. The griffins were as stern as before.

"Can you manage?" Agatha asked.

Miranda still hadn't moved toward the first step. Fatigue hung around her shoulders like a lead blanket. The python squeezed her chest so hard she dreaded every breath. "I think so," she told Agatha. A lie, but she hated how utterly weak she had become.

"There's a ramp," said Agatha. It offered a gradual approach on the left-hand side of the stairs.

Miranda shook her head. The ramp's length frightened her. She couldn't imagine making the journey of a few dozen yards around the porch and up the ramp. "I can do the stairs," she said. She'd managed to get out of her apartment building this morning, after all. But that was down, and it had been two days since she'd last made an ascent.

Agatha picked up the suitcase. Still holding onto her arm, Miranda started forward.

"What do you think you're doing?" a cheerful voice called.

Miranda looked up. She had been staring at the first step as if it were a rattlesnake. A nurse strode out of the entrance, pushing a wheelchair. She came down the ramp at a brisk pace, as if racing to stop Miranda from sprinting up the stairs. As she arrived, the clock tower of Miskatonic University chimed ten.

"You're early," the nurse said, smiling to show she wasn't scolding. Her cap sat on top of tidy curls of red hair. She had a kind face, one that seemed equally disposed to serious purpose and to laughter. "Professor Ventham, isn't it? I *am* sorry. I was going to be waiting for you when you arrived. But all's well, all's well. Sit yourself down like a good girl."

Miranda would normally have bristled at the infantilization. And the nurse couldn't have been more than five years older than her. Yet Miranda suddenly felt ten years old, and embraced by a grandmother's care. She sat down in the wheelchair with a sigh. She had been standing for less than a minute. It felt like an hour.

"I'm Nurse Holden," the woman said, turning the chair around and pushing Miranda to the ramp. "Let me officially welcome you to the Stroud Institute. Though I'm sorry for the struggle you're having, we're still glad to see you."

"I'm glad to be here," Miranda said. Relief washed over her. She'd reached the end of a hard journey, the end of the ordeal of the last few weeks. She had arranged a leave of disability with the university, feeling guilty about abandoning her students so close to the end of term. Knowing that she had made the right choice for them as well as for her did nothing to ease the irrational, gnawing shame, a shame that seemed to be the only emotion to cut through the numbing fatigue.

Tuberculosis. The word and the reality it signified were hard to face. She had to, though, and being here, at last, made that task easier.

When she had inquired about the Stroud Institute's rates, she had been pleasantly surprised. She could easily afford to stay there, closer to home, and in an environment she hoped would be less depressing than that of St Mary's Hospital.

Less depressing, and most of all, new. That mattered.

They reached the door where Agatha met them, carrying Miranda's suitcase.

"Here we are, Professor Ventham," said Holden.

Miranda's eyes widened at the size of the entrance hall. She had not expected a setting this grand. Two stories high, with a marble floor, it collected the echoes of footsteps and bounced them around for its amusement. Sunlight came in red and blue through stained glass windows, dappling the floor with color. Corridors branched off to the left, right, and straight ahead. Holden went straight, nodding to the nurse stationed at the circular, polished oak reception desk in the center of the lobby.

"Would you mind waiting here?" she asked Agatha. "Professor Ventham and I just have some paperwork to deal with before we can get her settled in."

"Of course." Agatha walked over to the wooden bench that ran along the entire perimeter of the entrance hall and sat down.

Holden took Miranda down a few more corridors, moving at such a clip that Miranda grew disoriented. The halls were more institutional than the lobby, though still more welcoming than a hospital. Above oak wainscoting, the walls were painted a cream color with a slight tinge of green. The effect refreshed, and reminded Miranda of spring as it might be, warm and lush instead of gray and drizzling. Pleased, she didn't mind losing her bearings. When they stopped at a small office and Holden settled herself behind a desk, Miranda no longer had any idea where she was in relation to the lobby.

"Now," said Holden, "we already have most of what we need from you, and we have your case history. You'll be getting a full examination later today. So just a few consent forms for you to sign. We also need to go over some of the basics of your treatment at the Stroud Institute. With me so far?"

Miranda nodded. "In other words, you're going to tell me the rules." She'd done some reading about the rest cure in St Mary's tuberculosis wing and elsewhere. She knew what was coming, and dreaded it. Still, Holden was a lot friendlier than she'd expected. She'd heard the St Mary's crew were dour enough to be gravediggers.

Holden laughed. "I suppose you might call them rules. But I don't think you'll find them all that bad. We're here to take care of you, Professor, not torture you."

That sounded promising. Miranda sat up a bit straighter in the chair.

"Our director, Donovan Stroud, believes that the established approaches to the treatment of TB should be questioned precisely because they *are* established. I know he'll want to meet you, and I'm sure he'll tell you more about his philosophy then, so I won't do him the injustice of getting it wrong now. What you need to know is that though we do practice the rest cure here, we do it with some differences."

"Will I be allowed to read?" Miranda asked. She knew what the answer to that would be at St Mary's. She had spent the days since her diagnosis picturing herself confined to a bed, denied her books, denied any activity of the mind whatsoever, forbidden even from talking. *That's not resting. That's rehearsing death.*

"The Stroud Institute has a very fine library, if I do say so," said Holden. "You're more than welcome to use it. In fact, you'll be encouraged to do so."

Miranda almost wept. "Oh, thank every god above," she said.

"Director Stroud has made reading *The Yellow Wallpaper* a compulsory part of our training."

"I'm impressed," said Miranda.

"So was Director Stroud, by that story. He has ensured that its lessons are not lost on any of us. He believes that a cheerful mind is essential to the success of any kind of rest cure. If the mind is not at ease, neither is the body, and the mind that is not allowed to be active is an uneasy one."

Miranda fought to hold back the sobs of relief. They wouldn't do her cough any good. She felt her body already beginning to relax. She hadn't realized how taut she had been, despite her exhaustion. "You have no idea how much hope you've already given me," she told Holden.

"Oh, I think I might," said Holden. "You are part of our initial intake of patients, but you aren't the first to arrive, or the first to express those sentiments."

Holden spent a few more minutes going over the first stages of Miranda's treatment. "Even though this is the 'bed rest' phase," she concluded, "you'll still have some upright activity, if you feel up to it. We'll monitor your progress and move to total bed rest only if the circumstances dictate it. You're free to converse with your wardmates, but do not raise your voice. No strain is key. We do have a silent ward, but believe me when I tell you that we view it as a last resort."

"I do believe you," said Miranda.

"Splendid. I'll be taking you in a moment to the west wing, the women's wing. Women in the west, men in the east."

"And never the twain shall meet?"

Holden favored her with a wry chuckle. "Only in carefully monitored situations. We do have some rules, Professor Ventham, and they must be respected. They're there for good reasons."

That caution sounded a little more rehearsed than the rest of Holden's delivery. "I wasn't planning on challenging them," Miranda promised. She didn't feel she could ever walk again, never mind cause trouble for the staff.

She signed the last of the forms, and Holden wheeled her into the halls. When they reached the lobby again, Holden waved to Agatha to join them. "We're taking Professor Ventham to her bed," she said.

"Will I be able to visit her?"

"Of course. There are visiting hours on Wednesday, Friday, and Sunday afternoons."

Holden took them to an elevator at the entrance to the west wing, and it brought them to the top floor.

"You don't remember me, do you?" Holden asked Miranda as the elevator doors opened.

"Oh dear," she said.

"Not the first time you've been asked that, I guess."

"It's an all too frequent event. I have the worst memory for faces and names. Did you take a course with me?" Miranda tried to call up the memories of students from years past, but drew a blank.

"I wouldn't expect you to recall," Holden reassured her. "It was more than ten years ago."

"My survey course?" Miranda guessed. "Please tell me I didn't put you off poetry forever?"

"You did not, and you weren't my first-year professor. I took the Romantics with you in my third year. My minor was in English literature."

"Is that right?" Agatha sounded impressed.

"Director Stroud told me it was one of the reasons I was hired," Holden said, not hiding her pride. "He wants his staff to have curious minds too. We aren't resting on our laurels here. The Stroud Institute is committed to continuously finding better ways of treating tuberculosis."

"That would be a feather in Arkham's cap if a vaccine came out of here," said Agatha.

"Don't be surprised if it does."

Miranda let their conversation fade into a comforting background as she took in the surroundings that were going to be her home for the months to come. *Maybe even longer,* she thought, and then chased the idea away before it depressed her. Her nose prickled with the familiar antiseptic smell of hospitals. The halls weren't the stark white she had been expecting, though. They were green-tinged cream instead, and though the lighting was bright, the prevailing atmosphere was warm, as if washed with amber and gold from a source she couldn't quite locate.

She also found the same paradoxical meeting of old and new that had struck her and Agatha about the exterior. Again, she couldn't put her finger on the reason for that impression. The brass railing that ran along the walls gleamed with newness, and so did all the fixtures. The paint on the walls was spotless. The floor was unmarked. She could almost believe no one else had been wheeled down these corridors before her, even though she saw nurses walking briskly from room to room.

At the same time, when she looked up at the slight curve of the ceiling, or let her eyes travel down the full length of the hall, she found herself thinking of catacombs beneath cathedrals, and of cloisters fallen into the silence of ruin. She didn't know why. Nothing here resembled the images that rose in her mind.

Maybe she was feverish. Nothing more than that. Maybe.

She thought about the night the vortex swallowed her, and shuddered.

"Are you cold?" Holden asked.

"No," said Miranda. "No. Just tired."

"We'll have you in your bed very soon."

"That will be nice."

Holden paused outside a room at the intersection of two halls. "Your bed is in here," she said. "We'll leave your things here, get you bathed, and then settled." She looked at Agatha. "Bed B," she said. "To the left, next to the window."

Agatha nodded. "I'll unpack her things."

"Thank you," said Miranda. It felt good to be taken care of, good not to have to decide or do anything for herself for a while. She could let herself go. Embraced by a soul-deep warmth of well-being, she could almost pretend the cough wasn't waiting for her just around the next labored breath.

Half an hour later, Miranda lay in her bed. The formalities were over. She had arrived. A few of her favorite books sat on her nightstand, ready to keep her company – William Blake's collected works, a copy of the 1805 version of Wordsworth's *The Prelude,* Ann Radcliffe's *The Mysteries of Udolpho*. Commanded to rest, she was more than happy to comply. Agatha sat in a chair beside her. They spoke quietly so as not to disturb the other three women in the room, two of whom appeared to be asleep.

"Well," said Agatha, "this seems nice, as far as sanatoriums go."

"I think so too."

They both paused. Their eyes met. Miranda tried to smile. They had both caught the hint of forced cheerfulness in the other's voice.

"It is, though, isn't it?" Miranda asked, needing reassurance as the moment of being left alone in the belly of the Institute drew near. Alone, with three strangers and bare walls for company. The books that gave her friendship and warmth, her prints that gave her eyes joy, she would miss them all terribly. She would miss home. Except she couldn't stay there, and here, she would be looked after. Here was where it was good for her to be. She kept telling herself that, and for the moment, the comfort of the bed made her believe it.

"I'm impressed by the staff," Agatha said, her tone emphatic. "You're going to receive good care here. *Humane* care. So you're absolutely in the right place."

Insofar as anywhere in Arkham was the right place. Miranda couldn't remember when she had first begun to feel the sense of wrongness, like a background electrical hum, covering every corner of the city. Much of the time, she didn't notice it consciously. She had grown used to it, and it wasn't an acute sensation. It had just enough strength to impinge on her thoughts in those moments when silence became a little too thick.

"What do you think of the building?" Miranda asked. She needed reassurance, but she needed her friend's honesty even more.

Agatha cocked her head slightly, thinking. "It's architecturally interesting," she said at last. "More so than you'd expect from a medical facility."

"The old and the new together," said Miranda. "The interior is the same as the exterior."

Agatha nodded. "I'm not sure why that is, but yes."

Miranda turned her head on the pillow to look past the other beds, to the doorway and the long corridor on the other side. She'd noticed something when Holden had been helping her into the bed. She had put the impression down to a fatigue-induced optical illusion.

She had hoped when she looked again, her perception would have changed.

It had not.

"Look down the hall," she said to Agatha. "Do you notice anything?"

Agatha cocked her head. She eyed the walls with a skeptical squint. "Yes," she said after a few moments had passed. "The hall is straight, but…"

"But it doesn't *feel* straight."

"You're right. It doesn't."

"Like there might actually be a curve in the walls."

"Maybe there is," said Agatha. "Just very subtle."

"Maybe."

"When was the last time you saw a truly straight line in this old town?" Agatha asked. "I can't remember. That could be our problem. We don't know how to look at something that actually is straight and new. We're out of practice."

Miranda turned that idea over. She liked its comforting possibilities. "Do you really believe that?"

"Do we have compelling evidence to the contrary?"

"No."

"No," Agatha repeated, leaning into the word. "So you're going to rest, and you're going to recover, and you're not going to worry."

"Because you'd tell me if I should."

"I would."

Miranda had spoken a fair bit with Agatha about the older woman's research into parapsychology. From the mere fact of living in Arkham and being curious, Miranda knew enough about the history and current events of the town to believe that Agatha's studies were important. She hadn't, as yet, had any direct experience of parapsychological events herself.

As far as she knew. And believed.

And Agatha would tell if she had reason to worry. That reassured her. Even Agatha's preferred word, *parapsychology*, was reassuring, unlike *supernatural*. Miranda liked *parapsychology*. The word had the power of rationality behind it, and stripped mystery away from the supernatural, forcing it to stand up to scientific scrutiny.

So much power in words, and so much treachery. That she knew intimately from her own research. Agatha's hardheaded approach imposed order on the chaotic and kept it at a distance. More than ever, Miranda needed the mere notion of things stirring in darkness kept far away.

But what about that night, the night of the maelstrom?

Delirium caused by fever and weakness. She'd experienced spinning sensations before when she'd been sick.

But not like this. Not with such intensity. Not with the abyssal plunge.

Then again, she'd never had tuberculosis before, either.

She shut the door on such speculation. It wasn't restful. Agatha said she was in good hands. Agatha said she could rest. If Agatha said it, then Miranda believed it.

Miranda sighed. She felt herself sink deeper into the bed, in a good way. "Thanks. I think I really will sleep well here."

"You look like you're going to conk out any minute."

"I just might."

"You really haven't been getting much sleep, have you?"

"I don't know when I last managed longer than four hours."

"Any recurrences?" Miranda had told Agatha about the maelstrom.

"No."

"Good." She stood to go. "Get to work on catching up on those lost hours."

"You'll come by Sunday?"

"Count on it. And I'll keep an eye on your place, so don't worry about home."

Miranda watched her go. She fell asleep before she saw Agatha reach the end of the corridor. On the edge of dreams, she wondered why it took Agatha so long to walk to the elevator.

CHAPTER THREE

Miranda woke shortly before the evening meal. She felt as weak as ever in body, but refreshed in mind, enough to take an interest in the room and in the women who shared it with her.

At first glance, the space struck her as a typical room on a hospital ward, as antiseptically impersonal and predictable as what she would have found at St Mary's. White walls, floor and ceiling, white sheets, iron bedframes. Gradually, she saw that it had a bit more character. The ceiling had a gentle curve, less pronounced than in the hall, but enough to conjure the gentle echo of a dome. The arched windows each had at least one pane of stained red or green or blue glass. Lying down, Miranda could see nothing through them but the sky. She looked forward to seeing the view of the grounds of the hospital when she stood up again.

Not now, though. Not right now.

The windows were shut against the dank, cold spring. That had to be another departure from the norms of tuberculosis treatment elsewhere. Miranda had done her reading and understood that conventional wisdom called for fresh air year-round, regardless of cold or rain, wind or snow. Not so here. The room felt warm, though not overly so. The temperature seemed calibrated to be comfortable when up and about, but just cool enough to give delight in curling up under the covers. *How can they regulate it so precisely?* she wondered. Maybe they couldn't. Maybe she just had the luck to arrive on a perfect day. By purpose or by chance, the air invited her to snuggle down and rest.

I'm going to be okay.

She hadn't been able to tell herself that yesterday.

"Is it always this comfy?" she asked no one in particular.

"It sure is," said Cleo Whitten, the Black woman in the bed opposite hers.

The woman on Miranda's left gave a sniff expressive of disagreement and contempt. Her name was Frieda Fleet, and she wore the whiteness of her skin like a badge of pedigree. When she coughed, which was often, she coughed pointedly. That hacking announced the fact of her illness and demanded that attention be paid. Cleo seemed stronger, her coughing fits ragged, but less frequent. Her eyes were brighter too, and not with fever. Miranda thought Cleo looked like someone making real progress in her fight against the disease.

You show it what's what. I will too.

Esme Garth, in the bed across from Frieda's, said nothing. She was even paler than Frieda, whiter than her sheets, her face sunken in on itself with weakness and exhaustion. She rarely coughed, but it seemed to Miranda that she rarely breathed, either. Miranda hadn't yet seen her open her eyes.

The only evidence she had that Esme still lived was that no one had taken the body away. She only knew the woman's name because Cleo had told her.

After less than five minutes of conversation, Miranda had a sense of the dynamics in the room. She liked Cleo and her expression of knowing amusement. Frieda was going to be much less fun. She had a face chiseled out of ice with harsh, severe strokes. She clearly resented not having a private room, and resented sharing space with Cleo even more. The social leveling of the disease presented itself to her as a personal insult, and no one else in the room had the grace to recognize that fact.

Miranda shrugged inwardly. If Frieda froze the rest of them out, they weren't going to mourn the loss of her sparkling conversation.

Dinner arrived at six, brought in by patients doing well enough to take on light volunteer duties. Cleo greeted one of them, Jennifer Wong, by name, and introduced her to Miranda.

"Jennifer's our good luck charm," Cleo said. "She's been getting stronger by the day."

Jennifer smiled at Miranda. She looked like one of those cheerful people for whom, Miranda thought, smiles had been invented in the first place. "It's true," Jennifer said. "I can't believe how much better I feel. Do you remember what it's like to take a deep breath?"

"I remember the concept," Miranda said.

"I can actually do it again! And you will too. I promise!"

Normally, Miranda found people that bubbly hard to take. Jennifer's enthusiasm and good wishes were so heartfelt, though, that Miranda found herself grinning too. "If you're the guarantee of that promise, then I'd say it's good as gold."

Jennifer took her by surprise by hugging her, and then finished distributing the meals.

Miranda looked at the plate of breaded veal, mashed potatoes and corn on her plate. It looked much nicer than hospital food should, she thought. It tasted nicer too, she discovered. *And* it was hot.

"I'm starting to think I'll just stay here," she said, then regretted the joke. "I'm sorry. That was in bad taste." No one in the Institute would have been there long, but some of the patients had likely been transferred from St Mary's, and might have been there for months or even years.

"They do make our stay as easy as possible," said Cleo, "and I thank them for it."

"Have you been ill long?"

"Four months trapped in my bed at St Mary's. Don't ask me how long I was sick before that."

"I don't know for sure how long I've had this, either," Miranda admitted.

"It's sneaky." Cleo pointed at Esme. "I knew her at St Mary's. She was there before me. Been like this all along." She didn't have to add that she didn't like the tiny woman's chances.

Frieda sniffed again. "I have no intention of spending the entire summer here," she announced. She gave Miranda a pointed look, as if Miranda had already offered a contrary diagnosis. "There are events, you understand."

"I certainly do," Miranda said with a straight face, careful not to exchange looks with Cleo.

"I won't have them badly run. I won't."

"Nor should you."

Frieda nodded, pleased that Miranda understood. "My husband is Reginald Fleet," she said, and paused.

"I see." *Should I genuflect?* Miranda thought. She knew the name, vaguely. It often headlined the society columns that Miranda flipped past in the newspaper. She knew Fleet owned more than one factory in Northside, and one of the newer, more ostentatious mansions in Uptown.

"I think it's very important that things be done correctly," Frieda said, stating a general principle and implying that this precept was not being followed by the Stroud Institute, at least as far as she was concerned.

"Words to live by," Cleo said, her tone studiously devoid of irony.

Frieda gave her a frosty look.

"I'm going to try to be adaptable," Miranda said. "Whatever I was doing at home wasn't enough to get me well, was it? So I'm going to assume they know better here."

Another unimpressed sniff from Frieda. "I'm sure you hope you're right," she said.

Miranda kept her polite smile in place and turned away from Frieda. She looked across the room to see Cleo's eyebrows raised in amusement. Miranda grinned a little bit wider, turning her smile into satire, and Cleo grinned back.

Miranda dosed fitfully through the evening after supper. When she roused herself with coughing, she and Cleo chatted a bit more. Occasionally, Frieda would hold forth on another of the Institute's shortcomings for their edification. Esme never said a word.

Music began to play from a ceiling-mounted speaker at lights-out. The "Moonlight Sonata" wafted gently through the room.

"Beethoven for bedtime?" Miranda said, pleased.

"The Institute has its own radio station," said Cleo. "Sometimes we get music. Sometimes a reading."

"A story?"

"More like a homily," said Frieda.

"Things for us to think about," said Cleo. "Nice things."

The music wasn't loud, but neither was it so quiet that Miranda had to strain to hear it. The piano soothed her. She turned onto her side and stared sleepily at the open door and the dim lighting of the hall.

She closed her eyes.

She still saw the corridor, in every detail.

Am I asleep? She didn't know.

The corridor twisted. Floor and walls and ceiling turned over and over, a ribbon of madness. The vertigo seized her, and she spun counter to the rotation of the hall.

She had to be asleep. She had to be dreaming. *Wake up! Wake up! Wake up!*

An old reflex kicked in, a desperate childhood defense against nightmares. If she hyperventilated, she might escape. She tried to take deep breaths.

Immediately, a flood of black water roared down the hall. Her breath, caught in her chest, turned into a scream, and the water swept over her and silenced her.

Down again, dropping and spinning as she had that night in her home. She flailed at the dark. Drowning. She was drowning. She couldn't breathe. Her chest burst with pain.

She surfaced, gasping and coughing.

Darkness around her. Motionless shapes in the other beds, shapes she sensed without seeing. The hall lay before her, an expanse of gray and dim amber.

Miranda didn't know the hall, didn't know the room, didn't know where she was.

She felt the rub of the cotton sheet against her arms, and the pain in her chest from another day of coughing.

She was awake. Had to be. But why didn't she know this place? Her mind fumbled in total disorientation.

A dull roar, and then the black water foamed down the hall again.

She couldn't make a sound. The scream stayed inside her skull. The water carried her away into the depths of the nightmare once more.

She surfaced again, praying that this time she was awake, that she had broken through the strata of dreams.

She faced the room, the hall, the disorientation. And then, to her despair, the black water.

Over and over, spinning and drowning, a false waking that felt completely real, and then the night flood churning and foaming as it came to swallow her.

The cycle did not end until dawn found her. Limbs tangled in twisted, sweat-soaked sheets, every breath a punishment; she didn't trust the reality of wakefulness until she heard Esme cough, and the Stroud Institute settled itself around her for the day.

CHAPTER FOUR

Agatha kept her promise. She arrived in Miranda's room on Sunday, just after lunch.

"Would it be all right if she took me to the library?" Miranda asked Nurse Revere. "I feel up to it." She did, in spite of the bad nights. She knew better than to believe she was on the mend after barely forty-eight hours, but she was sleeping well during the days, and the lack of teaching and marking and not worrying about working was making a difference. The nights were the nights, and she needed to talk to Agatha about them. Other sources of stress had been lifted from her, though, and that mattered.

Nurse Revere didn't answer right away. She scrutinized Miranda's chart as if there were already months of data on it. Miranda did her best to look meek. Revere was older than Nurse Holden, and carved from much sterner rock. She had eyes of flint, and the face of a granite axe. To Miranda's relief, Agatha picked up on her strategic approach and adopted an expression as close to innocence as she could manage.

Whether Revere believed in Agatha's act or not didn't

matter. After making them wait a full minute, she gave a curt nod. "You've been resting," she said. "That's good. You're going to behave yourself, Professor Ventham, aren't you?" The question sounded like a command. "You're not going to be a patient who doesn't want to get well."

"I *do* want to get well," Miranda reassured her. "I'll do anything to kick this. Show me the hoops, and I'll jump through them. I want to feel normal again."

"Then you'll behave."

"I will."

Another curt nod. "No exertions," she said. "Not too long." Then she turned to Cleo's chart, dismissing Miranda and Agatha.

Miranda made sure to take her time getting out of her bed and into the chair, accepting help from Agatha. Nurse Revere glanced back once, and seemed satisfied that there was no misbehavior.

"Which way to the library?" Agatha asked.

"This floor," said Revere. "Follow the signs."

Agatha pushed Miranda out into the corridor. "Do you see any signs?"

"Not here. Don't ask again." That would be asking for permission to be revoked. "Let's just go."

At the end of the hall, they found the first sign. Agatha turned right, down another long corridor. At the next intersection, they were sent left.

"These halls…" said Agatha.

"I know," said Miranda. "Just pretending to be straight, all of them. I think I'm getting used to them, though. Almost. I try not to focus just on what's immediately in front of me.

That helps, anyway. And it's not like I'm out of the room much."

"How have things been?"

"I feel taken care of. Had more tests and my X-ray done yesterday. Now all I have to do is keep resting."

"And they're helping you do that?" Agatha asked.

"They are. The food is good. There are enough little things happening in the day to keep things interesting."

"Such as?"

A coughing fit seized Miranda, and it was a long, painful moment before she could speak again. "Puzzle sheets that come with lunch," she said, her eyes watering. She rubbed them clear. "I hear there are counseling sessions for those well enough to attend, so that's something to look forward to."

"That doesn't sound like a lot happening," said Agatha.

"Weirdly, it's enough. There hardly seems to be enough time for all the napping I want to do between meals."

"You really are resting then. That's good."

"Plus, we get piped-in music in the evening."

"This place has its own radio station?" Agatha sounded surprised.

"Seems it does."

"Have you been doing any reading?"

"Not really," Miranda said. She thought about her little pile of books with a pang of guilt. "I haven't felt up to it yet. This will be my first visit to the library. But we get things to read with the meals along with the puzzles. Quotations for the day."

Agatha laughed. "No doubt very inspirational. Lifted from *Reader's Digest*?"

"Want to know what today's was?"

"Tell me."

"'I saw from afar and from before what I was to see from behind'," Miranda recited.

Agatha was quiet for a moment. They reached another junction and turned right again. The complexity of the route struck Miranda as excessive.

"Can't say I've heard that passage before," said Agatha. "Doesn't sound very *Reader's Digest*."

"It's from Thomas de Quincey's *Suspiria de Profundis*."

"I see," Agatha said slowly. "And what are you supposed to do with that line?"

"Think about it, I supposed. Puzzle it out. It does give us something meatier than a platitude to ponder."

"Granted. What did your roommates make of it?"

"We didn't talk about it. It made Cleo frown, I think. Frieda barely looked at it."

"And the other one?"

"Esme? I'm trying to think. I haven't spoken to her at all yet. She sleeps almost all the time. She *did* surface for the meals, briefly. I didn't notice if she read it."

They turned another corner, and at the end of a short hall the library entrance waited for them, wooden doors open, the high, wide space beyond inviting.

Miranda read the inscription on the lintel. "'The unexamined is the unquestioned'. Magnus Stroud."

"Stroud," Agatha repeated. "Is the director immortalizing his thoughts?"

"His first name is Donovan, I think. I'm going to guess these are the words of an illustrious ancestor."

The library had a high ceiling, much higher than anywhere else Miranda had been in the Institute, with the exception of the lobby. A row of arched, floor-to-ceiling windows poured daylight into the center of the space, where leather armchairs clustered. Bookshelves took up the other walls, resting in cool shadows and the gentle, warm light of lamps mounted along the ceiling's periphery.

Agatha brought Miranda to the window. There were other armchairs here, with plenty of space between them for a wheelchair. Agatha sat down next to Miranda. They looked down into the grounds together.

"Huh," Agatha grunted.

"Yeah," said Miranda. "Did you keep track of all the turns we made?"

"I thought I had. I must have miscounted."

The library was in the central tower of the Institute, and faced in the same direction as Miranda's room. From this vantage point, she would have guessed that a single corridor would have taken her straight back to her bed. "I wonder what the architectural reasons were for that route," she said.

"Someone thought they were very sound," replied Agatha. She took Miranda's hand. "You said the days helped you feel rested." She gave her friend a searching look. "How are the nights?"

Miranda sighed. "Not good." She told Agatha about the dream of her first night. In the daylight, it was easier to think of it as a dream. She also distrusted that ease. She wanted the truth to be that she was just having nightmares. She could deal with that reality. But their insistence and repeated imagery were new, and that disturbed her.

Agatha listened carefully. She prodded Miranda for a few more details, then asked, "What about last night? Any better?"

"Different," said Miranda. "Again, I couldn't tell if I was asleep or awake, but I wasn't drowning or spinning this time. I was just staring down the hall the whole night."

"The hall that you try not to look at during the day?" Agatha asked, eyebrows raised.

"I know what that sounds like, but yes. I couldn't help myself. So I'm lying on my side, eyes open, looking down its length. Then I'd wake up and realize I'd been dreaming of looking at the same thing I could see with my eyes really open. Or so I thought. Then I'd wake up again. And so on and on until morning."

Agatha had taken a pen and a reporter's notebook out of her handbag. She wrote in it, then frowned.

"You know more about this kind of thing than I do," Miranda said. "Are these more than bad dreams?"

"Do you think they are?" Agatha's tone was carefully neutral.

Miranda's instinct was to say yes, unequivocally. But a gut response was not what Agatha was interested in hearing. So Miranda thought through her answer. It was still a yes. "I've never experienced anything like them before," she said. "And though there are differences, there is also a consistency to them that I don't associate with dreams. I do think they're something more."

Agatha jotted down a few notes. "All right," she said. "You might be right. Then again, you might not be."

"I understand."

"This isn't me saying that I doubt your word."

"I know that's not the issue, Agatha."

"Good. We have to approach the problem with rigor. If we don't, we're being fantasists, not scientists."

Miranda almost pointed out that she *wasn't* a scientist. She decided that a plaintive cry of "But I'm in the Humanities!" wouldn't be helpful.

"Agreed," she said instead.

"Before we can seriously consider the possibility that you're experiencing a parapsychological phenomenon, we have to eliminate all other explanations," Agatha went on, almost as if Miranda were one of her pupils.

Miranda didn't object. Agatha had often expounded on her frustrations with the emerging discipline of parapsychology. There were too many self-styled researchers who didn't know the first thing about the scientific method. Too many proponents who believed in everything they encountered because they wanted to, without even consulting stage magicians to see if they didn't have ways of duplicating the reported wonders. Agatha feared the disrepute that hovered around parapsychology, not because of what might happen to her own academic reputation, but because of how that ridicule could bring down the entire field and destroy the good that it could do.

"We don't dismiss the parapsychological possibility," Agatha insisted. "But we don't make it our first assumption."

"Things happen in Arkham, though," Miranda said quietly.

"Yes." Agatha was somber now. "Yes, they do." She took a breath, straightened up in the armchair, and put pen to paper once more. "Tell me everything again," she said. "Let's start at the beginning. Go through it slowly. We want every detail."

Miranda relived the nights again, breaking them down, under Agatha's prompting, into phases, and the phases into beats.

"What is it?" Agatha asked after Miranda paused for an extended period.

"I was thinking about the corridor," said Miranda. "It feels like a fixation."

"Why do you think it might be one?"

Miranda shrugged. "Maybe because there's something about the hall that's significant."

"The one you see in… let's call them dreams for now, or the real one in this building?"

The question made Miranda feel queasy. She made herself examine it. She was going to beat TB, so she was going to beat whatever these dreams were too. "Maybe both," she said. "They both feel weird."

"Maybe they are," said Agatha, and Miranda did not find that answer reassuring at all. "And maybe that's the answer. Maybe a quirk of architecture is affecting your dreams."

That was more like it. That was reassuring. Except… "But my first hall dream was before I came here."

"And that's something we can't ignore. All right. Think about how you experience the hall. Tell me its defining features in the dreams."

Defining features? "Length," said Miranda. "It's too long, or longer than it seems." She remembered watching Agatha's departure on the first day. "I think I might have had one of the dreams right after arriving," she said, and told Agatha about the endless journey she had appeared to make. "And it twists," Miranda said, details becoming clearer as she thought about them. "Even when it isn't spinning around, somehow there's still some kind of twisting." She shook her head. "No, that's not quite right. *Coiling.* Yes, that's more like it. And it's old. Too old."

"How do you mean?"

"I can't say. That's just the impression I have." Miranda looked around the library. She eased herself up out of her wheelchair.

"Easy," Agatha warned. "Where are you going?"

"Nowhere." Miranda took a step forward and touched the wall between the windows. "Feel this," she said. She sat back down and wiped her palm against the dressing gown. The wall had been dry, but her hand suddenly felt clammy, as if she'd run it down a slimy surface. "Feel it," she insisted.

Agatha followed her example, and then she too was rubbing her hand against her coat sleeve.

"It's wrong, isn't it?" Miranda said. "I don't know why, but it is. Like the contradiction of the new and the old. In the dreams, the corridor seems ancient."

"I see," said Agatha.

They sat in silence for a few minutes. "Do I need to worry?" Miranda asked.

"I always worry," said Agatha. She gave a brittle laugh, then sighed. "I'm sorry. That's not what you were asking. Do you need to worry about this place specifically? I don't know. I would like to think that our initial impressions were correct, and that you don't. I want to think that the new that we see here matters more than the old. There's so much of the old in Arkham, and not just here. And you're clearly receiving good care."

"So I don't need to worry."

"I didn't say that."

"No. I was sort of hoping that you had."

"I wish I could too."

"Right," said Miranda. She drummed her fingers on the arms of her wheelchair. "So what's the plan?"

"For now, we monitor your dreams closely. And we learn what we can about the Stroud Institute."

"Just to be on the safe side."

"Exactly."

"Shall we start in here?"

"Why not?"

No one else had come into the library while they talked. They had the place to themselves. Agatha wheeled Miranda around the shelves, and they scanned the spines. Miranda expected to see a lot of popular titles, and she did. Mary Roberts Rhinehart, Edna Ferber, Zane Grey and Rafael Sabatini jostled for space. Their competition surprised Miranda. "I wouldn't have thought *The Waste Land* to be comfort reading," she said.

"Plenty here from your field," said Agatha. "Lots, even."

She was right. At first blush, Miranda had the impression their shelves held more Blake, Byron, Keats, Wordsworth and the other Romantics than any type of literature.

Then there was the philosophy.

"Boethius," said Miranda. "Hume. Kant. Light, bedtime reading." She took the Hume down to bring back with her.

"I don't know whether to be impressed or confused," said Agatha.

"I'm starting to think the quotation over the lintel is a real statement of intent for this library."

"Agreed." Agatha turned them back toward the doorway to start the return journey to Miranda's room. "I'll say this. I have a few questions I'd like to put to Donovan Stroud."

"You'll have the chance."

"Oh?"

"I meant to tell you. Friday evening. The director has invited me and a guest, and that's going to be you, to his quarters for a personal welcome. The invitation is on fancy stationery and everything."

"Now that is an evening I don't want to miss."

Miranda felt lighter for the first part of the way back. She felt as if she had taken concrete steps to deal with the bad nights.

Her mood faltered as they retraced their steps through the halls. It seemed to take even longer to return to the room than it had to reach the library.

CHAPTER FIVE

Miranda had two nights of something that could almost have passed for respite. No spinning, no drowning, no visions of twisting halls. No dreams of any kind, as far as she could remember. But not much rest, either, at least none that she could feel in the mornings. The threat of the nightmare's return simmered just below the surface of reality, waiting to stab through and set the world to howling.

Miranda actively dreaded the nights now. The possibility of nightmares was enough to trigger her anxiety. The days were good. They *were* restful, and she thought she was feeling a bit better. She had longer periods between coughing fits. A little energy had returned, and she could read for more than five minutes at a stretch now. She kept up her journal again. She was so used to the sounds of women coughing in her room and others that she barely noticed it any longer. And she could keep thoughts of the coming night at bay for most of the daylight hours. She could make it until after supper before she really became anxious.

But the worry was growing stronger. Soon it might become terror.

Miranda controlled the fear by taking notes. If Agatha wanted documentation, then she would have it. If, through meticulous observation, Miranda could help Agatha prove that her visions meant nothing more than that she was tired, sick and worried, then she would anatomize each day down to its component seconds. And if she was experiencing something worse than bad dreams, then they would need every detail she could glean if they were to learn how to fight it.

Fight it, she thought. *Fight what?*

She had no idea. The very thought of there being something that had to be fought bothered her. She had always found Agatha's research fascinating, but something to be examined at a remove. Just like the low-grade awareness she had that there were things that were not right in Arkham. That was knowledge she had taken seriously, while also filing it away as something that did not apply directly to her. In that, she believed, she followed the everyday practice, conscious or unconscious, of most of the population of the town.

Tuesday night, she was on her side, facing the hall at the moment of lights out. The hall's illumination dimmed, and the room went dark. The light seemed to rush out of the room, pulled down the length of the hall as if it were a physical thing being sucked into the depths of a throat.

Miranda jerked up. She swung her legs over the side of the bed, got up, and shuffled to the doorway as if to follow the fleeing light.

Nurse Revere would be angry to see her up. She didn't care. She would even welcome a scolding. The pain in her chest and the strain of her lungs kept her grounded in the real. She knew she wasn't dreaming.

Miranda held on to the doorway. She looked down the hall into dim stillness. No nurses walked by. The entrances to the other rooms yawned blackly. She heard coughing and moans. She saw no further plays of light.

Beneath the stillness, the dreams waited, even closer to the surface.

She did not want to go to sleep. She also knew she had to. Her body demanded it. Her legs threatened to buckle and drop her to the floor.

Miranda turned around to start the long voyage back to her bed. And Esme spoke.

"You shouldn't look."

Miranda jerked her head to the left. She could barely see Esme. The woman was a bundle of shadows, her face turned away from the hall.

"What do you mean?" Miranda asked.

Esme said nothing. She didn't move. Her breath deep and slow, sounding like sleep.

Miranda left her. Passing a snoring Frieda, she made her way to her own bed and struggled back under the covers.

"Did Esme speak to you just now?" Cleo asked.

"Yes," said Miranda, grateful not to be the only one awake. "At least, I think so."

"It's spooky when she does that, isn't it?"

Miranda rubbed at the gooseflesh on her arms. "Yes," she said. "I'd say so. Has she spoken to you?"

"She used to all the time at St Mary's. In the early days. She hardly does at all now, and when she does, it's upsetting."

"Because of what she says?"

"Because it's so rare," said Cleo. "She goes so long without saying anything at all, I just give up. And then, once in a while, she whispers." Cleo sighed. "We were friends at St Mary's. Now she just reminds me of death. She makes me think of what might be coming for all of us. Is that awful? Am I terrible for thinking that?"

"No," said Miranda. "I'd feel the same. I'm pretty close to that after just a few days, and you've seen her change."

"Thanks," said Cleo. "Still feel guilty though."

"Can I ask you something?" Miranda said after a few moments.

"If it changes the subject, I hope you will."

"How are your dreams?"

"My dreams," Cleo repeated. She paused, then said, "Not sure that I've had any, recently. Huh." She sounded surprised. "I used to. Haven't in a bit. Kind of a relief not to, you know? I need the rest."

So do I, Miranda thought. Cautiously, she said, "So you're getting that rest here? You feel good here?"

"I do," said Cleo, emphatic. "I feel something here that I never did at St Mary's."

"Which is what?"

"That I'll get to leave. Because I'll be cured."

Tuesday night, Wednesday night, Thursday night. The hours of darkness passing without relief. Always, the sense of the nightmares poised to strike, their claws inches from Miranda's throat, the jab and tear held back out of a dark sense of amusement.

By contrast, Wednesday and Thursday mornings and afternoons were measured out by blessed naps and the soul-deep joy of being looked after, and of feeling safe. Wednesday meant another visit from Agatha, and this time they stayed in the room, talking about ordinary, comforting things. Miranda's apartment was fine. Agatha brought a get-well card from the members of the English Department. The weather was still miserable.

Thursday brought the visit of a dignitary. With breakfast came the word that Councilman Payton Wallace would be touring the wards.

Frieda looked ready to clap her hands with glee. Miranda had never seen her in a state of unbridled joy before. The effect was jarring.

"Payton is a close family friend," Frieda confided to the room after Holden had left.

The way she said *Payton,* with too much emphasis on the first syllable and a bit too much of a stretch of the first vowel sound, turned the name into something unctuous. Miranda was sure she had had Paytons as students in the past. She had never had anything against the name. Until now. With one sentence, and one utterance of the name, Frieda had turned her against the very concept of men called Payton.

"He and Reginald went to college together," Frieda continued.

"Let me guess," Cleo deadpanned. "They were fraternity brothers."

"Why yes they were, as a matter of fact," said Frieda, missing the veiled sarcasm completely and delighted the question had been asked. "Reginald says you learn a lot about a person in a fraternity. Really get the measure of a man."

"Which is what going to college is all about," Cleo said. She turned to Miranda. "Isn't it?" she asked, raising disingenuous eyebrows.

"So I'm told," said Miranda. If Cleo was going to try to make her laugh, she would fire right back.

"Yes," said Frieda. She nodded sagely. "That's right. Payton gets things done," she said, her tone implying that Getting Things Done was humanity's highest calling. "He has great things ahead of him. He'll be mayor before long. Mark my words."

"That's nice," Miranda said. "What Things has he Got Done?"

"Well!" Frieda puffed up, as if Payton's accomplishments were her own. "This sanatorium, for one thing."

Miranda mused of that statement for a bit, fascinated by a world where a civic politician somehow deserved credit for the vision governing a medical facility, and where Frieda could bask in some sort of reflected glory as if she, too, had had a hand in the Stroud Institute's foundation.

"That's pretty impressive," said Cleo, who was not buying anything Frieda was selling.

"How did he manage that?" Miranda asked, and this time she was genuinely curious.

"Payton was a big supporter of the Institute from the start," said Frieda. "He pushed hard when the rest of the Council was slow to see the benefits. He kept pushing, and he brought them around."

"I guess he must have," said Cleo, looking around the room as if surprised to find that it existed.

"Why was he so keen on the Institute?" Miranda asked.

"It should be obvious, my dear," said Frieda. Her smile was

patiently understanding and condescending. "Think what it's done for the economy."

Miranda had no idea what that meant, and she suspected that Frieda didn't, either. If that was what Payton had used to make his case for the Institute, and if that was what he really believed, then that said nothing good about him. This was taking the concept of doing the right thing for the wrong reasons to the point of absurdity.

The great man arrived shortly after the lunch trays had been cleared away. Nurse Revere acted as his escort. He stepped into the room with a broad, very pleased smile.

That was the look, Miranda decided, of a man who believed congratulations were due for the accomplishment of being himself. Napoleon arriving in Egypt could not have been more certain that he was the conquering hero.

Payton Wallace was a man who, she guessed, had been very thin in his youth, had come to think of that condition as eternal, and still thought of himself as a thin man even as middle age proved him wrong. His blue suit was expensive but too tight, his pants squeezing his midriff because he refused to admit he needed a larger size. The orange of his ascot, brighter than it needed to be, declared his love for the flourish. His face was handsome in a self-conscious way that made Miranda's skin crawl. He struck her as a man who believed in his own beauty as an article of everyone's faith. His thick black hair, slicked back with Brilliantine, and his small, perfectly trimmed and waxed moustache, were more than carefully thought out grooming. They were the official presentation of Councilman Payton Wallace to the world, delivered with an expectation of applause.

"Ladies," he said, with a knowing smile and nod after Revere had introduced him. There was more oil in the word than in his hair.

Miranda wished she had the energy to get up and belt him.

Cleo stared back at him, stone faced. Frieda, though, blushed and simpered. Even Revere seemed, by her standards, disarmed. She didn't exactly smile, but she looked out across the room with an air of smug pride.

Esme, as ever, did not react at all. Miranda thought her eyes opened briefly, but the moment passed too quickly for her to be sure.

"It's a real pleasure for me to see the Stroud Institute in action," said Payton. "It's so good to know that our faith in Director Stroud has been well-placed. And what an honor to have so informed a guide as Nurse Revere to show me around."

The corners of Revere's mouth twitched, as much of a smile as she could allow herself. Her cheeks took on a hint of color.

"And it is *so* good of you to come and see us," said Frieda. "I can't tell you how much it means to see a friendly face."

Payton looked at Frieda. "I'm so glad," he said, smooth as plastic. "And how are you doing?" he asked, the inquiry about as genuine as a three-dollar bill.

Miranda watched the exchange carefully. *He doesn't recognize her.*

"Reginald will want me to give you his best," said Frieda, and Miranda heard the desperation in her voice, the need to prevent, above all other things, the moment where Payton asked her name.

Miranda *almost* felt a twinge of sympathy for the

councilman. She had wrestled with remembering faces and names most of her life, and though, by the end of each term, she was usually pretty close to knowing which student was which, all it took was to see one out of context, at the movies instead of in class, for instance, for her to stare blankly at the young person chatting happily about running into each other.

But then Payton said, "Dear Reggie," and turned around to announce to the room, "Now there's a man with a wicked backhand!" He spoke with such easy practice, such perfectly tailored but false enthusiasm, that Miranda's sympathy shriveled into contempt.

He didn't know who you were, Frieda. That's how much your friendship means to him.

"Do tell Reggie I'm ready for a rematch whenever he is," Payton said, addressing Frieda again, leaning forward slightly over her bed in a show of intimacy.

"I will!" Frieda promised. "Oh, it really is so nice to see you, and to have the chance to thank you for everything you've done."

Payton shook his head. "Now aren't you just the kindest?" Modest as a peacock. "But I really can't take any credit for the wonderful work being done here, and the vision it represents," he said, taking all the credit. "I have to congratulate Director Stroud on his accomplishment."

Miranda noted that Payton used the word *vision* in a way that separated it from Stroud, who merely had an accomplishment.

"But most of all," Payton said grandly, "the praise should go to Nurse Revere and her sisters. They are the beating heart of the Stroud Institute."

"Merely our duty," Revere said, unable to keep every trace of pleasure from her voice.

Payton smiled at her, and then toured the beds. He hesitated at Esme's, his mouth open to spout something meaningless, but her immobility stopped him. Marginally off his stride, he swerved to Cleo. "Taking good care of you, are they?" he said. "Good, good," he added before Cleo could answer.

Then he was at Miranda's bedside. He patted her stack of books. "My my," he said. "Lots of reading to get through there, I see. Taking the opportunity to improve our mind, are we?"

"Absolutely," Miranda said, her voice high and sweet. "We little women have to keep busy or who knows what trouble we might get into."

Payton blinked. His smile wavered, then steadied. "Good, good," he said, grasping for the first words he could find. Then a spin on his heel took him out of danger and back into the comfort of Frieda's worship. He took her hands and gave them a visibly hearty squeeze. Miranda choked at the display and started to cough, but Frieda glowed.

"You will tell me if there's anything I can do," Payton said.

"Oh I will," Frieda reassured him. "I will. You're too kind."

Payton waved off the praise.

"Reginald will never forgive me if I don't invite you over for dinner," Frieda rushed on, gushing. "Once I'm out of here, of course." She reddened.

"I'll be there with bells on," said Payton. "How could I refuse, after what you served last time?"

And just what did she serve last time? Miranda wanted to ask.

Frieda giggled at the empty praise.

His poise reestablished, Payton left as he had arrived. "Ladies," he said, bowed, and swept out after Revere.

Frieda glared at Miranda. "How could you be so rude?" she demanded.

"He was your husband's frat brother, he's eaten at your house, and he can't remember who you are," Miranda said. "What does that say about him?"

"That's just nonsense," Frieda said. She turned on her side, away from Miranda, ending the conversation.

Cleo shook her head. "That man," she said. "He could take credit for a sunset."

"And make the sunset dirty," said Miranda.

And then Friday came. In the afternoon, Holden helped Miranda to the shower room, ran the water until the chamber filled with steam, and left her to it. For several minutes, Miranda reveled in the privacy and the luxury. The water beat against her skin, hard and soothing with warmth. She was in no hurry to leave.

When she turned off the water, the steam coiled in patterns a little too distinct for her liking. Now she was in a hurry. She toweled off as quickly as her weak arms allowed, wrapped herself in her robe, and wheeled out of the room. The coughing that hit her as soon as she breathed the cooler air of the corridor undid all the therapy of the shower.

Agatha arrived just after supper for the evening visit to Donovan Stroud.

"So they're letting you stay up past your bedtime," she said.

"I'm sure Nurse Revere has opinions about this," said Miranda.

"Not her place to have them in this case though, is it?"

Miranda grinned. "Not when my invitation is from on high."

Agatha had stopped by Miranda's apartment and brought the simple black dress Miranda had requested. She didn't want to feel like a patient for a couple of hours. It took her a long time to get into it, and triggered another coughing fit. Her weakness alarmed her. But she triumphed over her body, and then sank into the wheelchair.

Agatha took her through the tangle of corridors that led them to the central block of the Institute.

"Does the layout bother you?" Miranda asked.

"You've been thinking more about it."

"I have, and you didn't answer my question."

"It seems more convoluted than it needs to be," said Agatha. "But I also don't want to assign malign intent to something that may just be bad planning, or an architect's whim. What about you?"

"I am fascinated," said Miranda. "All these straight lines, but so few straight paths. Are you ready for me to sound pretentious?"

"Always."

"Have you read any EE Cummings?"

"Can't say that I have."

"He's one of a number of poets who have been making quite a splash recently. He does fascinating stuff with typography and grammar. He uses the typewriter, this machine designed to regularize print, to defamiliarize words, and even letters and punctuation. And he'll use language to make us acutely aware of the rules we take for granted, because he uses those rules to produce combinations of words that are beautiful, but whose meaning we have to come at sideways. Do you follow?"

They had reached the tower, and they waited for the elevator that would bring them to Donovan Stroud's quarters.

"I think so," said Agatha. "But I don't see where you're going with this."

"Goethe said that architecture is frozen music," said Miranda.

The elevator arrived with a clanking hum. Agatha pulled the gate aside and Miranda wheeled herself in.

"I think it can also be embodied poetry," she went on. "The floor plan of the Institute makes me think of a Cummings poem. It has straight lines like the rules of grammar or the regularity of a typewriter's print, but the lines are breaking the rules."

The elevator jerked into motion.

"All right," said Agatha. "I see what you mean. The question is, do we conclude anything from that?"

"I don't know," Miranda admitted. "It just feels important."

Donovan Stroud greeted them as they emerged from the elevator on the top floor. Dressed in a dark brown suit and sporting a brown, polka-dotted bowtie, Donovan was old enough to come down on the right side of the boundary between dignity and foppishness. Miranda placed him in his early seventies. Yet with his gray hair neatly trimmed, and his sharp eyes looking out fiercely from his thin face, he looked like a man still just getting started with the projects of his life. Within seconds of meeting him, Miranda had the impression of a young man with much to prove. Nothing in him suggested a man looking back on the accomplishments of a lifetime.

"Welcome," he said, smiling broadly. "I'm so glad to meet you finally, Professor Ventham."

"Thank you," said Miranda, and she introduced Agatha.

Donovan shook her hand and ushered them down the short hallway to his apartment. "I hope you don't think I'm trying to be flattering when I tell you that I've been really looking forward to this evening." He spoke with an animation that made his sincerity palpable.

"You may not be trying to flatter, but you're doing a nice job all the same," Miranda smiled. "Don't let me stop you."

Donovan laughed. He brought them through the open door of a vestibule and into a lounge whose windows looked out over the front grounds of the Institute. Donovan had apparently jumped with both feet into Art Deco. The room was richly furnished, and bathed in warm reds and blues from light filtered through stained glass lampshades. Logs crackled in a fireplace, and Miranda felt cozier without having realized she'd been cold.

An oil painting, set off by a gold-leaf frame, hung over the mantle. It was the portrait of a young, early-nineteenth-century nobleman. He stood with his left hand behind his back, and his right appearing to gesture to the landscape behind him. Moody cliffs brooded beneath dark clouds. At the top of a cliff, the ruins of an abbey jutted up, tumbled and vacant. The man had a look of quiet satisfaction. At the same time, it seemed to Miranda that his eyes held a sparkle of wonder. The family resemblance to Donovan was unmistakable.

"An ancestor, I take it," Miranda said, pointing to the painting as Donovan invited Agatha to sit on a red velvet sofa with its back to the window.

Donovan helped Miranda out of the chair and onto the sofa next to Agatha. "That's right," he said. "Professors, I'd like you to meet Lord Magnus Stroud, my great-I-forget-how-many-times-grandfather. You see him with a backdrop of his estate in Galloway, Scotland." Donovan spoke with pride.

"Lord Magnus of honored memory, I gather," said Miranda.

"Indeed. He set an example that all of us since have tried to follow. Can I offer you a drink?"

"Is that allowed?" Agatha asked.

"If I say it is," Donovan said, and he smiled. "Don't worry. I'm not being cavalier. I've checked Professor Ventham's charts, and a little cognac won't do her any harm."

"In that case, yes please," said Miranda, and Agatha joined her.

Donovan served them, then took an armchair facing them on the other side of the fireplace.

"You said you try to follow Lord Magnus' example," Miranda prompted.

"Yes, I did." Donovan glanced up at the portrait. "I think you might appreciate this, Professor Ventham, given your field." He nodded at Miranda's raised eyebrow. "Oh yes," he said. "I've read some of your essays on Blake."

"Really?" Miranda asked, surprised. No one outside the walls of Miskatonic University had ever told her that.

Donovan nodded. He pointed to the middle shelf of the bookcase that took up the wall opposite the windows, and she recognized the spines of *The Review of English Studies*.

"I'm flattered," she said.

"I'm genuinely interested in your work," Donovan went on. "My family history makes that rather inevitable. You teach and study the Romantics, but Magnus knew them personally."

Miranda's jaw dropped, and Donovan laughed, delighted by her response. "Lord he may have been, but he was a radical. Cut from the same political cloth as Byron, if you will. He believed in the promise of the French Revolution. A poet in his own right, too, though, as he would be the first to admit, in a very minor way. He was friends with Wordsworth for a time. In fact, unless I'm mistaken, Wordsworth visited him in Galloway around the same time this portrait was done."

"Friends for a time?" Agatha asked.

"Yes. Magnus stayed true to his radicalism throughout his life. He and Wordsworth inevitably drifted apart. I do often wonder what they might have accomplished together, if Wordsworth hadn't tacked into more conservative waters."

"Together?" said Miranda. She sipped her cognac, enjoying the warmth in her chest. It eased the pain that lingered after the coughs.

"Magnus invited Wordsworth to collaborate with him in the creation of a community of writers. A physical one, founded on the Stroud Estate. Wordsworth declined, in the end."

"Did Magnus succeed anyway?"

"He tried." Donovan gazed into the fire with a regretful, melancholy air. "In the end, he failed. But I think the fact that he tried at all is important, don't you?"

"I think it matters," Miranda said.

"It does matter. It does very deeply, at least for those of

us who count ourselves as descendants of Magnus. I like to think that we're following his example here at the Institute."

"How so?" Agatha asked.

"By not being afraid to challenge conventional wisdom. By thinking radically. Always for the good of our patients, of course."

"Of course," said Agatha. Her tone, Miranda noted, was carefully neutral, scrubbed clear of any possible trace of sarcasm.

Donovan smiled at them both, then raised his glass in a silent toast to the portrait, and took another sip.

"I hope you don't take this the wrong way," he said to Miranda. "I don't mean it to sound like I am celebrating your illness. Having said that, though, I am glad you're here." He smiled.

"What do you mean?"

"I mean it's a privilege to have a mind like yours within these walls. I feel you might be able to help the Institute almost as much as, I hope, it will help you."

"I don't see how I could," said Miranda. "You're saving my life, after all."

"I'll tell you what I mean," Donovan said. "We can talk about details much later, when you're in the next stage of your convalescence. When you're up and about, and more active again. Part of our treatment, you see, involves discussion groups for the patients. Those who are up to it. The active mind."

"The active mind is important," Agatha agreed, still innocently neutral.

Stop it. Miranda didn't want to start laughing. It wasn't that she even disagreed with Donovan. He just sounded a little too evangelistic, and a little too much as if he had invented the concept of thinking.

"The active mind," Donovan repeated once more, nodding sagely. "Keeping busy even when the body cannot. Good for morale, and for mental energy. You'll be invited to take part in due course, and I can't help but hope that perhaps, down the road, you might think about leading some. Again, once you're at the more active stage of your cure, naturally."

"I will think about it," said Miranda, and she meant it. Donovan's delivery aside, what he said made sense.

"I can't ask for more, and I won't," said Donovan.

Fatigue caught up with Miranda a few minutes later. First, she left Agatha and Donovan to carry the conversation. Then she began to have trouble following it. When the painting began to writhe at the edge of her vision, she knew it was time to go and face what the night would bring to her.

"You look tired, Professor Ventham," Donovan said, preempting her.

"Yes," she said. Speech came with effort. Breathing felt like a boulder rested on her chest.

She barely took in the goodbyes. The next thing she knew, Agatha was wheeling her out of the apartment. She looked back to wave at Donovan. Leaning against the mantle, he waved back.

Above him, in the background of the portrait, the ruins of the abbey squirmed.

CHAPTER SIX

Miranda spent Saturday quietly. Her bed held her in an embrace of heavy comfort. She felt herself sinking into it as if the Earth's gravity had suddenly tripled. Her exhaustion worried her. Was she really this weak? Was this what even a short evening of conversation would do to her? Had she set herself back? Recovery became hard to imagine. The illness had become her life. It defined her existence. She could not see beyond its horizon.

And she was too tired to care.

The bed was soft. It took care of her, as did the staff of the Institute. She didn't have to worry. She didn't have to think. She could drift through the leaden sea of the illness, floating on numbing tides.

So unlike the woman she had been. The old Miranda would be bored stiff, desperate to find something to occupy her mind. Traces of the old Miranda had been present as recently as last night.

She didn't mind. She was safe. All was well.

Distantly, the old Miranda called to her. Rest, she said, but don't forget you have to fight, too.

Even when the evening came, she didn't have the energy to become anxious about the night. She barely stayed awake long enough to be aware of lights out. When she woke on Sunday, she realized, gratefully, that she had slept through the night. There had been dreams. She had a vague impression of long, twisting movements, but nothing specific. The night retreated with nothing worse than a faint, residual shudder.

Miranda felt refreshed, too, more like herself, and actually restless. Energy, that had seemed an impossible mirage the day before, a delusion that had vanished and would never return, was back. The fear that tuberculosis was forever receded. She could imagine getting well.

Up and down, she told herself. She should get used to this. Up and down, weak and strong, resigned and hopeful. There were no forevers. *Keep hold of that.*

"You look bright this morning," Nurse Holden said when she came by on her rounds after breakfast. "I think that's some actual color in your cheeks, and not the feverish kind."

Miranda touched her face as if her fingers could feel the color. "I had a good night," she said.

"You have a question," said Holden, reading Miranda's face.

"I was wondering if I could be up for a bit today."

Holden picked up her chart, gave it a scrutiny, and took out a pen to update Miranda's readings for the morning. "All right," she said.

"Thank you."

Holden held up a finger. "With conditions."

"Of course."

"No more than half an hour," Holden said, and now she

enumerated the restrictions with her fingers. "You stay on this floor. And you stay in your chair. No walking. Are we clear?" She sounded almost as stern as Revere.

"I understand."

"Good." Holden smiled, and the angel of the ward returned, reassuring Miranda that she was still a good patient, and that the strictures were for her benefit, and not a punishment.

After Holden had left, Miranda put on her dressing gown and settled herself in her wheelchair. She ignored Frieda's stare and disapproving frown. When it was clear that her silence wasn't going to have the desired effect, Frieda cleared her throat. Even that sound was sculpted by breeding.

"Do you think you're accomplishing something?"

Across from Miranda, Cleo snorted. Esme had her eyes open, or as open as they ever got, their lids half down, shielding her from the world.

"I hadn't actually set out to accomplish anything at all," Miranda said. If she'd been speaking louder than a murmur, she would have used a bright and artificial tone. Instead, she gave Frieda a wide, false smile.

"You should be resting," Frieda said. "We don't want this room to have a reputation."

Miranda's eyebrows rose. "And what reputation would that be?"

"That we can't keep still. That we're difficult patients. Troublesome."

Miranda stared at her until she was sure she could speak without laughing. "I wouldn't worry," she said. "Your reputation is secure. I'd wager my lungs on it."

Frieda sniffed. "I should hope so."

Cleo made a choking noise. Miranda wheeled herself out of the room before she lost her composure.

She had lied to Frieda, though. She did intend to accomplish something. She had had enough of disorientation. Her sense of her room was of an island in the middle of a tangle of corridors. She had no real conception of where the library was in relation to her room, and that was just one instance of her frustration. She had always had a good sense of direction. When she visited a new city, it usually only took her a few minutes to get its cardinal points fixed in her mind, especially if she was getting around on her own, and on foot. Like the first time she had been to New York City. She had been six, on an outing with her parents. Manhattan's grid between rivers had clicked into her mind so completely that, when a woman had approached her mother and asked for directions, it had been Miranda who had answered.

It offended her vanity not to know her way around the Institute. She told herself that her confusion was due to having been wheeled from place to place by other people. It always took her longer to get her bearings in an unfamiliar place if she was a passenger. So today she would start to sort out the vague tangle of the Institute's geography, beginning with the route to the library.

She started off by looking for a map of the floor, hoping to find one posted at a hallway intersection. No luck. Plenty of signs pointed the way to the library, X-ray lab, surgery, elevators, and every other destination she could imagine, but no map. When Miranda started following the signs to the library, she stopped after the first few turns. She felt like she was being taken around again, invisible hands pushing her chair and giving her no say in where she went.

She worked her way back to the hall leading to her room and started again. She took note of signs, but instead of following them, she concentrated on choosing the corridors in a systematic fashion. She took her time, not heading down another until she felt confident about the relation of the current one to the previous hall. If the Stroud Institute refused to post its floor plans, she would create her mental one.

She went past the doorways of rooms of coughing women. She smiled to the staff she encountered, and most of the time received smiles back. The overall atmosphere of the Institute was as cheerful as she imagined it was possible for a tuberculosis sanatorium to be.

I'm lucky to be here. I am.

She took her time. Mindful of Holden's admonitions, she took care not to tire herself. She would be the good patient. She would do what she must to get well.

Most of all, she didn't want to have future wanderings forbidden.

She took her time, too, to make sure she learned the floor plan. But when she finally made it to the library again, her mental construct of the layout collapsed. She had made some progress, but she was still confused. There were gaps in her understanding of the corridors. She felt as if she had arrived sooner than she should have. And she had a growing conviction that the walls of the Stroud Institute were too thick, the halls too spaced out from one another.

She checked her watch. Her half-hour was almost up. Time

to be good and head back. No point fighting the maze any longer today. She followed the signs to return to her room, Ariadne's thread leading her back to rest. Every intersection seemed to be a false choice, as if no matter which direction she chose, her path would always be between the library and bed.

She returned to the room a minute before her half-hour. She passed Holden in the last hall, who gave her an approving nod. *Good girl. Good patient.*

She spent the rest of the day retracing the halls in her mind, fighting to turn the web into a map. The web fought back.

And the halls followed her into her dreams that night.

On Monday, Agatha Crane marched up the steps of the Miskatonic University's Orne Library, determined to become acquainted with Count Magnus Stroud. Gray gargoyles lined the roof of the gray building, ancient guardians of still-older knowledge. Rain dripped from their jaws like venom. The damp came in through the door with Agatha, clinging to her bones as she made her way into the stacks.

She was worried about Miranda, worried about more than her health. The quality of care at the Stroud Institute struck her as excellent and progressive. Miranda was strong. She would beat the TB. But her dreams and visions concerned Agatha; they were not to be ignored.

Agatha considered herself a rationalist. That position was core to her identity. She hadn't set foot in a synagogue for more years than she could recall, but she treasured the tradition of asking hard questions that was the gift of her ancestors. Investigation, interrogation, the demand for evidence as extraordinary as the theories it meant to support – these were the tenets she lived by. Parapsychology had to hold itself to the most rigid of standards if it wanted to take its place among the established scientific disciplines. And it *needed* to reach that status. It *had* to be taken seriously. The matters it dealt with were too important, and too dangerous, to dismiss. The more Agatha encountered in the realms of the paranormal, the harder she found it to credit traditional conceptions of the divine, and the more she worried about what these forces, unopposed, might do.

She hadn't come to any conclusions yet about Miranda's night visions. They might be more than nightmares; they might not. She had to find out, and not just for Miranda's sake. She had to be sure.

Agatha began her search on the ground floor of the Orne, in the reference section. She gathered armfuls of biographical encyclopedias. Sitting at a wooden table scuffed and scratched by generations of researchers, surrounded by her stacks of thick volumes that smelled of dust and dry, crackling years, she started off on the trail of Magnus.

The initial volumes did no more than confirm that there had been such a person, that he had been born in 1770, and died in 1858. Older editions, though, referred briefly to the fact that he had been a writer as well as a friend to writers.

Agatha found nothing by him in the card catalogues. She consulted with the one of the librarians, Abigail Foreman. Severe in posture and dress, her hair in a bun so tight it seemed to be pulling her straight, Abigail got back to Agatha after an hour of searching and informed her that the archives had no record of any works by Magnus Stroud.

Agatha kept looking. She followed some pathways that Miranda had suggested, looking for references to Magnus in books about people connected to him. She had her first real luck in Besselman's biography of Wordsworth from 1896. It touched on Wordsworth's friendship with Magnus. Agatha learned the count's nickname among his friends was "Merrick", because of his habit of climbing the Merrick in the Range of the Awful Hand alone to look out towards the land in Galloway that would, eventually, be his.

Agatha went back to the card catalogs, and then to the librarian, this time looking for works by Merrick.

Her prize emerged from the archives. She took it back to her table. The reading lamp cast an amber glow over the book, and the gloom of the hall pressed in closer. Agatha turned the pages of the *Miscellany of Merrick,* which had received limited publication in 1806. The black covers contained a smattering of poems, some satirical jabs at politicians, philosophical musings, and journal entries.

Agatha started to read.

The afternoon darkened. The light coming in the Orne's stained-glass windows turned sullen. Through the words on the page, the past shifted uneasily.

CHAPTER SEVEN
Scotland, 1805

They were about a mile south and east from the summit of the Merrick, and the wind had turned ferocious. It no longer felt like August. The light rain turned into a horizontal attack. William Wordsworth squinted into the stinging wet and pulled the collar of his coat tighter. The footing was becoming treacherous, so he walked steadily and with caution, putting more weight on his walking stick.

"William! Keep up!"

Count Magnus Stroud had put a good fifty yards between them. No caution in his stride, he hurried up the slope, at times almost running. He laughed, giddy, and waved, urging speed.

William shook his head, grinning. "I'm not as young as you are!" he called back.

"We're the same age!"

"You're still younger!" Magnus raced on with the remembered energy of a child. He kept laughing, growing younger by the moment in William's sight. He didn't set a foot wrong. William wasn't surprised, though he was envious. Magnus knew the Range of the Awful Hand in Galloway like he knew his own hand. The Merrick, in particular, had been the count's home of exile, the land that gave him succor while he was denied the freedom of his true home.

Today, the exile was coming to an end, and William was glad Magnus had asked him to share the moment. He loved these hills too. If only the rain wasn't driving quite so hard and trickling cold inside his collar. He tried to find the enthusiasm of the child who ran through the hills and didn't care about the rain. It usually came to him a bit more easily. Maybe it was seeing that exultant freedom of movement in Magnus that made him feel a bit older and a bit more distant from his former self.

Or maybe it was just the years and the experiences. Maybe it was what he had seen in France. Magnus had been there too, more than once, in the last fifteen years. He must have seen the curdling of the Revolution's dream into the Terror and the Empire. Didn't that weigh on him?

Today, apparently nothing did.

Look around, William thought. *Look at these hills.* They elevated his soul, even with the wider view shrouded by the rain and clouds. He moved faster to catch up with Magnus.

"Are we not heading for the summit?" William asked. They were not taking their usual route.

"Not today," said Magnus.

"I thought you'd want to look out towards the estate." Stroud Hall and its grounds had been the possession of Hugo, an elderly cousin. Complex lineages had granted Magnus the title of count and possession of another house in

Yorkshire. But that mansion had been a place of cold comfort for Magnus since childhood. His heart belonged in Galloway. With Hugo's death, he was coming home.

"We wouldn't be able to see the grounds today," Magnus said.

"True," William admitted. The horizon had drawn close. Even the nearest hills were pale gray shapes, becoming insubstantial in the squalls. The estate, on the coast, would be invisible.

"We'll be walking the grounds soon enough," said Magnus. "We're here because I have to pay respects to their guardian."

"Their guardian?"

Magnus winked.

They came around a bend and over a rise, and William understood.

They approached the Grey Man of Merrick from its east side, the perspective from which the illusion was most convincing. On this side, the rock formation of a cliff face became a man's profile. Aged, contemplative, serene, the Grey Man gazed downslope into the distance and rain, unmoved by the turbulence of the world.

William slowed, savoring the sight. Magnus ran forward. He reached up, reverently, to touch the Grey Man's pointed chin. He bowed his head, and William held back, giving him the space for his moment of communion with stone.

Magnus lowered his arms. He looked up at the Grey Man, grinned, then called to William. "What say you? Is there a family resemblance?" He turned to look down the hillside, and William had to concede some parallels in the profile. The heavy brow, the pronounced bridge of the nose, the pointed chin; yes, the two could have been hewn by the same artist.

"There is no doubt," he said as he joined Magnus. "You are brothers."

The count took a deep, happy breath of air. He took off his hat and lifted his face to the rain. The wind gusted. He didn't flinch any more than did the Grey Man.

"You called the Grey Man a guardian," William said.

"He is." He pointed into the limbo of the rain. "He looks directly toward Stroud Hall. He has watched over the estate for me all this time. He watches over it even now when we can't see it."

William nodded. "You were right to give him your thanks. He has been a good friend to you."

"He has," Magnus said with feeling.

Two hours later, they were back in Magnus' carriage, rattling along the uneven road toward the estate. The rain had let up, giving way to rolling patches of mist.

"This day has been a long time in coming for you," William said.

Magnus shrugged. "I knew it would. I didn't mind the wait."

"Even though you and Hugo didn't get along."

"Hugo didn't get along with anyone. I did not take his animosity as a personal attack."

"But what about what he might have done to the Hall?"

"What of it?" Magnus' serenity was unbreakable.

"Aren't you worried? You told me that he had spent himself into bankruptcy."

"He did, yes. And yes, his taste was abominable. But I have my own fortune, so Hugo's sins on that front die with him. And I'll tell you this, William. As for the crimes he might have committed against the Hall, he could have burned it to the ground and it would not trouble my happiness one jot. What is the Hall? A building, and so by its very nature, ephemeral. The land, though. The land persists. Hugo could not make that vanish."

"He might have sold it."

"Not without my consent, and I made sure the funds to prevent that, at least, were present. The grounds are intact. They are as they were in my childhood."

William leaned forward to shake Magnus' hand. "Then you have my congratulations."

"And your approval, I hope, old friend."

"That goes without saying."

The day was failing when the carriage came to the wrought-iron gates of the estate. An attendant had been waiting for them, ensuring the gates were open before the carriage had time to stop. Magnus shouted his thanks to the man, and the horses carried on up the oak-lined drive, and to the graveled forecourt of the Hall.

The ancestral seat of the Strouds thrust its square battlements up into the gathering gloom of the late afternoon. Descending from the carriage, William looked up at the Hall, and it glared back at him, sullen, glowering. It was more a keep than a mansion, its walls built for defense, not comfort. A few of the windows glimmered with the light of fireplaces in their rooms, but many others were glazed with darkness. The hulk of a building felt cold, unwelcoming.

The servants waiting at the entrance seemed pleasant enough, though. Three came forward, accompanied by the butler, to take down the luggage chests from the carriage.

"My lord," the butler said, "welcome to Stroud Hall."

Behind him, the other servants were lined up, waiting for inspection.

"Thank you, Phillips," Magnus said. "It's good to see you again."

"It has been a long time, my lord."

It would have been, William thought. Magnus hadn't been here since his early adolescence. White-haired but rigid of posture, Phillips seemed as old as the oaks on the drive, and as unlikely ever to fall.

"You can all carry one," Magnus said. "Mr Wordsworth and I will stretch our legs a bit before coming in. I'd like to see the grounds while we still have some light."

The wind blew hard from the nearby coast. When William turned into it as he and Magnus left the carriage behind, it roared at him with greater ferocity than it had on the Merrick. He embraced its challenge, more eager to test his mettle against it than venture into the cold arms of the hall.

Past the small woods that circled the hall, the land became open and barren, and the wind howled in unbridled freedom. Midway between the trees and the cliffs overlooking the Irish Sea, huge shapes grouped together, behemoths whispering secrets to each other.

"Are those standing stones?" he asked.

Magnus just grinned.

"No," William said, answering himself. "They're too large."

Magnus' grin became even wider.

"But there's something about their arrangement…" William trailed off.

Magnus clapped his shoulder. "They're one of two things

I wanted you to see here before the day is done. Come and see!" He broke into a run, darting like a deer over the moor. William followed.

He slowed as he drew near the boulders. They were immense, the smallest at least thirty feet high, the largest twice that. Some were rounded, almost spherical, while others, narrow and tall, loomed over them like sentinels. They were clearly natural formations, yet William was sure he saw a pattern in their positions.

"What is this?" he breathed.

Magnus urged him on, and they passed beyond the nearest stone and into the embrace of the cluster.

"I call it the Stroud Spiral," Magnus said. "That's what it's always been for me, and no one has told me otherwise. Maybe it doesn't have a name, though that would be strange."

"Strange indeed," said Wordsworth. His voice had dropped to a whisper. He felt as if he had crossed the threshold of a cathedral. He stared up at the boulders. They leaned toward him, wise and secretive. On instinct, he reached out and ran his hand on the moss-covered flank of the nearest. A profound sense of touching the ancient struck him. He didn't want to let go. He walked around the curve of the rock and removed his hand only when he could transfer it immediately to the next behemoth. He moved from boulder to boulder, losing himself in a waltz with stone.

This was a spiral, and it had caught him in its coil. He followed it willingly, breath held in anticipation of revelation.

And then, as he felt the possibility of a center to the spiral approach, he pulled back. He wasn't ready. He shouldn't look. He didn't want to see.

The effort of pulling his hand away from the rock sent him stumbling, and for a moment he didn't know where he was.

Had he been released, or had the coil flung him away?

Magnus took his arm to support him. "It is an experience, isn't it? Do you think Coleridge would like it?"

William rubbed his eyes. "I don't think it would be healthy for him." He looked about. The new surroundings had come upon him by stealth. The ground was barren rock, with no trace of heather or moss. The land rose to the cliffs. It ended suddenly, and the booming of waves came from far below. On the highest point, ruins cut a jagged silhouette against the darkening sky.

"The abbey," said Magnus.

"Does it have a name?"

"No more than the stones, and don't you think that's fitting?"

"I do," William murmured, uneasy. The abbey seemed to flow up out of the rock on which it stood, as if it too were a natural formation. It declared its kinship with the boulders of the Spiral. They were one.

William looked back and forth between the abbey and the Spiral. He shuddered with awe. His throat went dry.

"Such a wonder," said Magnus, his face ecstatic.

A wonder? Yes, it was. And it upset William that he could not share his friend's joy. He did not want to be here.

He believed in the inherent goodness of nature. Every landscape could be a balm to the soul. But he also believed in the presence of the land, in a sense of being so huge that it called out terror that was the necessary element of awe. He thought about the strongest, most frightening sense of that presence he had ever felt. As a child, he had taken a boat out one night on Ullswater. Partway across, the mass of Glenridding Dodd had appeared to rise up before him from behind other peaks. The peak came for him. It was not a question of changing perspective. The mountain advanced. It rose higher and higher, and it *saw* him.

He had rowed back across Ullswater with fear driving his strokes, the mountain's silent pursuit bearing down upon him.

That had been the fantasy of a child. In the years since Glenridding Dodd had hunted him, he had looked back on the incident with fondness, the terror softened by memory to a delicious shiver. The experience came back to him now, primal and real, and there was nothing delicious about it.

The fear was there again. The cliffs with their ruins and the spiral of boulders knew he was there. They had him between them. If he stayed where he was, the trap would close.

"I would like to go back," he said.

Magnus didn't hear him. The count stared at the abbey, his face frozen in rapture.

"Magnus," said William. He spoke louder, and could not keep the tremor from his voice. He shook Magnus by the shoulder.

Magnus jumped. He blinked, coming back to himself.

"I'm sorry, William. What did you say?"

"I would like to go back." Urgency squeezed his chest. In another few moments, it might be too late. A coil he could not name would have them.

"Of course," said Magnus. "It is getting late. We won't have the light much longer."

They started back. William did not breathe easily until they were on the other side of the Spiral. The sense of danger receded. The fear that he had been seen did not.

Even when caught by the most violent storms in the Alps, he had never wavered in his belief in the benevolence of nature. He held firm to that tenet even now. He had to.

But this place was wrong. It was evil. Nature had been distorted into something else.

"I've long had dreams of what I might be able to do here," said Magnus.

William glanced at him uneasily, then concentrated on the land ahead. He strained to see some hint of light from the Hall shining through the woods that waited for them.

"Now you can realize them," he said. The response came automatically. He hated the idea as soon as he spoke.

"I will tell you my plans tonight," said Magnus.

William nodded.

He didn't want to know.

He wanted to run.

CHAPTER EIGHT

Agatha's studiously neutral expression made Miranda brace herself. She waited until Agatha had sat down at her bedside and they could speak quietly before saying anything.

"You've either made no progress, or the progress you've made is worrying," Miranda said.

Agatha grimaced. "Are you up to a visit to the library?" she asked.

"Not today. I overdid it the other day. I'm to stay put and rest until the weekend." The prospect didn't bother Miranda as much as she would have expected. The effort to map out the floor had taken so much out of her, physically and mentally, that she had accepted the strictures from Nurse Revere without complaint. Even getting up for visits to the washroom was an ordeal.

"I see," said Agatha. After a moment's thought, she shrugged. "Maybe it doesn't matter."

Miranda followed Agatha's gaze around the room. Esme was asleep, as usual. So was Frieda, her snoring coming out in sharp gasps and snorts. Cleo was reading a magazine. Agatha looked at her a few moments longer, then back at Miranda, her eyebrows lifted in a silent question.

"She's okay," Miranda mouthed. The subterfuge felt surreal. What reason did she have to worry about what Cleo or the others overheard? Did she think they were spying on her? For whom? For Stroud? Why? Was he responsible for her dreams?

Of course not. Ridiculous questions, all of them.

But at night, when they waited for sleep and the possibility of dreams lurked, murmuring in the dark, the questions would come back to make her heart pound. Better to face them now, in the daylight, and try to strip them of their power.

Did she believe Cleo meant her harm? No, she did not. Impossible to conceive of the other woman as dangerous.

Agatha seemed to be wrestling with the same debate. Then she nodded, ready to speak.

"You've found something?" Miranda whispered. No need to wake Frieda or Esme. No need to bother Cleo.

There. Good, sensible, *thoughtful* reasons to be quiet.

"Some material by and about Magnus Stroud," Agatha said. She took a notebook out of her leather briefcase and went through her findings. Miranda listened, struck by the fact that she had somehow never heard of this figure from her field of study. A friend of Wordsworth, another Romantic idealist, another *writer*, it seemed, no matter how minor, and, somehow, he had been completely forgotten.

"The lands that form the background to the painting reverted back to Magnus in 1805. He describes visiting them with Wordsworth," said Agatha.

"It's a shame Wordsworth never wrote about that visit," Miranda said. "At least, I'm pretty sure he didn't."

"You would know."

"I've never encountered any reference to Magnus in either Wordsworth's poetry or his correspondence. Which is strange, given their friendship. You'd think there would be some letters somewhere."

"Destroyed?" Agatha asked.

"That's what I'm thinking. The absence feels telling."

"But absence isn't evidence," Agatha pointed out. "And evidence matters."

"Granted. *Did* you find anything?" She still didn't know what she expected to uncover. Something sinister about Donovan Stroud's ancestor? Or maybe proof of his benevolence? What would that prove or mean in the present? And would any of it stop her worrying about her nightmares?

"I don't know if I'd call it evidence," Agatha said. "Have a look at this. Tell me what you think." She took an old compass from her briefcase, flipped open the cover, and passed it over.

Miranda frowned. She turned back and forth in her chair, holding the compass in different directions. "That's not north," she said. The needle, defiant, pointed south-west.

"Keep watching," said Agatha.

After a few seconds, the needle began to jerk wildly, then settled to the east. After another few moments, it sprang to life again.

"That looks unusual," Miranda said.

"Doesn't it?" said Agatha. "And listen to this. That behavior only starts once the compass is inside the Institute itself."

"It's normal otherwise?"

"It is, until I'm close to the Institute. At that point, the needle swings from the north to point at this building, and doesn't budge until I'm inside."

"What does it all mean?"

"I don't know," said Agatha. "It's suggestive, at least. Something real is affecting magnetic fields in the Institute. That doesn't necessarily imply parapsychological phenomena. The explanation could be something completely mundane. But it's a start. I'm going to perform some other tests. If you are having more than dreams, and the reason for has to do with the Institute, then there must be a way of physically registering its influence."

"That's fine," said Miranda. "But what does all this have to do with Magnus?"

"That remains to be seen. Maybe nothing. As for him, though…" Agatha produced a sheaf of papers from her briefcase. "Have a look at these. I transcribed some of his journal entries."

Miranda read them. Her stomach clenched with unease. "He's obsessed with that abbey," she said. The ruins came up over and over in the entries. Magnus visited them day after day, and each time he felt that they were suggesting new mysteries to him. They teased revelation but never delivered, offering instead always another secret, a different configuration of shadow. When Magnus wasn't writing about his explorations of the abbey, he was musing about it, speculating about its origins, regretting that Wordsworth hadn't wanted to share the experience with him, and anticipating his next visit.

"The full manuscript is more varied," Agatha said. "Theories of art, plans for his community, but it was the way he hammered on about the abbey that really struck me.

And as best as I can tell, Wordsworth's friendship with him ends after their visit to the estate. At least, Magnus doesn't mention any further visits."

"So these regrets that Wordsworth won't be part of things is the end of it?"

"As far as I can tell."

Miranda let the papers drop on her blanket. "Suggestive," she said.

"But not conclusive."

No. Nothing to tell her to worry, or to stop worrying. She might be looking at the traces of a friendship that sadly fell apart, and Magnus was not the only Romantic to wax enthusiastic about a Gothic ruin. He would have been a rare one not to have done so.

Suggestive. Sure. Only if read while also thinking about the Institute's unmappable geography.

She told Agatha what had happened to her. "Maybe I'm just too weak to be exploring right now."

"Maybe."

"Too many maybes," said Miranda.

"And nothing that says the mundane answers are the wrong ones."

"We need to know more."

Agatha gave a short, emphatic nod. "I'll keep digging."

"You said he writes a lot about that community of artists he wanted to establish. It would be good to know what happened with that, if anything."

"It would," Agatha agreed. "And you should try exploring again when you're able. And you'll tell me if anything else happens."

"You know I will."

They chatted a little longer, letting their voices rise a hair above a whisper now as they stuck to banal topics. When Agatha got up to leave, Miranda made herself get up too.

"I thought you were supposed to stay lying down," said Agatha.

Miranda eased herself down into her chair. "Just going as far as the doorway to see you off," she said. "To see if I can."

She managed it, but when she had said her goodbyes to Agatha and turned around again, the distance back to her bed looked like miles.

She was about to begin the trek when she saw that Esme's eyes were open and staring at her. Miranda smiled. Esme did not. Her cracked lips parted, and she formed words. Miranda wheeled herself next to the head of the bed and leaned forward.

"I'm sorry," she said. "I didn't catch that."

"What were you doing?" Esme's whisper was softer than air, thin as tissue, weak as a sigh.

"Just visiting."

The tiniest movement of Esme's head. A little bit more than a tremor, just recognizable as a shake, *no*. "Don't," Esme whispered, her eyes wider now, urgency flickering in their exhausted depths.

"Don't what?"

"Questions," said Esme. "Stop." Each word came out with the effort of hauling a boulder up from a well.

Miranda leaned in closer. "Why are you afraid?" she asked. She spoke as quietly as Esme.

Another shake of the head. "Don't... Quiet... Just be quiet..."

Esme closed her eyes. Her shallow, rasping breath slowed. She had willed herself back to sleep.

Chilled, Miranda left her. Esme might have been rambling, delirious. If they had been in a clinic in Manhattan, Miranda would have dismissed the warning. In Arkham, she could not. She crossed the room and put herself back to bed as silently as possible.

By then, Frieda was awake. She and Cleo were both looking at her.

"So," said Frieda. She glared at Esme and then back at Miranda. "You're worthy of conversation, then."

"We barely exchanged two words."

"Two words more than she has ever said to *me*. What did she say?"

Miranda could say that it was none of Frieda's business. She could tell her off, and wouldn't that feel good? It also would do nothing to douse Frieda's curiosity, and the next thing that might happen was her going over to Esme and confronting her with indignant shouts.

No one needs that. Least of all Esme.

"She asked what Agatha and I were talking about," Miranda said, deflecting Frieda's interest away from Esme.

"Which was what?" Frieda demanded.

"Wow!" said Cleo. "How have you never had that nose of yours broken, Frieda? Shove it into my business like that and it's pulling out bloody."

"We have a right to know," said Frieda, tilting her head up, the wounded party, the picture of aggrieved dignity, "if she was talking about us."

"We weren't," said Miranda.

"Then there's no need to be coy, is there? That will only make us think the worst."

"*Us*," Cleo repeated, disgusted.

Miranda wondered if she should come clean. If she should ask if they had dreams that frightened them, dreams that might not be dreams. She could ask if anything at the Institute didn't feel right.

But she already knew the answer. Frieda would be shrieking in terror or anger if she saw so much as a spider. Cleo had already said how good she felt being at the Institute, and Miranda believed her.

Nothing to be gained in frightening them. She might set their recovery back, and she didn't even know if there was a reason to frighten them. Warn them of what? Of the misfiring fancies of her subconscious?

And Esme said to be quiet. Esme urged silence, and lived by that principle.

Be small, be unnoticed, draw no attention.

No attention from whom?

Could she trust the others?

The question startled Miranda. *Why am I even thinking things like that? What's wrong with me?*

What if there was nothing wrong?

But no. Cleo was definitely not the problem. Frieda was *a* problem, but not one that worried Miranda.

"We're planning a trip to Scotland," she said. She lied so they wouldn't worry. She lied because Esme feared questions.

"Scotland?" said Frieda. "Why Scotland? Now, Monte Carlo, there's a place. Reginald took me there the summer before last." Frieda took off on an extended list of recommendations, their details endless, the personal anecdotes epic in their self-regard. Miranda watched her take pleasure from the belief that no one else in the room would ever be able to replicate the experiences she had had thanks to dear Reginald.

Good. That was Frieda deflected. Cleo wouldn't pry. Miranda could relax a little. Because the sun had not yet begun to set, all was still well. Miranda didn't have to think about the night and dreams – not just yet.

Miranda knew she was dreaming. Floating through the corridors of the Institute, she saw them from a perspective wrong for her memories. She was too high, too tall, only a few feet down from the ceiling. She had left her body and the chair behind. A being of pure awareness, she flew with effortless freedom toward Donovan Stroud's apartment.

She knew she was dreaming. But the details were so precise. The geography of the Institute did not distort. She heard the coughing from the other rooms. The antiseptic tang stabbed at her absent nose and throat. And the dream did not let her transport herself without transition to the apartments. She came to the elevator. Though she had no fingers, she felt the touch of the button. Her spirit had to wait for the Institute's automatic elevator to arrive, and, clanking and whirring, take her up the tower.

The apartment doors opened to her on their own. She flew more quickly now, hurrying to her destination. She tried to hold back, realizing the goal of her journey and frightened of it.

An ethereal rip tide had her, and it yanked her toward the

painting. The canvas filled her vision, and she passed into it. Brush strokes resolved into reality, and now she flew over the grounds of the Stroud Estate.

The abbey ruins loomed ahead. A sense of being watched made her look back. She saw no one, only a cluster of huge boulders. The eyeless shapes gazed steadily at her.

Twenty feet above the ground, she sailed toward the ruins, ensnared by their command.

Before the orphaned archway, the entrance to roofless emptiness, Magnus Stroud capered, spinning around and around in a spiral dance. He saw her, and he stopped. The end of his dance froze her flight. She hovered, suspended, directly above him, the threshold of the ruins hungry and waiting.

Magnus smiled. He put a finger to his lips. *Hush.*

The ruins heaved, the earth buckling with the promise of a monstrous birth. The walls, tall and majestic despite their gaps and wounds, swayed. Stone rippled, then began to flow like candlewax.

The abbey melted, becoming a river of rushing, foaming stone. It flowed back toward the ring of boulders, and it took her with it. She flew back, even faster than she had arrived, and Magnus laughed to see her flight.

She hurtled at the boulders. The moment that she understood this was where she had emerged from the painting, she plunged into the center of the spiral and shot out across Donovan's apartment again.

The river of stone came with her. It thundered out of the painting in a torrent, and it caught her, submerging her in mossy gray as it spread over the Institute. Crushed, suffocating and drowning all at once, Miranda caught one last sense impression before the darkness. A serpentine vastness shifted, tightening coils.

Miranda jerked awake, gasping. She sat up, clawing at her chest. Her lungs fought to draw air thick as molasses.

In her panic, and in the dimness of the Institute's night lighting, it took her almost a minute to notice that Esme's bed lay empty.

Part II

CHAPTER NINE

"Esme passed away sometime after midnight," Nurse Holden said. She stood near the foot of Esme's bed. From that position, she could address the entire room. She turned her head slightly with each breath, looking directly at Frieda, Cleo and Miranda in turn. She spoke calmly, matter-of-factly, but also with genuine sorrow.

Holden, Miranda thought yet again, was *very* good at her job. She had come to tell them the truth, to give them leave to grieve, and to reassure them.

"The night nurse discovered her during one of her rounds," said Holden. "Director Stroud thought it best to take her away without waking the three of you. It would not have done you or anyone else on the ward any good to be woken in the middle of the night to that news."

All very true, all very correct, but the reference to a night nurse made Miranda flinch. Of course every ward had a night nurse. It would be strange, and worrying, if they did not. It was just that Miranda had not thought about there being one before now. She had always felt alone during the nights, the halls empty except for the visions that haunted them. The sudden reminder that she was not alone, that someone walked the corridors while she slept, disturbed her. Instead of being a comforting presence, a guardian of the sick, in her imagination the night nurse became a faceless, roaming presence.

Esme had died and vanished, and Miranda hadn't known. This was how things were supposed to work. Nothing odd or abnormal here.

Still, she flinched. She wished Holden had given the night nurse a name.

"What happened last night is hard for you," Holden went on. "It is for all of us. The goal of the Stroud Institute is to cure everybody who comes through the door. The fact that this is impossible doesn't make the reality any easier to accept. Now, I don't say this to make light of what happened, but this is not just a day of mourning. We have something to celebrate too."

Holden turned to the doorway. "We're ready, Jennifer," she said.

Jennifer Wong stepped into the room. She was dressed in her own clothes and wore an overcoat. She clutched a suitcase in one hand and gave them a little wave with the other. "I'm going home," she said. "My lungs are clear."

Miranda and Cleo applauded. "Well done!" Miranda cheered, as loudly as she dared without straining her voice.

"Good for you," Frieda muttered, glaring at Jennifer as if her recovery were a personal insult.

"You'll all be going home too," Jennifer said. "I know you will. You should have seen me when I first arrived."

"We'll miss you," Holden said, "just as much as we're happy to see you go."

When Jennifer left, Holden became solemn again, though she spoke with a determination meant to be contagious. She was there to stiffen their spines, Miranda thought.

"TB is a serious illness," said Holden. "I don't need to tell you that. Not everyone recovers. Deaths happen. But because Esme succumbed, that doesn't mean that any of you will. All your conditions are different, and none of you are as ill as Esme was. When she arrived at the Institute, her case was already extremely advanced."

"I always thought so," said Frieda. "Yes, clearly very advanced. And she was weak." Frieda spoke with too much vehemence. Her relief sounded forced.

Cleo said nothing, but her shoulders dropped, her body relaxing. She *was* relieved.

Everything Holden said was true. Miranda had no reason to doubt a word.

But having seen the empty bed in the aftermath of her vision, she could not shake the idea of a causal link.

On Wednesday, when Agatha arrived at the start of visiting hours, Miranda felt stronger again, and Agatha took her to the library. They had the room to themselves once more.

"Does anyone else use this place at all?" Agatha wondered.

"Maybe it only exists for us," said Miranda, only half-joking.

They sat by the window, and Miranda told Agatha about the vision. "Does Magnus write about boulders at all?" she asked. "Arranged like standing stones, but too big?"

"He does," said Agatha, looking grim. "The Stroud Spiral, he calls it. I found an entry about it after I'd left you." She held a finger up. "And that, Miranda, is our first real evidence of the parapsychological. You saw something you had no prior knowledge of. Can you describe it in more detail?"

Miranda did, and Agatha's expression became more certain and more grim.

"So it wasn't a dream," said Miranda.

"No. I think we can be definite about that. And you didn't need me to tell you it was more than a dream, did you?"

"It helps to hear it from you." Miranda took a long, slow breath that rattled. "I feel less alone. When the visions come, I really am alone. It's hard, Agatha."

Agatha took her hand. "I'm sorry. I wish I could do more."

Miranda nodded, grateful that Agatha was there and believing her. "So what now? Have you made any more progress?"

"On a couple of fronts, maybe, but the progress isn't reassuring."

"I haven't been expecting any reassurance from your research."

"That's good. First, then, I thought it would be worth looking into this particular site, see if there's a reason why Donovan decided to build his sanatorium here."

"And is there?"

"I haven't found a direct connection between Arkham and Galloway, though I didn't expect to. Arkham itself is enough of a reason to draw the attention of people like the Strouds."

"What do you mean?"

"You grew up here. You went away, though, for your

doctorate. Did you notice anything when you returned? Did Arkham *feel* different after having lived somewhere else?"

Miranda thought about it. She remembered her first day back, after several years in New York City, when she had come to be interviewed for the post at Miskatonic. Arkham *had* felt different, yes. The ground did not feel the same as in New York. Even the air had seemed foreign. At the time, she had put the impressions down to the effect of having become used to the sights, sounds, and pace of a big city. She had stopped noticing the taste of the air, or thinking that the ground was somehow less stable. But the more she thought about it, the more Miranda had to concede that a faint, barely noticeable background sense of *wrongness* had never gone away. "Yes," she said, "it did feel different. It does now too."

"Good," said Agatha. "Not everyone can feel that, I don't think. Many who do, try to argue themselves out of their own perceptions. That's a mistake, and I'm glad you're not making it. There is something about this town that… I'm not sure how to put this… causes or invites certain kinds of events, and certain kinds of people."

"What something?" Miranda asked.

"I wish I knew. I've made it my life's work to find out. In the meantime, what matters is that Arkham is Arkham, and whatever that means, it's enough to justify Donovan's eye falling on our town. As to this location, though, I did find out something more specific. There was a pest house here at the end of the eighteenth century. Built in 1794. It was gone by 1840, as best as I can tell."

"A pest house," Miranda repeated.

"I wish I could say it was a proto-sanatorium," said Agatha. "It wasn't, not the Arkham one."

"Let me guess. More like a storage facility for the sick."

"Yes," said Agatha. "Tuberculosis, cholera, smallpox – the whole nine contagious yards. If you had it, and you could spread it, then you were quarantined here."

"Would I be wrong in thinking you just used *quarantined* as a euphemism?"

"You would not be. Not many of those who crossed its threshold ever came out again."

"What happened to the dead?"

"Buried on the grounds," said Agatha. "Unmarked graves. No graveyard for them."

"And now a sanatorium erected over their bones," said Miranda. "Were they exhumed before construction began?"

"I wondered about that too. I went through everything I could in city archives. No sign of any such order."

Miranda grimaced. "We saw how deep the foundations were dug during construction. If the bodies weren't removed…"

"Right. Then they were disturbed violently by the process. They'll have been scattered around. Some of them, or parts of them, hauled away with the dirt and disposed of who knows where. Others might still be in the grounds."

"Or ground to dust."

"That too. Now keep all this in mind while I tell you about the test I performed. I have an Atwater-Kent battery radio. I drove down here with it last night."

"Why did you do that?"

"It's an experiment I've preformed at or near other sights with reported phenomena. It's another way of trying to register their existence. I tune the radio to static, and see if I hear anything unusual."

"And did you?"

"Not exactly. I didn't hear anything *at all*."

"I don't understand."

"I set the radio to static before I left home. I had it on as I drove. I heard nothing but static all the way down. But when I came close to the gates, the static cut out. Dead silence."

"Dead silence," Miranda repeated.

"Sorry. Not the best choice of words, given what I told you about the grounds."

"Maybe exactly the right words," said Miranda. "Does that silence tell you anything?"

"Not yet, but it is a clear symptom. This is how we gather the evidence. Individually, the pieces might not look like anything. But I do believe, I *have* to believe, that eventually a picture will emerge."

Miranda thought again about the dead beneath the Institute's foundations. "Do you think building here, on this particular site, was deliberate?" she asked.

"On Donovan's part?" Agatha shrugged. "Did he even know about the bodies? Maybe. Could he have arranged for nothing to be exhumed? Not impossible, I suppose, but this could easily be explained as bureaucratic negligence."

"The innocent explanation we can't dismiss," said Miranda.

"*Innocent* might be a bit of a stretch, but yes."

"Only you don't buy that any more than I do."

"It's definitely not the first on my list of likely scenarios," Agatha said. "And there's something else interesting I found. The land originally belonged to the family of Payton Wallace."

Miranda felt her lips twitch in disgust. “The good councilman who worked so hard to get the city’s approval for the Institute’s construction.”

“He certainly did. You should see the transcripts of the debates. He was most eloquent.”

“Did he still own the land?” Miranda asked.

“I wondered about that. The archives weren’t much help on that front. Too many gaps. So I don’t know.”

“He could be involved with Donovan in some way, then.” Miranda examined the idea, and wasn’t satisfied. “Payton strikes me as too callow to be deliberately engaged in something sinister.”

“It may be a case of simple bribery, then,” said Agatha. “Or maybe not even that. I’ll see what he has to say for himself.”

“You’re going to see him?”

“I managed to get a late-day appointment. I’m not expecting much from our meeting, but I don’t want to leave any possible lead unexplored. And he has tied himself to the sanatorium, one way or another.”

For a brief moment, Miranda allowed herself to entertain the idea that they were about to uncover mundane corruption. It was pure pretense, one she just needed for a few seconds, a reprieve from the more terrifying prospects. Fiddled deals at city hall didn’t explain anything, and she knew it. But it was nice to pretend.

The moment passed, and she let the dream of a normal world flutter away. It had been sweet while it lasted.

Her mind went back to the pest house.

“It would be nice to take comfort in the fact that the Stroud Institute’s track record is better than its predecessor’s,” she said.

"It would be," Agatha agreed. "You might as well hang on to the comfort you can for now. At least the track record is real."

"You checked on the people who've been released?"

"I have. They're doing well."

Miranda sighed. "Well, that's something, anyway. And I guess we know why the Institute is here."

"Not exactly," said Agatha. "We have established a connection, a reason for Donovan to be interested, but we don't know his purpose."

"That brings us back to the Strouds, then. Any more luck with Magnus?"

"That's where the research hasn't been as productive," said Agatha. "I've gone through the *Miscellany* backwards and forwards. I've squeezed everything I could out of it. I haven't found any other promising sources. It ends with him going on and on about his dream of a community of artists. There's no indication if he actually did something about it."

"So that's a dead end."

"Yes. I don't think we've learned all there is to learn about Magnus."

"As far as what Arkham offers, you mean."

"That's right."

They sat without speaking for a full minute, both of them conscious of what had to happen next. Miranda didn't want to give voice to the words. If she did, she would hurry the moment of being truly alone. Agatha seemed just as reluctant to broach the subject.

Miranda forced herself to break the silence. "Galloway," she said. Speaking the word felt like putting wheels in motion.

She looked at the months ahead with a sharp spike of dread. The library seemed to grow dim, motes of darkness gathering in the air around her.

"Yes," said Agatha. "If we're going to learn more, that's where I have to go. And given your vision, I'd say my being on-site is imperative. The sooner the better." She grimaced. "I don't like saying this, but it seems to me that whatever is happening is getting worse."

"My visions sure are."

"And though we don't know that Esme's death is connected in any way…"

"We don't know that it isn't, either."

"And that's the problem."

"Yes," said Miranda. "We need to know."

Agatha squeezed her hand. "I don't like the idea of leaving you alone."

"I'm not wild about it myself."

"Maybe there's an alternative."

Miranda shook her head. *Come on now. Be strong.* "No. You have to go. We can't pretend nothing is going on."

Agatha gave her a tight, approving smile. "No, we can't."

"And I'm not alone, not really. Or at least, I won't be worse off with you gone. It isn't like you can be here during the nights, and even if you were, what could you do? I have friends here."

"We could see about having you transferred to the hospital," Agatha offered.

"No," Miranda said hesitantly, and then more emphatically. "No. The care here *is* good. And I'm feeling a bit better. Better than I was before being admitted."

"That's some good news, then."

"This is the thing," said Miranda. "We know something is happening in Arkham, and it looks like it's linked somehow to Magnus Stroud, but we don't know that it's centered on the Institute. My first vision was in my apartment, after all."

"The night before you came here," Agatha pointed out.

"I know," Miranda conceded.

"Tell me the real reason why you don't want to leave," Agatha said. "This is important. If you're making this choice, it has to be a clear one." She held up that finger again. "No rationalizations."

"Right." Miranda gave herself a moment. She needed to be sure. Putting the thought into words had consequences. "If there is something happening here, then someone has to fight it. There's only so much you can do from the outside. I'm here. If I don't fight, who will?"

There. She had said it. There could be no more pretending, ever, that nothing was wrong, and that she had just been imagining things. She couldn't hide behind that delusion any longer. No going back. Only forward now, into the gathering darkness.

Agatha squeezed her hand. "I'm proud of you," she said.

Miranda forced herself to smile. "Thanks." She knew she had made the right choice. She just wished she felt more proud than frightened. "How long will you be gone?" She had already begun the countdown to Agatha's return.

"Hard to say. Depending on the bookings I can make, let's allow for a week each way for the Atlantic crossing. Another few days of travel to and from Galloway, and that's assuming I can find an inn close to the Stroud Estate. As for how long the research will take me there, and what other travel might be involved, I don't know. Any guesses?"

"You might have to chase down records and look through archives in Edinburgh or Glasgow," Miranda said bleakly. "Or elsewhere." Agatha could be gone a month or more. An eternity, Miranda thought. She would be alone, and would have no idea when Agatha might be back.

"I'm not gone yet," said Agatha. She put her hand on Miranda's.

"No, but you must," Miranda told her. "If you don't, we won't be doing any good." She tried to shake her apprehension. "I'll be fine. It's not like the corpses are stacking up outside the Institute. Esme died, but Jennifer went home. This is still a place that's making people well."

"All right," said Agatha. "This is what we're doing, then. I'll head off as soon as I have tickets. I'll be back as soon as I can."

"Please do," Miranda said. "Please hurry."

A draft touched the back of her neck, the library breathing down on her, its teeth about to brush against her skin.

The councilman kept Agatha cooling her heels in the waiting room until the very end of the working day. The reception area had a carpet in rich red, and some gilt-framed paintings that were very passable pre-Raphaelite imitations. Agatha sat on a wooden chair, an antique clearly valuable, and strategically uncomfortable, and refused to give in to impatience. The struggle was hard. She should be home, preparing for the trip. Time wasted here was time she could not get back, and she had really hoped to be on a train by the evening. Yes, that might not be realistic, but she didn't want to dismiss the hope.

If she lost a day, that could mean a day longer for Miranda to be left on her own. Not necessarily, but maybe.

So many maybes, and so much time slipping away pointlessly.

Still, Agatha held her temper. Losing it would be a defeat. It helped that the receptionist was a young woman with, Agatha suspected, definite views about the utility of anyone over the age of fifty. She glanced at Agatha from time to time as if gauging whether the peasant had been taught her place yet. That gave Agatha someone to fight, so she kept her face placid. She barely moved, didn't even glance at the three-day-old newspaper insultingly set out on the low table before her.

Finally, more than an hour after Agatha's appointment time, the receptionist's phone rang. She picked it up, listened, acknowledged, and then begrudgingly informed Agatha that Councilman Wallace would see her now.

"Thank you," Agatha said without rancor, and also without the gratitude that was clearly due for being permitted to see the great and busy man.

Agatha had been surprised by the visual luxury of the waiting room. It turned out to be as nothing compared to Payton's actual office. Its polished dark wood, spacious dimensions and treed view were there for the clear purpose of creating envy and awe. So were the plentiful paintings and objets d'art. The councilman was not a man, it seemed, who had to rely on his salary as the sole source of income.

Then there was the larger-than-life portrait of Payton. Its scale and the heroic pose of the model made Agatha feel better. Instead of holding back her anger, she now struggled to suppress her laughter.

Payton stood up behind his huge desk. "Do please forgive me for the delay," he said. "Pressing business. I'm sure you understand."

"I do," she said, with enough edge to let him know he wasn't fooling anyone.

Payton smiled. "Please sit down." He gestured to the chair in front of the desk.

No, she thought, she would not sit in that. It was so low, she would barely be able to see over the top of the desk. Payton could have his little games with someone else.

"Thank you," she said. "I'll stand."

Payton missed a beat, thrown by her refusal to follow the script. "As you wish," he said. Another beat, as he debated whether to sit or stand himself. He sat, and from the look on his face, regretted his choice immediately. He was stuck now, though. He couldn't stand back up without looking ridiculous.

He folded his hands and leaned forward, making a concerted show of being comfortable in her presence. "Now, Mrs Crane–"

"Professor Crane," Agatha corrected him.

Payton coughed. "Excuse me," he said, the purpose of the apology ambiguous. "What can I do for you?"

"I was hoping you could fill in some research gaps for me," said Agatha.

"About what?"

"The Stroud Institute."

Payton's right eye twitched.

"Specifically," said Agatha, "why you fought so hard for it."

"Why would I not fight for what is so clearly a good thing for Arkham?"

"Your passion for this cause seems to me to have been of a different order than you usually display in council, I have to say. I've read the transcripts."

Payton smiled patiently. "I fight for what I believe in," he said.

"And your belief had nothing to do with your family's ownership of that land."

"That's outrageous!" Indignation reddened Payton's cheeks. He pointed a warning finger at Agatha. "You're fortunate there is no one else present to hear you say that, or I would be starting legal proceedings against you. I resent your implications about my character. And that land has not been a Wallace possession for a long time."

"That doesn't explain why there was no exhumation of the human remains."

Payton's jaw dropped. He recovered quickly and didn't even stammer, but Agatha knew she had struck home.

"The land is not a graveyard," he said. "It has never been zoned as such. There was no need for an exhumation. If there were any remains found, they were treated with due respect."

If there were any remains found. In other words, Payton had made sure not to know, one way or the other. Maybe his involvement with Donovan was one of basic bribery after all. How Payton expected Agatha to see the flaunted art in his office and presume him to be honest was beyond her. She gave the councilman a long look, and what she saw in him, she decided, was a mixture of ignorance and cunning. A dangerous combination, because it was also the right sort of politician's recipe for success.

Agatha found that she believed Payton's anger. He didn't

know anything bad about the Institute, and therefore didn't know anything useful to her. That didn't mean he couldn't be of some use himself, though. She wondered if the right words might turn another set of suspicious eyes on the place.

"I apologize," she said, and he leaned back in his chair, somewhat mollified. "Your conscience may well be clear when it comes to the construction of the Stroud Institute. Do you think the same will be true of your political record if something is wrong there?"

That got his attention. She finally saw genuine concern on his face. "What do you mean? What's wrong?"

"Possibly nothing, but then again, possibly much. This is what I am investigating."

"Surely the police…"

Agatha shook her head. "I'm not talking about criminal activity. What may be wrong there is outside the authority of the police." She braced herself. What she said next might have her thrown out of the office on her ear. "My particular study consists of the careful, scientific investigation of parapsychological phenomena." Better to multiply the syllables, hit him with words he might not understand but have to pretend that he did, and so couldn't easily dismiss. "I have evidence of such phenomena occurring at the Institute. The evidence is tentative at this point, but it is of concern." She didn't say to whom. Let him wonder if other people, perhaps ones he had to take seriously, were also taking a look at the Institute.

Payton said nothing for a long moment, his brow furrowed as he tried to parse what she had said, and what it might mean for him. "Has something happened to the patients?"

"Nothing that can't, *as yet*, be presented as natural causes." Everything she said was true. The presentation, though, she shaped to worry Payton.

I should have gone into politics.

Her tactic worked. He looked very worried now, and he hadn't even asked her what *parapsychological* meant. "I appreciate your bringing this to my attention," he said.

"My investigations are taking me away from Arkham for a while," said Agatha. "So I won't be able to provide you with any updates." She spoke confidentially now, as if he were a long-term ally and part of the small group that was in the know.

"I will be taking a closer look at the Stroud Institute myself," said Payton, his voice stronger again, closing in on being condescending again as he reassured her that he was now on the case.

"That's very good to hear," Agatha said. She gave him her best grateful smile. And she *was* grateful. She didn't think for a moment that he could do anything except make his scrutiny visible, and that might impede Donovan in some way.

Maybe.

If something was happening at all.

"If I may make a suggestion," she said, all deference. She even sat down.

"Please do."

"If there is, in fact, something going on, it will be well disguised. Be wary of what is normal and the easy explanation. Be especially wary of the explanations for things that bother you, even if you aren't sure why."

For a moment, Payton looked like a little boy who had been told a very scary bedtime story.

Good. The visit had not been a waste of time, after all.

"Did you get through?" Agatha asked Wilbur. Her husband had been on the phone in the apartment's entrance hall, calling the ticket offices of the shipping lines, looking for a last-minute third-class tourist booking that wouldn't bankrupt them. They had no children, and inheritances on both sides had left them comfortable in their retirement. Agatha's research called for travel, and they'd been able to afford her voyages up to now. She had never gone with such short notice before, though.

"Had some luck with White Star," Wilbur said. "You're on tomorrow's sailing of the *Leviathan*."

Agatha turned away from the suitcases opened on the bed and kissed Wilbur. He smiled, and lost some of the *this, again?* look in his eyes. He was a small, thin man, his bald head just a bit large for his slight frame. He was built for a quiet retirement, and Agatha loved him all the more for how well he had accepted that would not be their lot.

"So," he said. "Off again."

"Only because I have to." She went back to her packing. She stuffed another notebook into one of the cases. Better to have too many than not enough.

"An Atlantic crossing," Wilbur said. "In early spring, no less. Sure to be smooth sailing all the way."

"Lucky I don't get seasick, then."

"I was thinking about my own poor stomach."

Agatha paused, a sweater half folded. She looked at Wilbur.

He grinned. "Got us two tickets," he said. "Seemed like sense."

"Oh, you sweet old fool!" She threw her arms around him and hugged him tight before releasing him to become all business again. "You're sure you're up for this?"

"Well, I'm sure that I'm not going to be without you for this long again."

"On your head be it, then." She kept her tone light, but she wasn't joking. She went to her dresser and unlocked the small, dark chest that sat on top. She looked at the amulets and rings inside, thinking about protection for two.

"Are you doing something dangerous?" Wilbur asked.

"I don't know. I really don't." Just like she didn't know which object would help or why. Belief? Actual properties that obeyed a scientific principle she hadn't yet discovered?

"And if you don't go, will something bad happen?"

"I'm worried it might. Though I also don't know if my going will make a difference."

She chose two silver medallions. She had had them made two years earlier, commissioning a design that replicated one on a medallion in the special archaeological collection at Miskatonic. No one had yet been able to date the object. It appeared to be much older than the detail of the design permitted.

Agatha held the silver disks in her hand and felt comforted. She gave one to Wilbur.

"Keep this with you once we get to Galloway," she said. "*Always*."

"If you say so."

"I do." When he put it in his pocket with the care he might have given to explosives, she kissed his cheek. "You do put up with a lot from me, don't you?"

He shrugged. “I don’t understand any of it. Probably best that I don’t. But who is going to stop you? Not me. And I don’t think I should.”

He shuffled off to get his suitcases out of the storage closet.

Agatha moved to the bedroom window. She looked down toward the Institute. “Sleep well and be strong,” she murmured. “I’ll be back soon.”

She hoped she would be soon enough.

CHAPTER TEN

The first two weeks after Agatha left were quiet. Miranda's dread receded to the point that she felt the temptation to consider everything she had experienced as a dream after all. She hadn't had any further visions. She slept through most nights, and the few times she had woken up, anxiety crawling over her skin, there had been nothing to alarm her. She had calmed down and gone back to sleep.

She also felt better. Her sense of increasing well-being was real. She was sure of it. Her chest still ached, her energy was a fraction of what it had been before she fell sick, and fever gave her alternating chills and sweats during the night. But none of the symptoms were as bad as when she'd arrived. She sometimes went for half an hour or more without coughing. Breathing had become less of a strain. She had enough energy to be bored during the day, and even enough to do something about that boredom, crack a book, and read for entire minutes before falling asleep again.

Rested, feeling stronger, she found it easy to believe all was well. Easy to tell herself she had been imagining things.

Except she had seen the Stroud Spiral before knowing it existed. And Agatha had gone to Scotland. Agatha believed Miranda had experienced something real, and that worried the parapsychologist.

Even so, Miranda accepted the reprieve gratefully. She wanted to believe she was improving even more strongly than she wanted to believe nothing had happened.

Miranda took advantage of the calm to think about *why* she had the respite. The absence of evidence made it hard to theorize. All she had to go on was her experience, and she wondered if there was a pattern to the ebb and flow of night terrors. At first, she pictured the movements of a tide. During the one night that she did lie awake in the pre-dawn hours, she found herself imagining the whirl of a slow vortex with her at the center, terror spiraling to and away from her, tethered to her and following an arc she could not quite see.

Turning and turning in the widening gyre…

Yes, but in this instance the falconer was at the mercy of the falcon. It flew at her and away, responding to whims of horror. The center could not hold, and neither could she flee. The falcon would whirl and whirl, near and far, and always the talons would come again.

She did not like the image, or the way it resonated with her heart as truth. It kept her awake for much of that night, the fourth after Agatha's departure. In the morning, though, the conceit lost some of its power. It seemed too convoluted, too much the product of a fatigued imagination. She did not abandon it. She kept it in the back of her mind. But she did not feel its claws during the night.

Two days after Esme's death, Lupita Guerrero became the

new resident of the fourth bed. Lupita was in her mid-70s, her hair white and streaked with black, as if testifying to her strength. Intensely pious, she knelt by her bed to pray every night. She did so in silence, holding hard to her crucifix, and with an unshowy dignity that met with Cleo's approval, and annoyed Frieda, who somehow took it as a rebuke.

Ten days after the night of the vision, Nurse Revere informed Miranda that her tests were looking good, and that she now had permission to take short walks. Revere delivered the news with the severity of a judge pronouncing sentence, and Miranda took the message that she should not take her new privilege for granted.

"Thank you," Miranda said, with all due solemnity. Keeping a straight face was hard. She felt giddy. She really was getting better. She wanted to leap up and drag Revere into a dance. Instead, she said, "And thank you for your guidance."

Revere's stony gaze stayed on Miranda a few moments longer, as if scanning for sarcasm. Then she gave a curt nod and left.

Miranda's first journeys without the chair, just to one end of the corridor and back, went well. Her energy levels fluctuated, but her breathing remained steady. And so, two weeks after Agatha left, Nurse Holden told Miranda that she was well enough to start attending the counseling sessions.

"Is it mandatory?" Miranda asked. She had no objection to going; she was simply curious.

"No," said Holden. "It's up to you. I do recommend the sessions, though. They keep your mind more active than the mental exercises you've been doing here, and the active mind helps lead to a healthy body."

"I'll look forward to them," Miranda said.

Cleo and Frieda had just started going the week before. The privilege of doing something that Miranda was not yet part of turned the sessions into Frieda's new obsessive focus of conversation, even though she struggled to be specific about what was actually said. Cleo didn't help her out.

"They're interesting," she said to Miranda without elaboration. "You'll see. I know you'll be going soon too."

Lupita, much stronger than Esme, and – Miranda enviously suspected – stronger than she was herself, was also invited to start the sessions. On Friday, the four women wheeled themselves to what Holden had called the seminar room. As they made their way there, Miranda said, "I don't think I'll ever get the hang of the layout of this place." She kept her tone light. Just a casual remark, a random cast, nothing more.

She watched the others carefully.

Frieda clucked her tongue. "If you can't follow signs, then you deserve to get lost."

Cleo rolled her eyes at Frieda's remark and gave Miranda a sympathetic grimace. "Hospitals," she said. "I kept getting lost at St Mary's too."

Lupita bit her lip. She said nothing. Her reaction made Miranda feel a little less alone, and more than a little guilty for poking at a sore.

Miranda's first sight of the Stroud Institute's library had surprised her. The seminar room surprised her again. It had smaller windows than the library but seemed much airier and brighter. Cream and light green washes defined the wallpaper, with energetic lines and splashes of bright color conjuring irises, lilies, and entwining vines, a garden spare and lively, calming while bursting with life. Tall, potted ferns in the corners extended the soothing energy of the wallpaper into the room. A dozen leather chaise lounge formed a circle, with enough space between each to make it easy for the patients to park their wheelchairs and transfer onto the furniture. The circle surrounded a table, a pole raising its narrow surface to the height of a podium. It held a few books, some pens, and a sheaf of papers.

Once all the patients were settled, the door opened again and a woman walked into the room.

No, Miranda thought. That was wrong. She did not walk. She *flowed*. She moved with a dancer's grace, a dancer who never left the stage, and whose every gesture was part of a lifelong motion of grace. She had her black hair in a flapper's cut. Miranda put her in her late twenties, and her skin had the eerie perfection of a porcelain doll. She smiled at the group as she made her way to the center of the circle, and her teeth were perfect too, dazzling white between shining lipstick of a red so deep it was almost black. When she spoke, her voice seemed to be an extension of her body's endless grace, soft and low, the caress of a summer's breeze. She wore a black top and skirt; at odds with her haircut, the skirt was long and swayed with her movements, a partner in her dance.

"Welcome, welcome!" she said, making a graceful turn that extended her greeting to every woman in the room. Miranda felt seen. She felt cared for. The woman had only spoken four syllables, and Miranda couldn't wait to hear more.

"I'm so glad to see all of you back, and to see some new faces as well. To those just joining us, don't worry about catching up. We only just started this group of sessions last week. My name is Daria Miracle." She rolled her eyes. "I know. That last name is a bit much. But it's the one I have, so please be gentle with me."

Daria grinned, and Miranda grinned back. If Miracle was her name, then let her be one. Miranda was already halfway to believing Daria would embody her family's name.

She noticed the other women were grinning and laughing with Daria too.

Daria clapped her hands together in delight. "Splendid! We're all having a good time together, and we haven't even got going, yet. I think we'll have a fine afternoon. Don't you?"

More smiles. Everyone nodded.

"Good, good. So, for our new friends, let me tell you what we're up to during these hours." She paused and grew serious, her voice even more gentle, a balm for the soul. "TB is scary. Of course it is. It's a serious illness, and, well, all of you know what can happen. TB can make you feel like you've lost control. Or that you are lost, plain and simple. What I want to do is to help you feel stronger. Just because something *can* happen, that doesn't mean it *will* happen. After all, you're here to get well. Aren't you?"

"Yes," Frieda breathed. It was the closest to pleading Miranda had ever heard from her.

"You're not lost," said Daria. "You do have agency."

"We also have faith," Lupita said.

"That too."

Daria's agreement sounded genuine. Yet Lupita's lower lip trembled. Very slightly, very briefly. As if she had felt stricken, and then the moment had passed, virtually forgotten, but leaving a faint residue of confusion behind.

Why? Miranda wondered.

Lupita seemed to be wondering too.

Daria carved an arc in the air with her arm as she began to recite. "*In middle of the journey of our days / I found that I was in a darksome wood– / The right road lost and vanished in the maze.*" She lowered her arm. "Dante felt lost on his journey in mid-life. Some of you haven't reached that point yet. Oops, I mean *none* of you have."

More general laughter. Frieda looked schoolgirl-pleased.

"My point is," said Daria, "that we can feel lost on any stage of our journey. How did we get to this point? To every point? Is it fate or choice that decides?"

"God's will," Lupita murmured under her breath.

Daria heard, all the same. "Or God's will?" she added, and winked at Lupita. "These are big questions. I'm not the one with the answers."

The confidence in that last sentence suggested to Miranda that Daria didn't have the answers, but she knew who did.

"None of you chose to contract TB," said Daria. "Or am I wrong?" A chorus of "No!" answered her. "So it's understandable if you feel confused." Daria began to walk slowly around the circle. She came close to every chaise lounge, creating greater intimacy between herself and the patients. "If you didn't choose to get TB, why do you have it? Is fate cruel? Is God punishing you? Are you just the victim of meaningless chance? Does any of that sound right?"

More denials. Daria walked a full circuit in sympathetic silence. Then she returned to the center of the circle. She picked up two pieces of paper from the table. "Does anyone know the difference between a maze and a labyrinth?" she asked.

Miranda knew. She said nothing, growing more and more conscious of the performance nature of Daria's presentation. The initial seduction had worn off, and now Miranda was feeling played rather than seen. So she watched the session from a distance, curious instead of involved.

"Aren't they the same thing?" Frieda asked.

"They aren't," said Daria. "Many people think they are, and it's easy to see why." She held the two pages up and turned around slowly, showing them to the entire group. The illustrations on the sheets were similar. At first glance, the only difference between them was that one was a square, the other a circle. Both contained a density of lines.

Daria lifted the square higher. "This is a maze," she said. "The difference is not in the outer shape. That can be anything. It's what's inside the walls that matters. When you enter a maze, you must constantly decide what branching path to take. There are so many choices, but only one correct route. The maze is designed to be frustrating. The labyrinth, though, is soothing. The labyrinth has only one path. No matter how many times it turns and twists, there are no forks in the road, no wrong decisions to make. When you enter the labyrinth, you know you will reach the center. In a maze, you are lost. You might never find the way. In a labyrinth, you are never lost."

Riveted, Lupita said, "The labyrinth is God's plan."

"If you like," said Daria, "in whatever way you choose to understand that idea."

Again, Miranda thought Lupita looked a little betrayed, as if her revelation had met with dismissal.

Daria put the papers down. "You are at a point in your

lives where you seem to have no choice. You feel powerless."

Miranda had to admit Daria's bolt struck home there.

"I want to invite you to walk the soothing labyrinth with us. Think of your treatment as a labyrinth. There will be many turns. You can't see far ahead. You can only see to the next bend. But you know you'll make it to the center. That's what you came here to do."

Daria paused, her smile fixed and caring while she waited for her audience to take in her words. Then she went on.

"Maybe the image of the labyrinth is useful just for your time with us. If that's the case for you, then I'm glad it's useful here and now. But I encourage you to think about the labyrinth as the symbol for your entire path through life. You'll never know for certain if your outcomes are determined by choice or by destiny. But maybe that doesn't matter. Maybe you don't need to worry about that debate at all. What if you simply accept the twists and turns in your life as being the path of the larger labyrinth that you walk? After all, whatever choices you have made, and whatever chance events you have encountered, they have all been paving stones in the one route that is your life."

Daria paused again. She touched one of the books with a pensive finger.

Nice theatrics, Miranda thought. Was she not going to talk about the books at all? Were they just for show? They were good props, then, leather with old, cracked spines, ancient soldiers recruited for this mission from the library.

"If you see your life as a labyrinth," Daria said, speaking more slowly, delivering the lesson, "then you know that whatever happens, this is *your* route, and you can never be lost." Yet one more pause, and a solemn nod before she blazed with fervor again. "We're going to explore the labyrinth together. So you won't be lost, and you also won't be alone."

Applause all around, even from Miranda.

That was really good. Very entertaining. First rate show.

Daria never did do anything with the books. She did distribute pens and paper, though. The patients went back to their rooms with a maze and a labyrinth, and the challenge to find a path to trace.

The puzzles impressed Miranda. They reinforced Daria's points, and they made Miranda *feel* the argument. She solved the maze, but not without cursing under her breath as she crossed out one wrong route after another. When she reached the center, her paper looked a mess. *And this is why Daria gave us pens, and not pencils.* No erasing of mistakes. She had to live with the growing, unsightly mess of the dead ends.

Miranda could tell when the other women in the room were working on the maze. They frowned, bit their lips, glared at the paper, and did lots of angry scribbling.

The labyrinth, by contrast, soothed her, just as Daria had promised. The convoluted path seemed to take hold of the pen and gently pull her through to the end. As she traced the line back and forth, up and down, left and right in zigs and zags to its single end, she felt herself easing into a meditative state, less conscious of her tired, laboring body.

She finished by blinking, as if waking up from an unexpected nap.

Miranda looked around at the others. It was strange to see

Frieda thoughtful; Cleo and Lupita were deep in their own musings too. The room felt strangely quiet.

Miranda broke the silence. "What did all of you think about today?"

"Daria Miracle is a wise woman," Frieda pronounced. "Everyone would do well to heed her lessons." She nodded in agreement with herself, and in anticipation of a consensus. "I wonder if she speaks elsewhere. Reginald and his friends should hear her."

Cleo grunted. "She knows how to speak, that woman. She surely does."

"Does that mean you buy what she's selling?" Miranda asked.

Cleo made a face. "Don't like not having a choice." She folded up the two puzzles, creasing them with decisive energy. "I make my own choices and my own mistakes, thanks all the same."

Was she protesting too much? She spoke more loudly than necessary.

Lupita said nothing. She kept looking at her crucifix as if she didn't recognize it.

Miranda had another night without dreams. Lupita did, though, and her dreams woke Miranda. An hour before dawn, Miranda opened her eyes, startled awake by pleading and the sounds of loss.

CHAPTER ELEVEN
Scotland, 1806

Magnus walked through his grounds, trying not to look a fool by grinning too broadly. He had to work hard, and he almost didn't care. He felt giddy. He had turned the Republic of the Arts into a reality.

It had only been a couple of weeks since the first poets and artists had begun to arrive, and only today could he say that all of the cottages he had had built were occupied. The Republic had only just been born. But it lived. It no longer existed only in his dreams. People of revolutionary creativity lived together and worked here. He had created the conditions for his estate to become the artistic pole star for the young century.

The cottages were scattered by design. Some nestled in the trees closer to the Hall. Others braved the elements on the open moor. Magnus had directed that enough space be left between the thatched cottages that the inhabitants of one would barely be aware of those of another. The privacy and isolation necessary for artistic endeavor had to be preserved.

At the same time, the Republic should also be a community. So he had created what he called a village square in the shadow of the Stroud Spiral. It was a simple affair: a fire pit large enough for a proper bonfire, stone benches forming a semicircle around it. Anyone present would be facing the boulders and see them lit up by the flames and dancing with shadow. Magnus had ordered that a bonfire be lit every night. It initiated the gatherings, drawing the artists and writers to the heat and light.

They had need of both. Fall had come early, and the first days of September felt like mid-October. A chilly, rainy start to the Republic of the Arts, but Magnus didn't care. The weather created the need for more community in the evenings, and the days were warm enough for the work of creation to carry on uninterrupted.

Magnus stopped beside the fire pit for a moment, watching his servants prepare the wood for the evening. One of the poets, a slight, limping young woman named Christina Blackstone, sat on a bench, scribbling in her notebook.

Magnus sighed with delight and satisfaction. He had done it. He had told William of his hopes, and he had made them concrete in just over a year.

He wished that William had wanted to be part of it. He had been an eager collaborator in shaping the early forms of the dream when they were at St John's College in Cambridge together. But he had shown none of that interest when Magnus had brought him to the estate. William's mood had chilled; he had been uninterested in any of the schemes Magnus had tried to lay out for him, and he had left the estate the next day, in a sudden hurry to get away when the original intent had been for him to spend the week in Galloway.

William had not returned since. He wrote, but only when Magnus did first. His letters were civil but distant. Magnus grieved to think he had lost a friend without knowing why.

William, I wish you could see what I've done. Why did he draw away? Why wouldn't he rejoice in the realization of the project? The closer Magnus came to welcoming the first citizens of the Republic of the Arts, the slower and more curt William became in answering letters.

Maybe it was disillusionment. Magnus had noticed William turning more and more away from the promises of revolution. The souring of the dream in France had also soured William on its principles too, it seemed.

Magnus shook away his gloom. William's apostasy, if that's what it was, didn't matter. The Republic mattered. Its reality mattered. Magnus had created it himself. His dream, his accomplishment.

Arranging for the construction of the cottages had been the easy part. He had the means to hire whoever he needed to make small, simple, but comfortable homes. What had been more difficult had been finding a population for the Republic. That had taken time, research and patience. The Republic had nothing of interest for the more established or dissolute creators of revolutionary poetry, and that seemed, unfortunately, to account for a great many of the people Magnus thought of as the sort of poet or painter he wanted to support.

He tried courting William Blake. Magnus admired his work and knew he was part of a very select number to do so.

Blake was poor; Magnus could do a lot for him. Six months after William Wordsworth had departed the Stroud Estate, William Blake had come for a visit.

Things did not go well. Blake arrived late evening. During the night, he woke the entire Hall with his screams. The nightmare left him pale, shaking and weak, but he refused to talk about it. Refused, also, to set foot outside the Hall. For hours, Blake stared out at the grounds from the front windows as if demons lurked beyond the trees. He left for London without breakfasting.

Then, as if fate decided it had to make amends for the disaster with Blake, Magnus' luck turned. He combed through issues of *The Edinburgh Review* and *The Gentleman's Quarterly*, searching for hints of other poets, other artists, less well-known but still of the right sort. Disapproval from some quarters became signs of hope for Magnus. He would be the patron of the reviled and the abandoned. They would come to him because they would see that he shared their vision.

And they came. First one, then a few more. Soon, the Republic of the Arts counted twenty-three citizens.

I've done it.

The thought made him feel giddy again. Regrets about what had happened with the two Williams evaporated.

Magnus wandered over to where Christina Blackstone sat. She looked up at his approach and rose to curtsey.

"Please sit," he said. "I hope I'm not interrupting the flow of your composition."

"Not at all, my lord. I don't think that's even possible here." She sounded as giddy as he felt.

"So the grounds here aren't too sylvan for you?" Christina

was a poet of the Graveyard School. Her work that Magnus had seen was icy meditations on gloom and loss. "I'm sorry I don't have a graveyard to offer you." No Strouds had been buried on the grounds since the dissolution of the monasteries, and the earlier markers that must have been present had been removed when the abbey fell.

Christina smiled. She ran a hand over the page of her notebook. "I have been visiting the ruins of your abbey, my lord. There is fuel enough for a lifetime of inspiration there."

"I'm very glad to hear it."

"I was wondering if the abbey's crypt is safe to visit."

Magnus frowned. "The crypt?" In all his childhood explorations of the ruins, he'd never seen the entrance to a crypt.

"It's in what I judge was once the chapel," said Christina. "Near where the altar might have been."

Magnus knew where she meant. "You saw a way down?" There had been nothing there the last time he had been, just before the first citizens of the Republic had arrived.

"I did, but I did not know if it was safe, or permitted."

"Your caution does you credit," said Magnus. "I will have to see for myself, and I will let you know." He thought for a minute. "If there is something there, I find it remarkable that it has been hidden for so long, and even more remarkable that it suddenly became visible at this juncture."

"Like an omen," Christina breathed, her eyes shining with excitement.

"Quite so."

"I have been feeling, my lord, as if my entire life were a path leading to this place. It is a sense of destiny."

Magnus' blood thrummed with euphoria. Destiny. He wasn't alone in feeling it. The Republic was going to be more than a center of creation. It was something that was *meant* to be.

To what end?

He didn't know yet. He might never know. Its purpose might not be revealed until long after his death. But he had a new certainty now: the certainty of legacy.

He had to see what Christina had found in the abbey.

"I believe all of us are here in answer to a calling," he said. "You have just confirmed that belief. We will speak of this again soon."

She blushed and smiled with shy pride.

He left her, making his way toward the abbey. Midway between the Spiral and the ruins, he saw that Alfred Claymot had set his easel up on the moor, a short distance away from his cottage. He lived in one of the loneliest and most wind-battered homes on the estate. He had two canvases with him, one on the easel, the other leaning against its legs. Hands on his hips, Alfred looked from the canvases to the abbey and the Spiral, and then back again.

As Magnus drew close, he saw that the two paintings were unfinished landscapes. They looked like dreams of the moor, their details yet to emerge from a fog of colors. There was little indication of what the completed work would look like, and that, Magnus knew, would be impressive. Alfred's landscapes had a special weight to them, as though when he looked at the land, he saw more than its appearance. He saw its *meaning*. That insight was why Magnus had commissioned Alfred to paint his portrait.

The artist ran a hand through his long, disheveled hair. He had a soft, nondescript face pinched into a permanent scowl of dissatisfaction, as if his features were outraged by their own banality.

"My lord," Alfred said, bowing distractedly, his attention held by the problem he saw on the canvasses.

"What ails you, Alfred?" Magnus asked.

"I have been trying to settle on a backdrop for your portrait, my lord."

"I do like the idea of the moor," said Magnus.

"The problem is the perspective. I have been trying to experiment with either the abbey or the Stroud Spiral as a backdrop."

Magnus looked more closely at the two paintings. He couldn't make much of the blur of color. He wanted to squint, as if facing a thick fog. "I don't really see either here," he admitted. He had trouble making out a clear distinction between the two.

"Neither is there," said Alfred. "And both are. When I try to paint the abbey, I keep seeing the Spiral in my mind, and the reverse is true when I try my hand at the Spiral. Each refuses to be portrayed without the other, and so all that I produce is confusion."

"How very curious. Do you have a solution?"

"Not yet. I will find it, my lord. You will have a worthy backdrop."

"I am confident you will, Alfred." Magnus placed a hand on his shoulder. "Have faith in your skill. I do."

He carried on, marching up the slope that led to the ruins.

Though the abbey had lost its roof and none of the walls

were completely intact, its ruins were extensive, as if instead of being destroyed, it had transformed into a new kind of structure. It cut an imposing silhouette against the sky, its facade and shattered columns both massive and jagged. Magnus thought of it as the skeleton of a behemoth, the beast so huge it could not truly die, and instead slept, its new body as vital and even more imbued with meaning than its old one.

Magnus passed through the isolated entrance arch and into a space where stone, tumbled and standing, created the ghosts of chambers. The gaps in the walls formed junctions that had never been, and the concrete memory of the abbey's interior was a more complex web than it had been before the dissolution.

More arches stood on their own, inviting Magnus to go under them, though there was no need. It felt right to accept their invitation. Doing so made a ritual out of his path through the ruins, and the path felt like the true one, the only one he could trace despite the gaps and openings everywhere around him.

Magnus wended his way through the center of the ruins and to the biggest open area of the abbey, at the very edge of the cliffs. A jumble of fallen stonework took up the western end of the chapel's space. Magnus went up to the heap and examined it.

He found what Christina had seen almost immediately. Three large chunks of masonry leaned at angles against each other, leaving a dark gap between them, just large enough for Magnus to squeeze through, if he felt brave.

It had not been there before. He would have noticed. The abbey had been his special domain as a child. Every day of his stays on the estate, he had explored the fallen walls and archways. He had lived with every stone preserved in memory during the long years of his exile, and he had walked through and around it several times daily since his return. The abbey had always called to him. The ruins were a special kind of perfection, granting the site far more meaning than if the building had been intact. Destruction had profundity. In being broken, the abbey had changed character. For Magnus, it was no longer a site of something as mundane as Christian worship, but speaking somehow to mysteries more ancient.

More ancient than stone.

The mysteries were his to plumb, his to learn, *his*. He would have known if this secret had been visible before. It was for *him* to be the first to cross this new threshold.

The rubble must have shifted very recently, maybe even today. Christina was not the only artist to frequent the ruins. Someone else would have mentioned this before her, and maybe been foolish enough to venture down.

Which was it, brave or foolish?

What made the stones move, and why now?

What was he going to do?

Magnus supported himself against the stones and poked his head into the gap. Darkness breathed cold against his skin. It smelled of the sea.

He thought he heard something, the hint of a whisper, a trace of syllables.

He held his breath and strained to listen. Silence waited for him.

Magnus examined the stones. They seemed to be solid in their new configuration.

That meant nothing. The rubble had appeared unchanging all his life. And now it had moved.

But the darkness called.

He stepped away from the gap and looked around. The poets especially liked coming to the ruins at night for the atmosphere. He found some stubs of candles, and someone had left flint, steel, char cloth and some tapers in a bowl for the use of the night visitors. Magnus got a taper burning and lit three of the stubs. He crouched at the entrance and reached inside with a candle. The space beyond widened quickly, and there were worn steps just past the threshold.

He dropped the candle. It rolled down a few steps, gave him a hint of a long descent, and then the dark breeze snuffed it.

Magnus sucked in his breath. His heart beat fast with excitement. He would come back with a lantern. He had to go down.

He would go, and no one else.

This is mine.

He walked slowly from the chapel to the abbey's entrance. He looked down the slope toward the Stroud Spiral and, beyond it, the woods with their cottages. The bonfire had been lit, its orange glow growing brighter in the waning day.

This was his republic, spread out for his inspection. This was his dream made real. This was his destiny, he only now understood, coming into being. He was more than a patron for these poets and painters. The unheard whisper from beneath the abbey embraced him and showed him the truth. He was the conjurer of change. He had gathered the artists of true revolution. They would achieve, thanks to him, the promise that had been squandered in Europe.

The breath of the dark reached out from the crypt and touched his neck.

Look. See. You are the guide and the light.

You are inevitable.

But how? *How?* He didn't know what the revolution should look like.

The crypt called to him. His descent would reveal all.

Come and see.

Come and see.

CHAPTER TWELVE

Another week passed, another week where the night terrors lurked as a potential, but did not strike.

Grudging as ever, Nurse Revere gave Miranda permission to extend the length of her walks. Miranda practiced for her exhibition by repeating her now-familiar stroll up and down the corridor outside her room. She knew this hall. In the day, it held no surprises. It was a straight line. It was not a labyrinth.

Was it part of one?

What if she ventured down other halls and couldn't find her way back? Miranda pictured herself without her chair, collapsing in an unknown region of the Institute, calling for help and water while staff ignored her because she was not one of their charges.

A silly image, one she should laugh at.

One more length of the hall, she decided. Do one more length of her hall before she ventured further.

She thought about the confusing layout of the Institute. Was it a maze or a labyrinth?

The question refused to be set aside. Miranda couldn't stop thinking about labyrinths and their natures. Whenever she gave free rein to her thoughts, they ran down the paths Daria Miracle had opened. She saw labyrinths everywhere, the metaphor multiplying like twists in the road.

And there, now she was using the labyrinth as a metaphor for the metaphors.

In another context, she would have been amused or annoyed. She had been amused after the first session. She hadn't thought Daria's lectures had any real significance for her. She was too skeptical to take them seriously. But then the ideas wouldn't leave her alone, and she saw them at work on her roommates. There was nothing she could find objectionable in what Daria said. But the way her words lingered in the mind began to feel like a symptom.

Miranda wished she could speak with Agatha.

She reached the far end of the corridor again, hesitated, then forced herself to go further. Hiding in her room until Agatha returned was not an option. She had the responsibility to search for answers herself.

What answers? Where? Search how?

She didn't know. But she did know that she would find nothing if she did not look.

An experiment occurred to her: find the library without reading any of the signs. She had gone there and back enough times in her wheelchair that, if this were any other building, she would know the way without thinking. But no matter how much she had tried, she still had no mental image of the floor's geography. Maybe, though, maybe she had a better instinctive sense of where to go than she thought.

She headed off, keeping her eyes on the floor, carefully avoiding sight of the signs. At the first intersection, she was already at sea. Left or right? She had no idea. She went left before she gave in to the temptation to look up.

She kept up her momentum after that, taking each turn at random. If she didn't know which choice was the right one, then it was pointless to debate. Every hall was both unfamiliar and identical to all the others. She had no idea where she was.

Irrational worry nagged. What if she couldn't find her way back? That was stupid. All she had to do was stop being stubborn and follow the signs. Nothing to it.

What if the signs were gone?

Ridiculous. That was a thought for three in the morning, not the hour before lunch. But the fear that all the signs would have vanished when she looked for them kept growing.

That was the irrational trying to break her resolution. She refused to give in.

But she really did not know where she was.

And then she was standing in front of the library door.

Miranda felt no sense of victory. She couldn't pretend that instinct had brought her here, not when she had felt so completely disoriented.

She had set out for the library, and the halls had brought her here. As if all her choices were an illusion, and there was only one path.

It is a labyrinth.

One path. Leading where? To being well, Daria would offer. But that wasn't true for everyone.

Too many questions, and no answers. Not yet. Miranda promised herself she would find them. And she promised herself that she would not submit to the mercy of the halls. She would find her own way. She would learn to navigate the Institute. She would defy its will.

Determination renewed, she opened the doors and entered the library. In one of the chairs by the window, Lupita huddled miserably, her hands clutched in fists before her lips.

Miranda sat in the other chair. She leaned forward, offering comfort but not touching Lupita unless invited. "Are you all right?" she asked.

Lupita turned a tear-streaked face to her. "There's no chapel here," she said.

Miranda had never thought about looking for one. "You've asked, I gather," she said.

Lupita nodded. "I did. Why isn't there one? What kind of place is this?" She spoke as if she had woken to find herself in a burning speakeasy. "The hospital has one."

"It does," Miranda agreed. "But this is a private institution. It is not under any obligation to provide a chapel." Though that was true, she didn't want to push too hard to be convincing. She heard Agatha's voice at her shoulder, warning her not to leap to conclusions. Of either kind, she thought. She mustn't read malice into the banal. She also mustn't dismiss the threatening as banal.

"Private or not, shouldn't they be doing everything possible to help their patients? Don't they understand how not having a place of worship makes things for some of us?"

"I guess they don't," Miranda said.

Lupita wiped the tears from her cheeks. "I thought, if I came here to pray, I might feel better. I thought, this is a quiet place. I thought it would be better than nothing."

"Did it help?" Miranda asked.

"No!" Lupita choked back a sob. "It's been getting harder for me to pray in the room. But it's worse here."

"Do you know why?"

"The thoughts here are too loud."

Miranda's breath caught. Her skin began to crawl. "What do you mean?" she asked. She realized she was whispering, as if the walls might overhear.

Lupita looked stricken. She squirmed in her seat, trying to get away from her own words. "I don't know." She shuddered. "That didn't make any sense, did it?" She squeezed her hands together. "You shouldn't pay attention to what's coming out of my mouth. I'm babbling."

"I don't think you are," said Miranda. She held out a hand, and Lupita clutched it gratefully.

"I'm so upset with myself," Lupita said. "I keep trying to find things to blame. Why can't I pray the way I used to? Why is it so hard? Is it my fault?"

"I'm sure it isn't." Miranda found it hard to look at the pain in those eyes. "You should try to be kinder to yourself. Maybe you should stop attending the counseling sessions." Miranda had always doubted. She treated all orthodoxies with suspicion. Yet she was finding the sessions sinking hooks into her mind. For people who did not like doubt, the hooks had to be more painful, and sinking in more deeply. All her roommates had been looking more and more thoughtful, and, it seemed to her, more worried.

"I have to go," said Lupita.

"Why? They aren't compulsory."

"What if what Daria says is true?"

"What if it is?" said Miranda. "Why should that affect your faith?"

"I don't know!" Lupita wailed, her voice high and thin. She held Miranda's hand harder, then let go, embarrassed. "I'm sorry."

"Don't be."

"I have to go," Lupita insisted. "I have to follow her thread."

They were both quiet for a moment, conscious of the labyrinth that had crept into Lupita's words.

Miranda almost asked if Lupita was afraid of where the thread might lead. But she didn't, because Lupita's face made the answer clear.

Durstal's small cluster of houses huddled in the shadow of the slope that led up to the Stroud Estate. The nearest railway station was two miles away. A narrow road, badly in need of repair, twisted through until it reached Durstal's hollow and came to an end in the village.

"We should have waited for a cab," Wilbur said again.

"I didn't see any at the station, did you? If we had waited, we'd still be waiting. Spending the night on a railway platform wouldn't be comfortable." Agatha spoke gently. Wilbur was exhausted after the trek. He was entitled to a few grumbles. They were the first he'd made since leaving Arkham, and the trip had been a long one.

The ocean crossing had been pleasant, with no storms to trouble Wilbur's stomach. Once they had arrived in England, though, Agatha had pushed them hard. She didn't want to be away longer than she had to. Once she learned how awkward a route the journey to Durstal would be, she had realized that it would make more sense to stop at Glasgow and Edinburgh first. Wilbur only had a couple of days in each city to recover before Agatha bundled them on to another train.

She was tired too, but the call of the hunt kept her energized.

Agatha had hit dead ends in the cities. She found almost nothing about Magnus Stroud. The university holdings there had even less by or about him than Miskatonic. Frustrated, she wondered if the absence was significant, history erasing Magnus' presence, or Magnus erasing his tracks.

But absence was not evidence. And so she and Wilbur had come, at last, to Durstal.

Night was falling when the road took them out from the trees and down toward the village. They had been using flashlights to see their way for the last few minutes. Wilbur heaved a sigh of relief at the sight of lights glimmering in windows.

"It's very small, isn't it?" he said, clearly hoping for reassurance that it wasn't *too* small.

"There will be an inn," Agatha said. *There had better be.* "Come on." She gave her suitcase a bit of a heave. "Almost there!"

To her relief, there was a *there* at which to arrive. They found the Ash Inn at the edge of the village. The tree that gave the inn its name towered over the small buildings, its limbs thick and twisted with age. It stood out in the village, a moody sentinel waiting for the ephemeral humans to pass away and leave it in peace.

Inside, they found a pub on the ground floor. All but two of the tables were occupied. The volume of the conversation had not been loud, and it dropped further as they walked inside, but did not cease. The locals eyed them curiously, and with something that surprised Agatha. She had been prepared for hostility; she had not expected hope.

Agatha strode over to the bar, Wilbur shuffling behind her. The landlord, a small man with bulging, perpetually surprised eyes, regarded her with a wary, but not unfriendly, expression.

"We're hoping you have a room available," she said.

The landlord laughed. "Oh," he said. "I was worried you were going to tell me you were lost!" He reached over the bar to shake hands with them. "Tom Spalding," he said. "Let me get you your room."

A quarter of an hour later, Agatha left Wilbur gratefully collapsed on the bed. It was late for what she had in mind, and dark, but she was too restless to wait until the morning. She needed her first glimpse of her goal.

Tom had given her directions to the Stroud Estate readily enough when she asked, though he had not hidden his concern. "You'll hardly be able to see to find your way," he said. "You wouldn't prefer a seat by the fire and a brandy instead?"

"I would prefer such things," Agatha agreed, "and I'll look forward to them when I get back."

The landlord nodded solemnly. "Don't be long, then." He had to be fifteen years her junior. His worry made him sound like her father.

The bar's patrons watched her with open curiosity. When she had asked Tom how to get to the estate, this time the conversations *had* stopped. She smiled on her way out, and a few people shifted, as if about to say something to her. One old man gripped his pint with both hands. He looked at Agatha with pleading eyes.

What do they want?

Tomorrow. Find out tomorrow.

With her flashlight, she had no difficulty following the landlord's directions. There weren't many ways to choose from. Agatha felt a sick, vertiginous inevitability about the way her steps had brought her to the threshold of the Stroud Estate.

A dirt road wound from the center of Durstal and up the slope. With no trees to flank the road, Agatha had to walk slowly, careful not to step off the track and into the thick gorse on the hillside. Partway up, the moon came out from behind clouds, and the cold, bleaching wash of its light showed her the path ahead.

At the gates, she moved her flashlight beam back and forth, examining the obstacle. A chain and padlock held the gates shut. It would take heavy bolt cutters to break the lock, and she had no intention of leaving signs of her passage, if she could avoid it. The dry-stone wall, though, was not much more than six feet high. If she could borrow a ladder…

Easier said than done. How did she plan on acquiring one? Walking up to a random villager and explaining that she needed to break into the Stroud's property?

The villagers' desperate looks came back to her. The old man clutching his beer, on the verge of calling out to her. Maybe just asking would be the right approach after all.

Worry about that in the morning. Get some sleep, be less tired, and think more clearly. She had made it this far. She'd find a way in.

And then what? What did she hope to find?

She had no specific hopes. She had run out of leads, except the goal to stand on the ground depicted in the portrait of Magnus, and see what there was to see. Miranda's vision had meaning. Agatha had to find why it linked Galloway to Arkham, and the abbey to the Institute.

She went right up the gates and aimed her flashlight through them. The trees on the other side of the wall held on to the darkness, nurtured it, and thickened it. Silence coiled with the night.

Agatha took her compass from her jacket pocket. The needle pointed quite a bit west of north. It held steady, just as it did outside the walls of the Stroud Institute.

The air, still as a held breath, chilled her. The space beyond the gates felt hollow, abandoned.

It also waited, anticipating her arrival. If the chain slipped open and fell from the gates, she would not be surprised.

She turned back and hurried away before that could happen.

The moon painted swirls of shadow on the gorse. The secret paths grinned at her as she hurried down the hill.

CHAPTER THIRTEEN

Lupita calmed down, and, after a little while, she left the library, declaring she needed to lie down. Miranda believed her. She had the face-sagging look of someone feeling the numb exhaustion that comes after grief. Lupita paused at the exit, as uncertain of direction as Miranda. She looked up for the signs, then headed right, walking slowly. The door swung closed behind her with a soft sigh.

The walk here had tired Miranda, but not overly so. She didn't feel the need to head back just yet. She sat and listened to her breathing. It strained and rattled. The iron band around her chest seemed looser than it had been. Any better than yesterday? Hard to tell. Better than before coming to the Stroud Institute? Definitely. Again, a fact to remember. She was being well cared for, and she wasn't a prisoner.

Really? What if she tried to leave?

She hadn't reached that point. Especially not with her health improving.

And what if the night visions followed her home? What if they had no connection to the Institute?

The vision of the painting said otherwise.

When she became too conscious of her breathing, Miranda pushed herself up from the chair. Enough of chasing her own tail. Time to be useful. Don't leave all the research to Agatha. She moved slowly around the room, scanning the titles on the shelves, looking for the name that stood out, or the pattern that was less innocuous than a first look had suggested.

She found nothing.

Miranda started pulling books off the shelves at random, flipping them open to see if they were, in fact, what their spines purported. She found none in disguise. Someone had left a bookmark in a copy of *The Magic Mountain*, and it fell when Miranda riffled the pages. She knelt to pick it up, and noticed the carpet for the first time. It had barely registered on her awareness before, a deep burgundy with a pattern of black stripes. Up close, she saw that though the stripes gave the impression of being arranged in tight, angular, parallel formations, they actually connected. The positions of the links varied, never too close to each other, so they were easy to miss.

Miranda put the book back and focused her attention on the carpet. She picked the nearest connection and followed the stripes on the right to the next link. She frowned, crouching down to look more closely.

She'd been wrong again. What she had thought were links were a line making two ninety degree turns. The gap between the stripe that turned and the one above was so thin, so close to being indiscernible, that it looked as if two stripes were one longer one.

Miranda straightened. She swayed, fighting vertigo as

her understanding of the rug's pattern shifted, tilting reality. There were no links. A single stripe covered the entire carpet.

A labyrinth.

Now that she saw it, she had to work to pull her eyes away. The labyrinth called her gaze, inviting her to lose herself in its contemplation. She walked to the door on unsteady legs. The zig-zag path tried to capture her steps. She swayed, off-balance as if on a ship in a storm. The distance to the door stretched, endless, across a carpet as wide and treacherous as the sea.

Miranda closed her eyes to escape the labyrinth's grip. It held on. She felt the stripes beneath her feet. The soles of her slippers squirmed, trying to shift so they faced in the direction of the stripes. They wanted her to walk the labyrinth.

She dragged herself forward, pulling against glue. She opened her eyes and kept them focused on the door. She stared at it fiercely, making it her beacon, her lighthouse that would save her from the undertow of the pattern. It taunted her, unreachable, miles and miles away. She would never get there.

She put one dragging foot in front of the other, to no point, to no end. The labyrinth would take her. It would not let her escape.

One step, one step, one step, her breath scraping, exhaustion hauling at her. She would fall. She would sink through the carpet into the true labyrinth beyond its simulacrum.

One step, one step, one step. She couldn't go on.

She touched the door. The pull of the labyrinth ceased so suddenly that she stumbled. She breathed in, out, steadying herself. She risked a look at the carpet. The pattern was there, and that was all it was. No danger to her. Just a carpet.

"Nice try," she whispered.

She stepped into the hall and closed the door behind her. She would not be returning to the library.

She was more than ready to be in her bed now. And she would follow the signs. She wanted only a clear, rational reason for getting back.

First, though, she looked closely at the wall. She didn't believe the labyrinth only existed in the library.

There were no patterns in the paint. No stripes, no shifts in tone of the greenish white.

Miranda ran her palm along the wall. She felt a slight unevenness. She traced it with her fingertips. It was so slight, she almost lost it. It took her three tries to follow the bump, and learn that it became a ridge.

She pressed the side of her face on the wall. Deep age reached through institutional paint to chill her cheek. She looked down its length, focused on the line she had under her fingers, and there…

There. The ridge extending, then turning back, and turning again, and again. The endless switchback and relentless, single-minded advance of the labyrinth.

In the morning, Agatha left Wilbur to linger over his coffee at the inn and strolled through the streets of Durstal. Under the brittle sunlight of spring, she smiled at the people she passed, said hello when someone smiled back, and started conversations wherever she sensed an opening. She kept her initial comments banal while giving the villagers the chance to take things further.

"Durstal is very pretty," she said to an older, broad-faced

woman who smiled at her as she came out of a newsagent's.

The woman's smile became strained. "You'd think so." She seemed to be looking at something a long way off, an unpleasant memory ducking behind the mountains.

"You don't?" Agatha asked.

"Pretty to see and pretty to live in are two different things. You stay here for any length of time, and you'll see what I mean."

"Have you lived here long?"

"We all have. Our whole lives."

"I can't help but notice there aren't a lot of young people about."

"If they have the chance, they leave. More power to them. Best they're gone."

When she returned to the inn late in the afternoon, Agatha had put together a mental mosaic of Durstal. A cloud hung over the spirits of its people. She couldn't make out what lurked in the cloud and gave it shape and power. She didn't think any of the villagers could either. Again and again, they surprised her with the way they opened up to her, as if by being an outsider, by being someone who came from a place without a cloud, she had the means of lifting its oppression.

They had clearly never been to Arkham.

By four, the ground floor of the inn had filled again. Agatha ordered a round for everyone and did so again a couple of hours later, when she and Wilbur sat down to their dinner. The locals greeted her as one of their own.

"Are you planning something for tonight?" Wilbur asked, digging in to his fish and chips.

"Nothing frightening," Agatha told him. "I won't be heading out."

"Good."

"I'm going to spend some time here, talk to people."

"You've been doing that all day."

"Yes, I have. I've been making myself known. And now that the beer has been flowing, I hope I'll hear more. I think these people are frightened. I'd like to know why."

"That's very reassuring." Wilbur contemplated his fish as if it had suddenly spoken. "If you find out, does that mean we head home tomorrow?"

"No. I still have to get into the Stroud Estate."

Wilbur grimaced. "I keep hoping you'll change your mind about that. What if you get caught?"

"Then that will be a problem."

"What's the charge for trespassing here?" Wilbur asked. "Does bail work like it does back home?"

"I don't know," said Agatha. "With a bit of luck, you won't have to find out." She didn't say that being caught by the police was the least of her worries. "I'll be careful," she promised.

Wilbur didn't try to argue. He went back up to the room when he'd finished eating, and Agatha sent still another round for the company. She looked around the room, and met the gaze of an old man sitting in the far corner. She took her own beer over and sat down at his table. "Agatha Crane," she said, and held out her hand.

"Ben Laurie," he said, shaking her hand. "So, what brings you to these parts?"

"Events at home."

"Oh?" he looked surprised.

"I think there might be a connection between home and Durstal."

"Oh." He sounded guarded.

"I'm here to find out what that might be, if I can."

Ben took a thoughtful sip of his ale. He kept his eyes on the table. "You want to be careful, doing things like that," he said.

"I always am," said Agatha. "And I get the feeling that you would like to tell me more."

"Mmm," said Ben, very neutral.

"I'm curious as to why that is."

Another sip, another pause. Then Ben looked at her. "An outsider is a rare thing in these parts. When we see one, we like to hope they've come to help."

"Help with what?" Agatha asked.

Ben shrugged. "Not sure that we know."

"Then I'll tell you what I'd like to know. I'm curious about the Strouds."

"Ah." Ben made a sour face, his weathered skin wrinkling like a walnut.

"Do you like them?"

"We should." He looked ready to spit.

"But you don't."

"Well, they've spent enough money in Durstal over the years. Enough to make most kinds popular."

"But … ?" Agatha prompted.

Ben lowered his voice. "They're a wrong bunch. Have been for a long time. You know how some folk'll give you money but are laughing at you?"

"The Strouds are like that?"

"No, they're worse." He paused, then corrected himself. "*He's* worse, I should say. Only ever one Stroud at a time up at the Hall. Just the master. Don't quite know how they manage it. Must be wives and children, but all we ever see is the master and the servants. I've seen three different ones in my years, one at a time. Always one at a time."

"You said he was worse," Agatha said, bringing Ben back to his point when he looked like he was going to nod to himself and consider his piece spoken.

"Worse, aye," said Ben. "He's not laughing at you. But it doesn't half feel like he's bought something from you that you shouldn't have sold. D'you see?"

"I think I do."

Ben opened his mouth, then shut it again as Tom Spalding walked by. His attention shifted again to his ale. Agatha felt dismissed. Ben had said all he would.

She got up and went to the bar. Tom, cleaning some glasses, smiled apologetically. "Sorry if I made old Ben shut up," he said. "Didn't mean to."

"Why would he feel comfortable talking to me, but not to be overheard by you?"

"Not me specifically," Tom said. "Anybody but you."

"I don't understand."

"You're not from here. By your accent, you're *really* not from here. That makes people feel safe. They want to talk, and they can talk to you."

"But not to each other," said Agatha.

"Now you're grasping it. Any of us might be getting Stroud money to keep an ear and an eye open. No way of telling."

"I might be too."

"Maybe. Seems unlikely. And if you need to let something out, you're a safer bet than our neighbors."

Lucky for me. "So if I'm a safer bet, can I ask if you see Donovan Stroud much?"

"Hardly ever," said Tom. "And not at all for some months now. Not since all those lorries."

"Oh? What were they up to?"

"Who knows? I couldn't tell you if they were bringing things in or taking them or both, but there were a lot of them."

"That sounds like something was done on the grounds," said Agatha.

Tom wrapped his dish towel around a hand absently. "We've all been too scared to try to have a look," he admitted. After a pause, he added quietly, "All but one of us."

"Oh?"

"Our vicar, Peter Wilson."

"I'd like to speak to him."

Tom looked grave. "You can't. He went up to the estate, and then he went over the cliffs. I was with him at the end."

"I'm sorry."

"We've all been careful not to go near the grounds since."

"I don't blame you," said Agatha. "And I appreciate the warning. It does, however, make it even more important that I get over that wall."

Tom nodded. He gave the towel a nervous tug, then nodded again, this time to himself. "I'll help," he said.

"Thank you."

Tom held up a hand. "Don't thank me. I owe the vicar that much. And if you can do anything to help us, it'll be me thanking you."

"I won't make promises I don't know that I can keep, but I'll do what I can."

"Can't ask fairer than that."

"I don't suppose," said Agatha, "that you have a battery radio? It would be useful to bring along."

Tom blinked in surprise. "I do, at that. We don't like to use it much." He sounded uneasy again.

"Why is that?"

"Hard to get anything at all in these parts, and…" He hesitated. "To tell you the truth, the static gives us the shudders."

"Because you hear things in it."

Tom twisted the dish towel and said nothing.

CHAPTER FOURTEEN

The days passed, and the night visions still held off. Their absence ceased being a relief. It became a false recovery. Miranda felt her tension growing worse every day. She wasn't sleeping well again, lying awake waiting for the blow that threatened but never fell.

The arc of its path must be huge, she thought. Its momentum ferocious. The impact, when it comes, will be awful.

The Thursday after her encounter with Lupita in the library, Miranda revised her understanding of her vision of the abbey and the river of stone. The connection between the Institute and the Stroud Estate was profound. Somehow, she thought, the Institute and the abbey and the stones were one and the same.

She wished she could speak to Agatha.

She wished she could warn her.

This is much worse than we thought. Age and the labyrinth defined the halls of the clinic.

In the days before Thursday, she became more and more

aware of the malaise running through the Institute like a new infection. As she walked the halls, she would sometimes poke her head in another room and get to know other patients. Two more deaths occurred during this period, two more faces disappeared just as she was getting to know them. The change in the mood of her roommates, though, seemed independent of the bad news. It began before they heard about Ingrid Shelley and then Angel Hayden. Lupita's crisis of faith continued. Cleo was subdued, the closest to withdrawn Miranda had ever seen her. And Frieda had started crying too during the night. The sainted Reginald came to visit her, and she barely spoke to him.

Miranda took comfort in one thing: Cleo's health was improving, and quickly. She had already reached the stage where she would normally have been moved to another ward. No beds were ready for her yet, so she stayed in the room and spent most of her days taking part in the volunteer work, delivering food trays, collecting puzzle sheets, arranging ornaments on bedside tables. They all expected her to be going home soon. An iron determination to make that expectation a reality seemed to animate her. When Miranda looked at her, she saw a woman willing herself well.

Then Thursday came, and with it another of Daria Miracle's sessions, as hopeful and as metaphysically troubling as ever. Miranda now thought of herself as an enemy agent when she attended the lectures. She held herself as far as she could from the sweep of Daria's oratory and the hypnotic dance of her body. She had to know what Daria said. She told herself she rejected everything the woman said.

Daria's words flowed like her gestures, comforting

and seductive, and there was nothing wrong in what she said, nothing to take exception to. Her labyrinth of hope beckoned, and Miranda fought its pull as she had the pattern in the library.

If only she could identify the foe hiding in the loving platitudes. She couldn't fight what she couldn't see.

And on Thursday, after the session, she walked the halls at random, walking for exercise and the chance to think without interruption. She turned into a long corridor and saw, at the far end, Nurse Holden silhouetted by a window.

Holden stood perfectly still. She could have been a mannequin. Unnerved, Miranda slowed down as she approached. Holden did not move. Her arms hung down at her sides. She faced the window. Miranda had the sudden conviction that she did not want to see Holden's eyes.

She stopped half a step from Holden. She looked around. Some orderlies crossed from one room to another at the other end of the hall. Coughs and the occasional moan rasped out of the doorways. Signs of life and signs of illness, and Miranda felt profoundly alone.

"Excuse me," she said.

Holden did not react.

Miranda reached out. She didn't want to touch Holden. The nurse would feel like stone, like death. She made herself tap Holden's shoulder.

Holden jumped with shock and gasped. She spun around, her eyes wide and stricken, and for a moment they didn't see Miranda. The inward vista held them fast. Then they focused and Holden tried to recover herself. "I'm sorry," she said. "I was miles away. You startled me."

"I didn't mean to," said Miranda. "I apologize."

"No, no, I'm the one woolgathering on the job." Her lips stretched into a sick imitation of a self-deprecating smile. "Can I help you?"

"Can *I* help *you*?" Miranda asked.

Holden's professional mask fractured, then reassembled itself.

She wanted to say yes, Miranda thought. She wanted someone to help. She wanted to lean on a shoulder.

She could not.

"That's very kind of you, Professor Ventham. I'm quite all right. A long day. You know what those are like, I'm sure."

"I do." *And I know the difference between being tired and something worse.* She listened to a hunch and asked, "Does the staff have sessions with Daria Miracle too?"

"Are you enjoying them?" Holden deflected. She didn't wait for an answer but instead made a show of looking at her watch. "Is that the time? Duty calls, and I'm remiss!" She laughed with forced humor. "Must run!"

Miranda watched her go.

Later, after supper, when Nurse Revere came to take their temperatures, Miranda studied her. Revere's stony face gave little away. Her eyes, though, barely took in the patients and the thermometers.

"You're looking lovely today," Miranda said, probing for a reaction.

"Hm," said Revere.

"I saw fairies dancing in the grounds today."

Revere grunted, and moved on to Frieda.

Cleo stared at Miranda. "What are you doing?" she mouthed.

Miranda shrugged and grinned, hoping she looked more impish than she felt.

A preoccupied Revere disturbed her almost as much as a motionless Holden.

That night, in the dark, the thought came that she had been wrong about her vision. She had feared it was a prophecy. What would be worse was if it were history. An event that could not be prevented, because it had already occurred.

She thought of the river of stone flowing from the abbey to the Institute.

What if that was what really happened? What if, in some way, the abbey and stones had come here?

Miranda turned her head to face the doorway. Gazing at the wall outside the room, and the paint above the wainscoting, she could not see the labyrinth of barely raised texture. She knew it was there, though. She could feel it.

Feel it snaking across the entire Institute, capturing them all.

Daria's voice came to her, inviting them to walk its path.

Why resist? You're already here.

Tom carried the ladder to the wall of the estate. Agatha and Wilbur shared the awkward load of the radio. It was a rectangular console, not unlike her Atwater-Kent, and weighted a good thirty pounds. The men seemed eager to carry as much weight as possible, as if to compensate for a different weight, the weight of shame for staying on the other side of the wall. The burden was unnecessary, but she knew it would be pointless to tell them.

They reached the wall and Tom placed the ladder against it, about twenty feet down from the gate.

"Should we come with you?" Wilbur asked.

"No," she said, and they both looked guiltily relieved. "I need to do this alone." She had no idea what she might find on the other side of the wall. She had her medallion, as did Wilbur. Unlike Wilbur, she had some ideas of how she might use it, if she had to. Tom had no protection at all. "What you can do for me is monitor the radio." She turned it on.

"That's odd," said Tom.

The radio had been full of static when Agatha had tried it at the inn. Now it was silent.

"This isn't entirely surprising," Agatha said. She spoke as if studying a lab report, but her mouth had gone dry. "Let's leave it on. If you hear anything, anything at all, please make a note of it."

"We can do that," said Tom.

"I wish you wouldn't do this," said Wilbur.

"I wish I didn't have to," she said. "But it's why we're here." To Tom she said, "Thank you for lending us a hand. Again, I can't promise I'm going to find anything that will help you."

Tom shrugged. "I don't expect you to. We don't even know what it is we need help with."

Agatha gave Wilbur a hug, then climbed the ladder. Perched on the top of the wall, she pulled the ladder up with Tom's help, lowered to the other side, and descended into the estate.

The weather favored her again. With the full moon out, she didn't need her flashlight, except to check her compass, once she worked her way through the brush and onto the drive leading from the gate. She turned it off, hoping she could manage without it at least until she was well past the Hall.

Her sense of the estate's geography was two centuries old. She expected changes, and she crossed her fingers that they wouldn't be so extensive that she would get lost.

In fact, there were no changes at all until she reached the Hall. Moonlight reflected like cataracts on the windows. The house was dark, silent, and the east side looked as if a bomb had hit it. Only bits of walls still stood, broken and unwanted. The interior was gone. Agatha wondered if the entire house had become a shell.

No one would be living there. She relaxed and used her flashlight again.

She looked at the compass, wondering if the needle would indicate the Hall. It did not. It pointed in the direction she planned to go, as steady as it had been at the gate.

Beyond the Hall, a new gravel road cut through the woods in the direction of the Spiral and the abbey. If this was his doing, Donovan Stroud had made life easier for her. She would have to thank him.

What were you doing with all those trucks?

She found the answer a few minutes later. The road brought her to a quarry where the Stroud Spiral had been. The boulders had vanished, the ground excavated to the point where all trace of the stones had been erased. They had been extracted like teeth.

Based on the descriptions in the *Miscellany of Merrick*, the stones would have been much too huge to load onto trucks. Donovan would have had them broken down; he had done so cleanly. Agatha swept the beam across the shallow crater next to the road. She didn't see a single stray fragment.

The road carried on up the slope to the abbey. The ruins

were gone too, the top of the cliff unbroken by the silhouette of fragmented stonework. Agatha followed the road to its end, urged on by the compass whose north, she now realized, was the site of the abbey. She had to see everything, even if all she saw was absence.

Not every trace of the abbey had disappeared. The last remains of its corpse lay before Agatha, broken stones strewn like barren seeds. The abbey had become a carcass picked over by scavengers.

What did Donovan want with the Spiral and the abbey?

She knew, of course. She should have guessed sooner. She should have pieced it together when Miranda had told her about the vision of the abbey flowing through the Spiral and into the Institute. She should have realized because she had wondered about the sense of age the new building radiated.

The abbey and the Spiral had become the Stroud Institute.

A deep, circular shadow swallowed the moonlight. Agatha walked over to it, and shone her flashlight beam into a shaft. It looked like the mouth of a wide well, with a rough staircase carved into its sides, circling down and down into the night of the earth. Agatha peered into the depths. They kept their secrets, inviting her down.

She picked up a fragment of masonry and put it in her jacket pocket. Something to test back in Arkham.

She looked at the compass again. The tip of the needle was stuck flat against the housing, pointing down. It vibrated hard, as if trying to escape.

Agatha took a breath, then started down the stairs.

She walked carefully, one hand on the wall to keep her

balance on the narrow, uneven, treacherously smooth steps. She paused after a minute and looked up. The pale, moonlit circle above her had shrunk, as if her way back to the surface would close behind her.

"Don't be stupid," she whispered. Echoes slithered down the shaft ahead of her.

Which was stupid? To be afraid or to keep going?

She started forward again, more slowly now, making sure of her footing before each step. She could smell the sea. The salty tang grew stronger as she went down, and soon she thought she could hear the surf too, the rough, grating rhythm crawling up the stairs toward her, as if in answer to her whisper.

Instinct made her stop again. She listened carefully, eyes starting to water from the smell.

That was not the surf. The sound scraped too hard, too heavily, scales against stone. The indrawn rasp of the surf became a breath, a murmur, the expectation of words.

Agatha turned around. She headed back up, forced herself not to run. If she did, she would slip. She climbed, steadily, her movements calm but her heart pounding, the blood in her ears roaring as it tried to drown out the rhythmic scrape and hiss below.

The circle above expanded grudgingly. It taunted with the hope of light and air, so far out of reach as the sounds below grew louder, and Agatha did not look back. She must not see what might be closer.

She climbed, and the wall turned slick and clammy under her palm.

Below, the presence shifted. The hiss, the hiss that sounded like wave on rock but was infinitely older, began to shape itself.

Hurry, Agatha's panic urged. *Hurry, or you'll hear your name.*

If she hurried, she'd fall.

Maybe if she screamed, she would not hear the call.

No. She would not scream. She would not betray who she was, even now, even now with the hiss ready to form a first syllable.

The circle widened at last. She breathed clean air. She gave in to the panic and ran up the last few steps. She burst out of the shaft and now she really ran, leaping over the broken stones, rushing headlong for the road that would take her back through the grounds, back to the wall.

The road was true and straight. But when, behind her, the hiss became a snarl, and the snarl uncoiled into the laughter that lingers over dying stars, the road groaned. The gravel vibrated. The road strained against its path, trying to wrench itself into sharp angles and turns, trying to become a new journey that would spiral down into the depths and bring her back to the danger she had fled.

The flashlight beam bounced over the quivering road. Agatha clutched the silver medallion that hung around her neck. She felt squeezed, as if she would imprint its configuration of lines into her flesh. She used precious breath to chant a few words. They came from the Last Prayer of Evashallon, preserved on a few tatters of parchment, a fragment of a much longer work, as lost now as the language in which they were written. She did not know the meaning of the words, only their effect. They anchored reality, and they fought with the road, holding it back from the thing it wished to become.

Cracks opened in the surface, racing along the track, chasing after Agatha. The gravel rolled and squalled like an infant.

Agatha's shoulders tensed. The hair on the back of her neck bristled. The false sound of the surf thundered, close, so close, the entire sea rising above the cliff and waiting for her to look back, look back, and see the wave gazing down at her.

Don't look, don't look, don't look, don't look.

She ran past the gaping wound where the Stroud Spiral had been, and things slithered in the crater. She ran past the broken Hall, and though the moon still shone, the windows reflected nothing, darkness pressing close against them to witness her flight. As she left the Hall behind, the dark shrieked, harsh and high, like a fox, like hunger, like rage.

Then she had the ladder in her hands, and she went up and over the wall in a single breath.

"Did you hear it?" she asked the two men, shoving the ladder at Tom and hurrying down the road.

"Hear what?" Wilbur asked, jogging beside her. "The storm coming?"

"Storm," Agatha repeated, and held back a frightened moan.

"That wasn't wind?" Tom asked.

And then a snarl broke the silence of the radio, deep and long, grating low in a thing of many throats. Tom recoiled, then smashed the radio with the ladder.

Agatha grabbed him and Wilbur and pulled them after her down the slope. The sound behind the wall grew louder, a precursor to a more terrible snarl. Tom began to turn his head.

"Don't look back," Agatha said, and he snapped his head forward. "Don't ever go into the estate. Leave Durstal, so you will never be tempted. All of you, leave Durstal behind. The land here is blighted." She had none of her precious physical evidence. Only a stone to investigate later. And she had never been more sure of anything. "Run, Tom. Run."

CHAPTER FIFTEEN
Scotland, 1806

Partway down the shaft beneath the altar, terror almost sent Magnus rushing back up. He fought the urge. He leaned against the wall, the lantern swinging softly in his grip as he breathed in and out. He sought the excitement that had accompanied him on the first part of his journey. Why did the exhilaration abandon him? Every step of his descent made the discovery even more wondrous.

His discovery. It didn't matter that Christina had told him about it. No one else had gone in before him. His were the first feet to walk these stairs.

First for more centuries than he could guess. There was no record of what lay beneath the abbey in any chronicle he knew of, and he had read them all, many as a youth when he visited the estate, and many more in the years afterward, when they gave him leave to dream of the land that would one day return to him.

His land. His abbey. His discovery.

The fear receded enough to let him resume his way down.

New waves of it washed over him with every crash of the surf below.

"You behold the sublime," he said to himself, speaking aloud. "Terror is meet and right."

Sublime, said the echoes. *Sublime, sublime, sssssssublime.* The word spun down ahead of him into the shaft, distorting, becoming one with the next crash of the surf.

The stairs carried on before him into the dark, and into the endless turns.

Magnus examined the wall as he walked. It changed as he dropped down, becoming a greater source of wonder in its own right. At the top of the shaft, the walls had been stonework, in the same style as the abbey, and for the first twists of the staircase, Magnus had thought Christina right to think this was the crypt. Now, though, carved stones became rare objects, fading into the naked stone of the mountain. The shaft seemed neither artificial nor natural. It blended both states, an impossible construct. Magnus no longer believed it had been built with the abbey.

This is older.

Who created it? He asked himself the question with growing urgency and wonder. The Romans? The answer seemed absurd as soon as he thought it. He looked at the play of the lantern's light over the wall, at the way it was a cavern one moment, a well shaft the next.

"Human hands did not build this," he announced.

This, this, this, thissssssss, said the echoes, merging with the hiss-roar of the surf.

No, not the surf. He admitted that to himself. It was that knowledge, instinctive at first, that had frightened him. That knowledge now kept him going, dropping down and down to greater revelation.

He began to breathe in time with the hiss and crash. Then he imagined the sound changed, became precise, became a voice directed at him.

Mag... nussssssssss

Withdraw and crash, withdraw and crash.

Mag... nussssssssss

Destiny and revelation were one, and the one called him by name.

"I hear you," he said. "I am coming."

No echoes of his own words now, just the call.

Mag... nussssssssss

Around and down, darkness above and darkness below. Soon the sound surrounded him, and he lost all sense of progress. The stairs could go on forever. He had been here always, answering a call that would never cease. He became frightened again, but the wonder kept him going. How far had he descended? Hundreds of feet, miles and miles, a drop beyond measure without beginning or end.

He took the stairs faster. He knew he would not fall. He didn't have to look. His vision blurred. The walls rotated around him, their glistening black shadows at play in the lantern's light. Nothing changed and everything was change. He no longer had a body. He had become his soul, plunging through the forever toward the summons.

The voice in the depths roared his name once more, and then, louder and more demanding and more sinuous than before, it spoke new syllables, a new name.

Crothoaka

The name uttered, the light went out. Magnus stepped onto level ground. The jolt returned his body to him. He staggered in a half circle, then stopped, breathing hard. He could see nothing. Fully terrified again, conscious of the mass of earth above him, he tried to find the stairs. The roaring, hissing voice had fallen silent.

Alone, abandoned in the dark, he fell to his knees. He curled up and closed his eyes.

He tried to pray. He had admired the courage of the atheists of the French Revolution, and he had voiced that admiration sometimes, much to the consternation of William Wordsworth. He hadn't really believed in his ostentatious radicalisms, though. Not those ones.

But now…

The prayers fell into emptiness. No one heard. No one answered. The darkness took apart his certainties and left him with nothing but doubt.

No one heard his prayer. Some*thing* did, though, and when the dark had done its work, the voice returned, the voice of a god that *would* answer.

Mag… nussssssssss

Crothoaka

Magnus opened his eyes. Light, green and slithering, leaked over the floor to him. He stood and followed the trail.

The light bloomed. Magnus saw walls now, rising up to the hint of a vault. He could not say that the walls were stone, or that they ran straight or curved. They had been carved from doubt itself.

The floor sloped and then dropped steeply. The light intensified, and Magnus looked down into vastness and a serpentine nightmare. Below him waited the architecture that was the truth of the abbey. The ruins he had loved since childhood were, he now saw, the extrusion of the immensity below. Perhaps there had never been a true abbey. Perhaps there had only ever been the ruins, the pretense of ruins, waiting for the chosen Stroud to see more deeply, and to take the lure.

The twists of the structure below reflected the shape of the ruins on a grand scale. That was Magnus' first thought. Then he understood that the reverse was true. The abbey, the mere extrusion, was the poor, shallow reflection of what lay beneath, the monstrous and the sublime reduced to a scale that could be encompassed by human understanding.

The serpentine structures captured his eye, his mind, and his soul. Magnus sank to his knees again, in weakness and in awe, and because his body had become irrelevant. His consciousness fell down into the twists of the path below. He traced the convolutions of the halls, more dense than the surface of a brain. He traveled up the corkscrewing towers that reached toward him. He listened to the ocean surge darkly through the veins of the inhuman temple, and heard its commands. He heard, too, the shifting of the inhabitant of the labyrinth, the coiling of the thing that used the ocean for its voice.

He heard the summons of Crothoaka.

The dweller in doubt devoured all his beliefs but the ones that it had whispered to him before. It had planted in him the seeds of a cancerous truth, one that had strangled every other conviction with its roots. Now the truth had ripened, and Magnus understood that all his choices had

CHAPTER SIXTEEN

Cleo's suitcase sat packed on her sheetless mattress. She looked awkward in her street clothes, uncertain where and how to stand, as if the act of wearing anything other than the hospital gown were unforgivably rude.

If so, Miranda thought, Frieda shared Cleo's opinion. She sat up in bed with arms folded, lips pressed in a thin, sour line. She watched Cleo with sovereign resentment and judgment.

"I'm going to miss you," Cleo said, her smile unusually shy. She looked at Miranda and at Lupita when she spoke. Then, with a return of her spark, she cocked her head at Frieda. "You too!"

"It would be a shame if it turns out that you're being hasty," Frieda said, snipping each word. "You don't want to find yourself worse than before."

"Cleo isn't the one making this decision," Nurse Holden put in. She had arrived with supper, which included chocolate cake and ice cream for dessert for the farewell celebration. "Cleo has been given a clean bill of health. Her lungs are clear."

"Thank you so much for everything," Cleo said to Holden. "You've taken such good care of me."

Holden took both of Cleo's hands in hers. "It's been my pleasure," she said, and then, after a slight pause, "I know you'll walk the path in strength."

Sitting on the end of her bed, legs dangling, her plate of cake in hand, Miranda watched the two women carefully. Cleo's smile became strained. So did Holden's, as if her own words had thrown her off her stride. Her delivery had been mechanical, but at the same time emphatic. Her gaze becoming distant again, Holden said another goodbye to Cleo and left.

Cleo gave Lupita a hug, then looked around the room, awkward again, waiting for the right cue. "Well," she said. "I guess…" She picked up her suitcase and turned to go.

"Wait for me," said Miranda. She got up, linked arms with Cleo, and walked her to the door.

"Going to see me out?" Cleo asked.

"That might be a bit too long of a walk for me," said Miranda. "But let me take you to the elevator, at least."

Cleo squeezed her arm. "I really am going to miss you."

"I'm sure going to miss you," Miranda said with feeling. "You're walking away with all the fun in the room." Conscious of the invisible pattern on the walls, she lowered her voice as if the lines could hear her. "I am glad you're going, though."

"Me too," Cleo whispered back, and Miranda wondered if some part of her sensed the need not to be overheard. "I feel guilty saying that. I've been treated so well. I just… I just don't feel right here anymore." She shook her head. "You must think I'm silly."

"I don't," said Miranda. "I think you're absolutely correct. Things feel wrong to me too."

"Do you think you could leave?"

"No," said Miranda. "I'm too ill. I can't be on my own and I have no family. And I think I'm where I need to be. Do you think *I* sound silly?"

"You don't. I get you. I don't know why, but I think it's good for the others that you're here."

"That helps. Thank you."

They arrived at the elevator.

"I'll come and visit," Cleo offered.

"No!" Miranda hung on to her whisper. "When you're out of here, you're gone. Please?"

"Okay," said Cleo.

"Promise me," she said as the elevator doors opened.

"I promise."

They hugged. Cleo stepped into the elevator. They held on to each other's gazes until the doors closed.

Miranda listened to the hum of machinery taking Cleo away. She felt very, very lonely.

Miranda woke up around three. She climbed out of bed and padded quietly to the bathroom next to the exit from the room. She closed the door before turning on the light, and held her breath during the brief second of total darkness. The harshness of the overhead light always came as a relief.

While washing her hands, Miranda realized she was squinting. The light had dimmed from sharp yellow to a dirty orange. Miranda's face in the mirror became grainy. She dried her hands, and they became distant and grainy too. Motes of darkness danced in the light.

Miranda looked up at the light. She reached up to tighten the bulb. It dimmed to red as her hand drew near.

The motes swarmed, multiplied, thickened. They came together. They became worms, twisting angrily in the air.

A nightmare. She wasn't awake, just dreaming. Had to be.

Please, she begged to anything that would listen.

The worms grew longer. They coiled around the bulb and draped their bodies over the mirror. Some, grown plump and heavy, dropped into the sink and squirmed around in bunches at the drain.

The childhood reflex came again with the terror, and Miranda started hyperventilating.

Wake up, wake up, wake up.

But in the nightmares of her early years, she could breathe freely, even when drowning. Now her gasps hurt, and she lapsed into a coughing fit. It bent her over the sink. He lungs heaved, and a worm, coming up from inside, caught in her throat. She gagged. It wriggled on her tongue, slimy and furry at the same time. She tried to spit but choked. She couldn't breathe at all. She put her fingers in her mouth, tried to grab the worm. It was like trying to pull out her tongue. She gagged again, and this time the worm came out in a ball of phlegm, landing with a wet smack in the sink.

She moaned, eyes watering, and the dim red light flickered.

Wake up, wake up, wake–

No. She couldn't wake because she *was* awake.

A vision, a terrible vision, but just a vision, let it pass, know that it will end.

The worms gathered, fused, became longer coils, became serpents.

Miranda closed her eyes to shut the vision away. She could not. The growing serpents still writhed in the air before her.

Impossible. So this had to be a vision. The inescapability of the sights gave her hope, until a coil tightened around her wrist.

She opened her eyes again, and now that she wanted to see, she could see almost nothing in the dimming light, just the snakes, no, the single snake, and yet again no, it was not a snake, but something else and darker, not worm but wyrm, scales and muscle and a head she could not see and hoped she would not.

The wyrm pulled at her arm, and she pulled back, fighting a physical force. Nightmare or vision, it had flowed out of her mind and into reality, as the abbey had flowed into the Institute.

With a yank, Miranda hurled herself against the door. She grabbed the handle, but more coils wrapped around it, thinner than the greater mass and yet part of its single length. Her hands slipped on the slimy cluster. Long, glistening strength looped around her midriff and pulled her back. It had a path for her, and it would drag her down its dark road.

Whispers crawled up her spine. They squeezed into her skull. They searched for her certainties, bringing the venom of doubt.

But doubt was already hers. She valued doubt, and its shield against doctrine and dogma and pride. She doubted even the truth of the serpent and the pain of its grip. She clutched *her* doubt like a sword, and lurched forward to grab the door handle again. Both hands now, squelching through slime and gelid flesh, and she would not let go, not ever, and before the wyrm could constrict and devour, before the light failed and the snarling dark came, she pushed down with all her force on the handle.

It turned.

The door opened.

She fell out of the bathroom and hit the floor with a bruising impact.

The bathroom light blazed yellow into the room. In her bed, Lupita stirred and whimpered a complaint, shut eyes squeezing tighter.

Miranda got up, turned off the light and closed the door on the empty bathroom. She tiptoed back to her bed and nestled under the covers, breathing as deeply as she could without pain. She rubbed her hands, her blessedly dry hands, together, and interlaced her fingers.

She had survived the blow. She wondered, terrified, how much worse the next one would be.

She vowed, determined, to ward it off too.

CHAPTER SEVENTEEN

The storm hit on the third day of the *Leviathan*'s return crossing. The wind came up and the clouds gathered. The rain came down in angled torrents, chasing passengers off the decks. Then the swells grew. The rocking of the ship became noticeable by lunch. The people most prone to seasickness took to their cabins. Many people, especially children, had fun with the movement of the hallways, laughing as they teetered back and forth, banging into doorways and grabbing onto rails. By dinner, the waves were twenty feet high, and the novelty had worn off.

The Tourist Third dining room was half empty. Agatha had to keep catching her plate to stop it from sliding back and forth on their table. The folds of the white tablecloth brushed against her knees, drew back, and touched again, an insistent linen ghost. Wilbur stared at his food, his complexion a pale shade of green. Finally, he closed his eyes and shook his head.

"I can't," he said.

"Can you manage a bit of water?"

Another shake. "No." He breathed through his mouth. "I need to go back to the cabin."

Agatha stood up. "Then let's go."

She held his arm, and they walked slowly. Wilbur winced every time he swallowed, waging a last-ditch battle against nausea. He spoke with pauses for shaky inhalations. "Didn't I say… a spring crossing would be fun."

"You did, and I am sorry, my dear. This has been a rough trip all around."

"Was it… worth it?"

"I think so. I learned something important."

"Will it help?"

"I want to believe that it will." She didn't know.

The storm grew worse in the time it took them to reach their cabin. The ship climbed and plunged down such mountainous waves, Agatha and Wilbur had to clutch the rails with both hands to keep from falling. The struggle actually seemed to help Wilbur. He had to work so hard to stay on his feet that he forgot how sick he felt.

Once in the cabin, he tumbled, sick and relieved, into the lower berth. Agatha tucked him in, pulling the covers up to his chin. He looked so frail, and she cursed herself for having given in to the selfish impulse to have his company on the trip.

"Are you going to be all right?" she asked.

"I will be when we get home."

She stroked his forehead. "I'm sorry this is so hard."

Wilbur took her hand. "We will be all right, won't we?"

"Of course we will. This is a good ship, and the storm isn't *that* bad."

"That's not what I meant. I know the ship will make it to port. Will *we* be all right?"

"Yes," Agatha said, firmly, because that was what he needed to hear, and she needed to believe. "Why?"

"Is something following us?"

Her throat dried. "Have you seen something?"

"No," said Wilbur. "It's just… Sometimes I think you have."

Agatha bit her lip. She had felt tense the entire trip back from Durstal. She had kept checking behind them whenever she thought Wilbur wouldn't notice. She should have known he would pick up on her anxiety. From the moment she had come down the outside of the wall around the estate, her overriding drive had been to put as much distance between them and the blighted ground as possible. The trains had not been fast enough. They did not accumulate enough miles. No distance felt safe. Rationally, she knew she couldn't hope for that safety, not when the abbey and the Stroud Spiral had become the Institute, not when a link of that kind existed between Galloway and Arkham.

Irrationally, she felt the need for flight. And she did not have a reassuring answer to Wilbur's question. Was something following them? She couldn't lie and say no. She couldn't terrify him and say yes. She couldn't even give herself a definite answer. Several times on the train journey that took them to Southampton, she thought she saw something in the corner of her eye. A flicker of grey, the vibration of a thread, a cracked and fluttering angle. When she turned and looked directly, she never saw anything.

But her shoulders ached from the tension and the watching.

She hadn't seen anything since they'd boarded the

Leviathan. The last few days had been the first restful ones she'd had since the night on the estate. She didn't even mind the storm, though she wished it wasn't so hard on Wilbur.

"We're fine," she said. "I encountered something frightening and dangerous on the Stroud Estate, but it isn't here. We're safe."

Wilbur sighed and gave her hand a grateful squeeze. "Thank you," he said. "I think I'll sleep now."

"I thought I'd read in the lounge for a while." It was barely past seven. She wouldn't be ready for bed for another few hours.

"Good idea," said Wilbur. "I'll be fine here. Go and relax."

There were even fewer people in the Tourist Third cabin lounge than there had been in the dining saloon. Agatha had most of the lounge to herself. She settled in an armchair next to one of the wooden pillars. A potted fern nearby swayed gently with the motion of the ship, as if remembering the feeling of wind.

She hadn't been there more than a minute when two of the small handful of passengers present hurried out, hands over their mouths. The rise and fall of the ship leaned Agatha back and forth in her chair. She found the side-to-side motion almost soothing in its rhythm, and she sank into her book.

She had chosen to be in Leo Selig's company tonight. She had read *The Ascended Treatise* more than once, but the massive volume warranted return visits for new arguments. Agatha found Selig as interesting as he was frustrating. Selig, who eccentrically followed both Aleister Crowley and Helena Blavatsky, managed to avoid the worst features of his inspirations. That didn't prevent his book from being a mess of conjecture and foundationless theories. In spite of that, over the course of a thousand pages of dense, recondite prose, he kept giving Agatha interesting things to argue with, and insights that she had never considered.

Lost in the thickets of Selig's thesis, she didn't look up for a couple of hours.

The sound of gnawing broke her concentration. The noise seemed to be coming from inside the pillar. She tried to tune it out. Rats, she thought. Every ship had them. She went back to her book.

The teeth chewed through something that snapped like bone. A body rustled. Then it slithered.

Agatha put the book down. She looked around. There was no one else in the lounge.

Slither. Scrape.

She stood up, then backed a few steps away from the table, her eyes on the pillar.

A long scrape, the sound of a claw dragging down against the interior.

The wood rippled.

Agatha fled the lounge, moving as quickly as the heaving deck permitted. The sounds followed her, snaking out of the pillar, into the floor, and then up into the walls of the corridor.

Her first impulse, a primal instinct, was to find other people, as if nightmares could not exist in the presence of a crowd. She saw no one. The hall from the lounge stretched out before her, a deserted perspective to the vanishing point.

She hesitated. Go where? Run where?

A tongueless voice moaned like a dog. The slithering sounded familiar, and claws scrabbled at metal.

The walls began to ripple.

Agatha held her medallion. She whispered another portion of the Evashallon prayer, almost as afraid to speak those words as she was of the thing that had come for her. She did not know what cost might attach itself to the prayer, or what alliance she might invite.

The uttering of a few syllables seemed to push at the enemy. The rippling ceased. The clawing became frenzied, and it moved away from her.

Then it paused, and a liquid snarl came from the ceiling. At the same time, on her right, the slithering rushed ahead, leaving her behind.

Leaving part of itself behind.

Unless more than one being had come.

Agatha heard the sound of a long, sinuous body shooting down the corridor in the direction of her cabin.

Wilbur.

She hurried forward again, struggling up sudden inclines and then running down them as the ship climbed and plunged. She had to reach the cabin first, had to save Wilbur.

How?

Fight how?

Why had the thing chosen them as prey?

No, she thought. She had it wrong. They had not drawn the horror to them. Not directly. It was the stone she had taken from the abbey. She had created the same link between herself and the abbey as the one between it and the Institute.

You fool. You damned, damned fool. Why not summon it deliberately and get it all over with right away?

She chased the sounds now, racing to get to the cabin

first. And the heaving of the ship mocked her. It took her balance away, changed the direction of her momentum up and down, back and forth. The corridor stayed empty of people and hope, but no, it was not truly empty, because there were things here, things inside the walls, and the walls were rippling, ready to tear like bad skin.

The hallway reached to infinity, taking the cabin away, so far away she would never get there.

Except she did, with the walls bulging now, the metal thin as a film of surface tension, turning translucent, and Agatha saw the squirming within, the strong twitch of a coil, and the flex of claws.

She burst into the cabin, accompanied by a scraping cacophony of the long, slithering thing changing course to follow her from the inside of the wall.

"Agatha!" Wilbur cried. "What is it? What's happening?" Eyes wide, he had his covers pulled up past his chin. He stared at Agatha so he would not look at the walls. "What is happening?"

"It will stop," she promised. She flew across the cabin to her suitcase. She rooted through it as, above her head, the metal of the wall began to tear.

Her hand closed around the stone.

"Stay here," she ordered Wilbur and ran for the door.

"But..." he began.

A claw as long as her hand poked out of the wall between the berths. Wilbur yelped and tried to shrink down into his mattress.

"It will come with me," Agatha promised, hoping that was true.

She ran from the cabin and pounded down the corridor again, making for the door to Tourist Third promenade deck. A hiss, outraged and hungry, pursued her.

She did not know if one creature or many were in the walls. The snarling and the rasping of movement surrounded her. Clawed rents opened up in the ceiling and on either side of her, horror keeping pace, horror toying with the moment to strike.

Agatha threw the door to the deck open. The wind screamed at her, seized her, and almost lifted her off her feet. Spray lashed her like a whip. Skidding and stumbling, she hurtled across the deck to the railing.

Though the ship's bow aimed into the wind, the chaotic swells of waves slammed against the sides in fury. Their white anger blinded Agatha and left the deck soaking in water deep enough to pull at her feet as it withdrew. She weaved back and forth, and the railing hit her so hard it knocked the breath from her lungs.

She hurled the abbey stone overboard, then clutched the railing. The wind and waves surrounded her with their rage. They wanted to take her with the stone.

Behind her, horror tore itself out of the walls of the ship. It surged past her, a being not yet fully born into the material world. It howled through the air. She had a sensation of monstrous length whipping by in the spray and vanishing into the roiling depths.

Gasping, choking, her ribs a mass of pain, Agatha fought her way back across the deck and inside the ship. She slammed the door shut and leaned against it. She slid to the floor, soaked, drained with relief.

She did not want to think. Her mind betrayed her and leapt forward to the next terrible thought.

If this was what a single stone had called, what would the transported totality of the abbey and the Spiral summon?

CHAPTER EIGHTEEN

The Stroud Institute shifted. It changed. Its anticipation blew through the wards, an intangible yet insistent breeze that chilled Miranda. She could not feel the touch of the breeze, but she felt its effects. She could not get warm. The breeze followed her down the halls. It insinuated itself under her blanket. Darker than a promise, its smile wider than a threat. *Soon,* it whispered.

Soon.

Soon.

And sometimes, she thought, it laughed and said, *Now.*

She couldn't treat all change as sinister, yet with each change the breeze seemed to creep closer to being a wind, a storm to end all things.

She had expected the first change, inevitable with the departure of Cleo. Barbara Paul was her replacement, and she was not going to be nearly as much fun as Cleo had been. Not that Miranda felt humorous these days, but Barbara sucked the energy from the room. She lived and breathed her terror of her illness. She regarded every cough as a sign of terminal decline and imminent demise. "Am I going to die?" she asked endlessly.

"I hope so," Frieda muttered a few hours after Barbara's arrival, her words just audible enough to make Miranda wince, though Barbara gave no sign that she had heard. She was too consumed by her attempts to feel her pulse, to see if it was beating too strongly, or perhaps not at all.

"You are not going to die," Miranda told her. Tall, broad-shouldered, Barbara looked like she could take on a quarterback and come out the victor. "I guarantee it." With an inner sigh, she accepted that she had just committed herself to making that same guarantee on a daily basis, at the very least.

The other change came the day after Barbara's arrival. Exercise was not just permitted now. It was encouraged. At least, *encouraged* was the word Nurse Revere used. Coming from her, it sounded more forceful than a suggestion.

"How long can my walks be?" Miranda asked her. Revere had just announced the new regime to the room before doing the usual check of vital signs at each bedside.

"As long as you can manage," Revere said, whipping off the blood pressure cuff, her movements as brusque as ever, as if the cuff had offended her and needed punishment.

"Every day?"

Revere looked down her nose at Miranda. "Why?" she asked, suspicious. "You aren't thinking of shirking, are you?"

"No, no," said Miranda.

"You wouldn't want to be thought of as *difficult*."

"Of course not."

"This is how you get well."

"I know."

"You aren't going to pretend you know better than the doctors."

"I never meant that."

"Walk the path," Revere commanded.

Miranda said nothing. She just nodded. Did Revere mean what she had just said? Was she even aware of it, and of how out of character it sounded? The order had come out as a mechanical compulsion.

Revere looked at her, motionless, waiting for a satisfactory response.

"I'll walk the path," Miranda said softly.

Revere jerked back into motion. She gave Miranda a curt nod and turned to Frieda.

For the first time, Miranda doubted the wisdom of the care. That was a change that truly belonged to the cold, impossible draft.

She obeyed, though. She would not be difficult. She would not call more attention to herself than necessary. Not until she knew what she had to do. Not until she knew how to fight back.

Fight back against what?

Find out. Somehow, find out.

Miranda went out on longer walks. Everyone did. The corridors became crowded with patients shuffling along or wheeling themselves on journeys without destinations. Miranda changed her approach to the halls of the Stroud Institute. She accepted that she could not map the floor in her head. She shifted her attention to her fellow patients and watched them instead, searching for patterns.

•••

Miranda wished for larger groups at Daria Miracle's counseling sessions. She didn't like being part of a single circle of participants. Mentally, she had moved to the back of the room, where students could pretend the teachers did not see them. She wished she could really be there, lurking in the background of the session, observing without being observed.

Miranda maintained her camouflage instead. She knew what bored students looked like, and made sure to appear otherwise. With a bit of effort, she kept her face bright and interested.

Daria began the session by asking the circle how everyone was doing.

"I don't know," Frieda said, sounding genuinely upset instead of chagrined.

"What don't you know?" Daria said, moving to Frieda's chair with feline grace.

The question seemed to throw Frieda, as if it struck home in a way she was frightened to understand. It pulled the pain out of her in words. "What am I supposed to believe?" she cried.

Other patients nodded. Some leaned forward, hanging on Daria's answer. Lupita squeezed her hands together in distress.

Daria knelt beside Frieda. "Why ask me?" she said, soft and kind. She touched Frieda's hand. "This is for you to know. Your journey is yours. As it has always been."

"Where are you taking us?" a woman called Perla Todd asked.

Daria rose from Frieda's side. Pure dance, she turned and

moved to smile down at the teenager. "I'm not taking you anywhere," she said. "You're taking yourself."

"But we're asking questions we shouldn't," Lupita said, on the edge of a quaver.

Daria flowed in her direction. "Why forbidden?" Always gentle, always soft, always welcoming, never stern.

"Because…" Lupita said. She searched for words. "Because they're wrong."

"Wrong? But why? Is it because they don't have answers?"

"I don't know." Miserable, Lupita stared at her hands.

Daria leaned and touched Lupita's chin, soft as a breeze, a breeze from the ether.

Are you cold, Lupita? Miranda wondered.

Lupita jerked her head up to meet Daria's warm, piercing gaze.

"Is faith fragile?" said Daria. "Is yours?"

Lupita's breath hitched.

"You don't have to answer," said Daria. "I'm here to help, not upset you. And I don't think faith is fragile at all."

She did not say *your* faith, Miranda noted.

Daria moved to the center of the ring, carrying all attention with her. "We don't like doubt," she said. "No one does. It hurts."

"It does," Lupita whispered. She hugged herself against the cold.

"I'm sure you're not alone, my dear," said Daria. "How about a show of hands? How many people here are wrestling with doubt?" She raised her hand high.

After a moment's hesitation, so did everyone else. Miranda did too. Did it count if, instead of wrestling with doubt, she embraced it? That didn't matter. The point was not to stand out. Not yet.

Appear to be one of the flock.

"There," said Daria. She turned her smile on Lupita. "See? You're not alone at all." She went back to addressing everyone, walking slowly around the circle again.

Miranda watched her spiraling, spiraling.

"What should you do with doubt?" Daria asked. "You should ask yourself why you are encountering it. Let the questions come. Find the true source of the doubt. Get to its core. Can I let you in on a secret?" A conspiratorial smile. "Doubt is the path to certainty. Follow the doubt all the way, and you'll come out the other side. Walk the path of doubt to its center, and there you will find knowledge. There you will find truth."

The pattern of Daria's movements changed. Instead of circling inside the ring of chairs, she went back and forth across the circle, gracefully bouncing from one patient to the next. The directions seemed random at first. Then Miranda caught the way the tight turns created nestling lines. Daria was walking a labyrinth.

"Don't stagnate in dogma," said Daria. "You won't find certainty there. The harder you clutch on to dogma, the worse the doubt will become. Find your way to a living belief. It will change you."

Daria kept speaking, urging the audience on their journeys. Her voice pulled, and her words pushed. She created a powerful current. Miranda felt it, and even braced as she was, she had to fight hard to keep from being swept off her feet. She distracted herself and tuned Daria out by focusing on the others. The current had them. Their faces were rapt. They were happy to drown for Daria. The wind from the ether blew stronger, stronger, becoming a gale, and the waves it conjured could not be swum.

But doubt was her element. Miranda lived for the questions that troubled. That was why she could fight. She had always lived in this sea. She would battle the currents, and not fear the gale.

After the counseling session, after an afternoon rest, Nurse Revere called on them to go walking again. Miranda watched as she strolled slowly, noting the changes caused by the Institute's wind in the faces of her fellow patients. In some, she saw the look of gnawing obsession that haunted Lupita and Frieda's features. In others, she saw a kind of blank determination. Barbara had it, when she wasn't swamped by her health terror of the hour.

Beyond the shared expressions, Miranda finally began to see a pattern in the walks. Daria's ballet had taught her what to look for. No one moved with Daria's elegance, but the pattern was there. It defied easy definition. It lacked location or clear direction. Miranda found it concentrating on the turns she saw the other patients make. She kept herself a dozen steps behind Barbara and counted her left and right turns. When Barbara returned to the room to lie down, Miranda kept going, following another, and then another patient.

She counted, and she found the pattern. She found the labyrinth path they were walking.

Her legs ached with fatigue. She wanted to lie down. She

made herself keep going. She had to see how far the pattern went.

She took the elevator to the next ward down. There, as with her floor, every mobile patient was walking. She didn't stay long. She didn't want to be noticeable. She strolled casually, looked pleasant, and counted turns just long enough to be sure that everyone walked the same path here too. Then she took the elevator again.

The ward above hers was the one where Cleo would have gone, had she not recovered so quickly. Here were the patients closest to being given a clean bill of health. These were the volunteers, the active residents of the Stroud Institute, the ones learning how to adjust to active life once more.

They walked quickly, and there were many of them. Miranda shrank back next to the wall, fearing the traffic would carry her off at a pace that would overwhelm her. She could not keep up with anyone she chose to follow. She didn't have to. The sheer number of walkers, and the purpose of their stride, made the shape of the pattern so much easier to see. Miranda didn't have to count the turns. She knew what to expect from the floors below, and so now she could predict which way any of the patients would turn.

The intersections were lies, she thought. There were no choices here at all. Not a maze, but a labyrinth, a single path leading to the center.

What center, though? Where was it?

She walked for as long as she could, taking in the full force of the walk's flow, and the chill of the blank, straining faces.

She wondered how close to the center these people had come.

Perhaps because of the greater freedom of movement of these patients, with the chains of illness fallen from them, she caught the flaws in the walking more easily. They stood out more. Every now and then, a stuttering twitch interrupted their gait, a splice in the film of their movement. Miranda slowed down to a mere shuffle, watching closely. The twitches, she saw, happened when the patients passed particular spots of the walls. No features stood out about the locations. That meant nothing. Miranda knew about the lines of the labyrinth beneath the paint. They didn't stand out, either.

Miranda became conscious again of the wrongness of the intersections, of the Institute's skewed architecture. The rooms were not big enough. The corridors extended too far beyond the end walls of the last rooms before they turned.

Miranda ran her fingers gently on the wall starting a few yards away from one of the twitch points. She felt the lines, and walked as slowly as she had to so she would not lose them. Remaining wary of falling into its rhythm, she let the pattern draw her on.

She came level with the point where the patient ahead of her had jerked. Her fingers found a slight, circular depression. The lines coiled around it. She took her hand down and moved away from the wall before she attracted attention.

That night, Miranda waited until her roommates slept, and the night nurse had come by on her first round. She wouldn't be by again for at least fifteen minutes.

Miranda rose and, barefoot, padded silently into the corridor. She went down to the end of the hall, close to the intersection. Battling the misleading geography of the

Institute, she searched for the point equivalent to the one she had found on the floor above. It took her a minute or two of going back and forth for her fingers to follow the pattern to another depression.

Miranda took a breath. She checked the hall. She was alone.

She pushed.

The circle of wall went deeper in, then stopped with a faint click. A vertical line appeared and the wall parted before it, the two halves of the stone portal pulling back with unnatural smoothness of motion and a silence that sent gooseflesh up her arms.

A passage led into the dark. No paint on its walls; the stone was rough, damp, reveling in the glory of its age. The smell of the sea crept out and wrapped around her.

Miranda pushed the depression next to the opening again. It clicked back out, and the walls closed once more. She could see no sign that the portal had ever been there.

Still alone, she hurried back to the room.

The others were awake, sitting up, and staring at her.

"Sorry if I woke you," she said, slipping back into bed. *Please don't ask what I was doing.*

Lupita asked something worse. "Are we in danger?"

"No," Frieda snapped, and the danger was in her voice.

"But…" Lupita began. Frieda's glare stopped her.

"Is there something wrong with this place?" Barbara asked.

What could she say? Miranda wondered. How could she help them? If she took them into her confidence, what would that do? Could they fight, when she didn't know how? Would she just be putting them in danger?

"If you can leave," Miranda said, feeling a gamble in each word, "I think you should."

"Nonsense," said Frieda, brittle and angry. "Whatever is wrong with you?"

Lupita shivered and pulled her blankets up to her chin.

"Oh dear," Barbara whispered shakily. "Oh dear, oh dear, oh dear. My brother is a police officer. Maybe he can help. I'll speak to him in the morning."

He wouldn't be able to help, Miranda thought. But if the idea gave Barbara some comfort, or he could find a way of taking her out of the Institute, then well and good.

Miranda managed to fall asleep an hour later. She did not dream.

In the morning, Barbara was gone. A different woman slept in her bed.

CHAPTER NINETEEN

Breakfast came, and no one said anything about Barbara. Miranda recognized the new woman from the counseling sessions. Her name came back to her after a minute – Norma Reese. She had been in a room four doors down.

Frieda chatted with Norma as if she saw nothing unusual in the other woman's presence. Lupita joined in too, a bit shyly, but also with a dogged commitment to normality. Miranda couldn't manage more than some grunted agreements and noncommittal mumbles when one of the others spoke to her. How could they be talking about the orange juice, and whether it tasted more chilled than usual this morning, and how nice it was that the eggs were a proper over-easy with lots of runny yolk? How could they not ask Norma what she was doing here? How could they not raise the alarm and demand to know where Barbara had gone?

The questions shrieked in Miranda's mind. She did not voice them. She didn't do any of the things she wished the others were doing. Instead, she watched them closely, looking for signs of things that were wrong, or she hoped, that were still right.

Was there any hint that they knew something strange had happened?

In Lupita, yes, Miranda thought. Her contributions to the conversation were tentative and brittle. She reminded Miranda of a dog licking the hand of an unpredictably violent master.

What master? She didn't know.

Frieda, on the other hand, seemed resolute. She would impose normality on the situation through sheer, bulldozing belief. That was Miranda's more optimistic reading. She didn't want to think that Frieda really did believe all was fine. But if she had to face that reality, she would.

"Eat up," Norma said, eyeing Miranda's barely touched breakfast. "Got to keep your strength up for all the walking later." She laughed, and Miranda did her best not to cringe too visibly. Norma was one of those people who laughed at the end of every sentence. "We need to get lots walking today," Norma added, nodding at her own wisdom.

The other two nodded as well. Walking must be done. Consensus reigned.

Were they all mad? Miranda wondered. Could they hear themselves?

Maybe something had happened during the night. Maybe the effects of all the walking of the day before had sunk in, only these three had not woken with sore muscles because the walking had nothing to do with exercise, not really. Just like a communion wafer wasn't about food. The walking was a ritual, Miranda knew that. What kind, and to what purpose, she didn't know yet.

They were changing, she thought. Through the ritual

came transformation, one deeper and darker than transubstantiation.

Nurse Holden came by on her rounds after breakfast. Her movements seemed stiff, as if her body had become unfamiliar to her. When she smiled, the smile came from a distance. It looked like plastic.

"Where's Barbara?" Miranda asked.

"Who?" said Holden.

"Barbara," Miranda repeated, her pulse skipping beats. "She was here yesterday. Very frightened about every single symptom. Big, strong woman." She kept piling on the details as if that would force Holden to acknowledge Barbara's existence.

Holden frowned. She shook her head. That was when Miranda noticed the twitch. It had no rhythm between occurrences. She picked up on it this time because it happened twice in a few seconds. After Holden shook her head *no,* she shook again, so quickly her face blurred. And then, as she started to speak, the sudden, rapid shake happened once more. "I'm sorry, Professor Ventham," she said. "I don't know who you mean. Norma has been in this room since Cleo left."

Miranda stared at her. *Liar,* she thought. And then: *What if she isn't?* It might be worse if Holden believed she was telling the truth.

Worse yet if she was right.

Or perhaps Miranda should be hoping that was the case. If the problem lay with her, and her grip on reality, then there was nothing for the others to fear at the Stroud Institute.

No. She could not take refuge in that lie. That would be cowardice. She had made a promise to fight.

Frieda and Lupita were staring at her. Propped up against their pillows, they were very, very still. They didn't want to be frightened. Norma was looking at her in confused expectation. She needed her cue to laugh again.

"Oh," Miranda said. "I see." No, I don't, but I'll play along for now. "Sorry. Rough night. My dreams must have confused me." A weak explanation, but it seemed to satisfy Holden and the others. She had given them something they could choose to believe.

After Holden left, Norma decided she had her permission to laugh. "That must have been quite the night!" she said to Miranda.

Miranda gave her a weak smile. "Seems so." She braced herself for awkwardness.

None came. Norma chatted happily, bubbling on about how much she was looking forward to the day. "It's so exciting, isn't it?"

"What is?"

"Our journey! That is something I really didn't expect when I came here. I'm not just getting well in body! I'm walking the path! Isn't that wonderful?"

She laughed and laughed, and Miranda didn't have to answer.

When Norma went to the bathroom to get washed up and ready for her exciting journey, Miranda confronted Frieda and Lupita.

"Well?" she asked. "Did I really just imagine Barbara?"

Lupita squirmed and didn't answer. Frieda rounded on her with a ferocious, frightened glare. "Why are you being like this?" she demanded.

"You didn't answer my question," said Miranda. "What about Barbara?"

Lupita kept her eyes down. She pulled a rosary back and forth between her fingers, her lips moving in an unconvincing, heartbreaking mimicry of prayer.

"Just stop it!" Frieda hissed. "You aren't helping. You're being scary."

Miranda didn't reply. She saw that she would not get the answer she wanted from either of them. She couldn't even tell if they believed in Barbara's existence or not.

"Let's just do our walk," Lupita whispered. "We'll all feel better."

"Will you?" said Miranda. "Did Daria help you yesterday, or make you feel worse about your doubts?"

"We have to reach our center," Frieda said, pronouncing judgment from on high. "Once we get there, we'll be better."

"No more doubts?"

"Stop it!" Lupita pleaded.

Miranda took a breath, then nodded. She was doing no good. Lupita and Frieda were clinging to the labyrinth and the promise of certainty. If she insisted on asking about Barbara, she would only make their doubts more painful, and they would clutch Daria's promises with even greater desperation.

They had nowhere to go. They had to feel safe here. They weren't, but she couldn't save them through terror – if she could save them at all.

If she could save anyone.

After breakfast, the walking began. Frieda, Lupita and Norma threw themselves into the exercise with a fervor that gradually became a blank effort. Miranda stayed close enough to watch them. She saw their features loosen, their eyes become dull. The ritual had them, its grip stronger than yesterday. She could feel its power now, and it wanted her to take part. It would be so easy. She could walk the path to certainty too. She could stop worrying about Barbara. She could stop worrying about everything, if she walked the path all the way.

New doubts crept into her mind, squirming in like spiders, doubts inserted by a force outside her, but so perfectly shaped for her that, if she had not been on her guard, she would have thought they came from within. They were doubts about her doubts, insinuations that she had misread everything, that she and Agatha were sabotaging her recovery, to the point where she could no longer tell the difference between fever dreams and reality. How could she really believe she had found a secret passage in the Institute? Gothic nonsense, so obviously born of her research field that it was amazing she could credit the thought in the light of day.

It would be easy to walk the path. It would be restful, in the end, to let the doubts take her, and follow Daria's prescription to certainty.

Miranda shook herself. *No,* she thought. She pushed back at the doubts. The inside of her head itched from their scrabbling legs. *No.* She knew what she had seen. She knew what was real. She would not accept these doubts. She had plenty of her own to turn against the enemy and the blandishments of certainty. That, above all things, she distrusted. The Great War and the physical, emotional, cultural and spiritual devastations it had left behind had proven the wisdom of that perspective.

She resisted the currents of the ritual. She eyed the location of the hidden door every time she passed it. She wondered how many other entrances there were. At least one on every floor, she guessed. She pictured secret halls, thick with age and the smell of the sea, spreading out through the Stroud Institute, an inner rot. The scale of what might be present made her feel very small. She walked closer and closer to the edge of despair. How was she going to fight this all alone?

Where was Agatha? When would she be back?

The awful possibility: *What if she's dead?*

The rooms Miranda passed were largely empty. Almost all the patients in the ward were walking. Miranda thought the numbers were wrong. If there was no one in the rooms, she should be seeing more people in the halls. She wondered how many other Barbaras had disappeared.

She felt the crisis padding down the halls with her, gathering its forces, growing ready to complete its great work.

A desperate thought came. She could burn the Institute down. She pictured the flames rising high in the night, engulfing the roof, billowing out of the windows, roaring down the corridors.

She shuddered. Even if she could find a way to do this, how many patients would she kill?

Nauseated, she banished the idea.

She turned a corner and saw Donovan Stroud coming down the hall, against the tide of walkers. He smiled at everyone, stopping every few steps to exchange a word. His approach was casual.

It was also purposeful. Miranda knew he had come to see her.

He stopped in front of her. “Professor Ventham,” he said. “How nice to see you looking so much better than the last time we met.”

“That’s kind of you to say.”

“I was wondering, do you think Nurse Revere would object if I stole you away from your exercise for a little while?”

“I owe you and myself an apology,” Donovan said when they were settled in his lounge.

They sat as they had before, with Miranda on the couch and her back to the window. She tried to not stare too fixedly at the painting over the mantle. Had it changed? Had the abbey vanished? No, the ruins still loomed on the horizon behind Magnus Stroud, as if mocking her for believing in her vision.

She felt something had changed in the room, though. Something more concrete than her trust in the place.

“An apology?” Miranda asked, scanning the room.

“Yes, for neglecting my opportunities to talk with you.” Donovan pulled a wry face. “And after all my fancy talk of being delighted to have a scholar in residence, as it were.”

“Flatterer.”

“Not at all. Not at all. But it is good to see that color in your cheeks. How *are* you? I’m told you’re improving.”

“So I am,” Miranda said.

On the wall behind Donovan, that wood-engraving, its lines dense as a Doré. She didn’t remember it from before. She hadn’t noticed it, at least. In a storm of wind and waves and fire, a serpent and a dragon entwined in combat. The twisting of limbs and scales leapt out at her, rich with meaning. She saw in the print the symbol of the Stroud Institute's architecture. She saw two sets of corridors entwined, one hidden by the other, a double labyrinth, the true center concealed from the walking patients. For the moment.

"Does Agatha Crane still pay you regular visits? It would be lovely to speak with her again too."

Miranda tore her eyes from the print. She focused on Donovan. "Agatha's away," she said. "She'll be back soon, I would think."

"I'm sure you will be glad to see her." Donovan smiled.

How many layers should she read below the innocuous surface of his comments? How deep a threat?

The skittering, spider-legged doubts scratched to be let in, to tell her that in her paranoia, she turned pleasantries into murder.

"It will be nice when she's back," Miranda agreed.

"Tea?" Donovan asked. "I think it has steeped enough." He picked up the Wedgwood teapot from the table between them.

"No, thank you."

Donovan poured himself a cup. "I've been meaning to ask you," he said, "what you thought of our counseling sessions." He added a teaspoon of sugar, hesitated, then another. He looked up as he stirred, all attention.

"I didn't know what to expect," said Miranda, ready for a trap to spring, not knowing which word, look or hesitation could trigger it. "Daria Miracle is an extraordinary speaker."

Donovan chuckled. He wagged a finger at Miranda. "I detect diplomacy behind your words. You have your doubts about her teachings. I can tell."

"I always have doubts." So there would be fencing today. Very well. She would not retreat, in spite of the traps.

Donovan looked pleased. "That's what I thought," he said. "They're a necessary part of your pedagogical practice, aren't they? They're needed for critical thinking."

"That's right."

"You teach your students to have doubts."

"I do."

A wide grin. "I imagine that makes for some lively dinner conversations at Thanksgiving for them, when they trot out what they've learned from you."

"You're flattering me again," said Miranda. "You overrate the impact I have on my students."

"And I think you're being too humble."

"You wouldn't if you were nodding off at one of my lectures."

"I'm sure I wouldn't. I can't imagine anyone could."

"Then you would be surprised."

Donovan sipped his tea. "I suppose anything is possible," he said. "The fact remains that I know I would be riveted. We have very similar philosophies, you and I."

"Oh?"

"Yes. We simply apply them in different fields. I, too, firmly believe in the need to foster healthy doubt."

"Healthy," Miranda repeated.

"Naturally."

"So you think being wracked by doubt helps the body combat TB?"

Donovan raised his eyebrows in mock surprise. "Wracked?" he said. "*Wracked*? That doesn't sound like the language of someone who believes in the value of doubt." He raised a hand before she could answer. "But I see what you're doing. You're making me apply the principals of critical thinking to my own system. Give it a shake, eh? Make sure it isn't brittle dogma? Yes, in answer to your question. Because doubts and curiosity are intimately related. A curious mind is an engaged mind, as I have always maintained, and that is the way forward."

He wanted her on-side, Miranda thought. Why?

Donovan put his cup down. He brought his hands together and leaned forward, delivering a confidence. "If I could cure this century's ills," he said, "I would. And one of the greatest of those ills is misplaced certainty." He lowered his voice and carved his words out of solemnity itself. "Look what certainty has done to the world."

Miranda held her face still. *Don't let him see you're startled.* Donovan hit too close to her thoughts of earlier. The doubts from outside plunged through her defenses. Her lungs felt thick and cold. She struggled to breathe.

"Magnus saw the same thing," Donovan continued. "He saw what the cancer of certainty did to the French Revolution. He witnessed the Terror, and Napoleon's betrayal that became the Empire. He saw that he had to fight, to carve the path through the reeds of false certainty, wielding the blade of doubt." He leaned back with a theatrical grimace. "I am very sorry about that metaphor. That was a bit much."

"How did Magnus fare in his struggle?" Miranda asked.

"He made a start. It was always a project that would span generations."

"So the torch has fallen to you now."

"Yes, it has." Donovan's eyes burned as he spoke the boast, the promise, and the warning.

He knew she was fighting him. He was telling her that he knew. They weren't even pretending to be talking about the treatment of tuberculosis anymore. She still wondered why they were speaking at all. Barbara had mentioned a brother in the police, and she had vanished. Miranda's visions, when they came, were worse than ever. But she was still here, physically unharmed.

Donovan wanted her for something.

And the currents in the Institute kept trying to pull her down the labyrinth's path.

Donovan had all the advantages. He knew what was happening. She didn't.

I'll fight you anyway.

"And are you the one to bring Magnus' work to completion?" she asked.

"I am. And I will."

The impossible wind blew hard through the halls. It blew through the lounge. The windows rattled. Though it was spring, Miranda shivered with the coming of winter.

CHAPTER TWENTY

Agatha and Wilbur arrived at their apartment well after ten at night. The last task of the journey looked like it was going to break Wilbur. He tottered as he got out of the taxi outside their apartment building, and he carried his suitcase as if it were slowly pulling his arm out of its socket.

"Almost done," Agatha encouraged him. She hooked her arm in his, and they made their way up the porch and into the building.

When they unlocked their apartment, Wilbur went straight to the bedroom. Agatha heard his suitcase thump on the floor, and the squeak of mattress springs as he threw himself on the bed.

"Get into pajamas before you fall asleep," she called out.

"What are you doing?" he answered.

"I'll be there in a minute." She had an inspection to make.

Agatha moved through the rooms, turning on all the lights. The apartment exuded that chilly stillness that settled over rooms left empty for longer than a few days. The familiar had taken on a sheen of the uncanny. Furniture and possessions looked back at her, inviting her to wonder if any had changed positions while she had been gone. None had, but it took the tour, and several minutes of reacquainting her with her space, to make the home hers again.

She banished shadows and stood in each room, turning around slowly, until she satisfied herself that nothing had come here ahead of them, and nothing waited in the dark corners.

She ran her hand over the books, crammed and bursting from shelves, and stacked in precarious piles on every flat surface. She walked down the hall, with its lithographs of Paris, London and Prague, and asked herself if the lighting was not a bit dimmer than it should be.

No, it wasn't. She could see down the corridor's length as well as she ever had.

She had left a small, protective circle, drawn in salt, in every room. Nothing had broken the boundaries of the circles. She did not really know what, if anything, could shield her against what she feared was coming to Arkham, and that might still have its sights on her. But her home felt right, and she sighed, grateful. She went to her office, opened the large wardrobe next to her battered, cluttered desk, and opened the tool box inside. She took out a geologist's hammer, then went back to her suitcase in the living room to dig out her flashlight.

"Agatha?" Wilbur called, suspicion shaving the sleep from his voice.

She poked her head in the doorway. "You get some sleep," she said. "You need it."

"So do you. What are you doing? Why do you still have your coat on? You're not going out again?"

"Yes. Sorry, but I have to."

"But you must be exhausted too. Can't it wait?"

"I'm fine," she lied. She was ready to drop. "It can't wait." That was true. She had been racing against time since her flight from the estate. What worried her was the growing conviction that the race had started much earlier.

Tuesday night in Arkham, after eleven. The streets of French Hill and Rivertown were quiet. Nothing unusual in that. But the quiet felt deeper than normal to Agatha. She saw no one else. No cars passed her. The streetlamps created pools of stagnant light. It had rained earlier in the evening, and the water from the eves broke the silence only to have it return with greater force after every echoing drop.

The night was taut with anticipation. It watched her, muscles coiled, coiling tighter the closer she came to the Stroud Institute. A current ran through the dark too, picking up strength and speed, trying to rush her to the Institute. She had to pay attention to each step, had to work to ensure her approach was on her own terms, her action, not a passive acceptance.

She would not be swept through the gates by the unseen river. She was heading to the Institute, but she would leave it again.

It would not devour her.

The gates were shut when she arrived. She hadn't expected them to be open, not at this time of night. Still, irrationally, the barrier felt like an angry response to her resistance. The current flowed hard, and the night was ready to pounce, and now she would have to work to get in.

"If I want to," she whispered to the Institute. "If I choose to."

The gate's pillars were made of the same stone as the Institute itself. She might not have to go any further.

So she told herself. It was the right kind of comforting lie for this moment. She didn't know if she had the energy to try to enter forbidden grounds again. The symmetry of the effort made her uneasy.

And yet. And yet. She knew she shouldn't make do with "good enough", not with so much at stake. She eyed the wall. It was higher than the one around the estate in Galloway. She didn't have a ladder. She could not climb it, and she could not squeeze through the pickets.

No way in. Not tonight, at least.

With a tired sigh of relief, she moved into the shadows of the left-hand pillar and pulled out her hammer. She looked up and down the street. She was alone.

Water plinked. The night watched.

Agatha struck the pillar. The hard *crack* of the hammer sounded like an explosion in the deserted street. She hit the pillar three more times before she could lose her nerve. The fourth hit dislodged a small piece of stone. She snatched it up, put it in her coat's pocket, then listened for the sounds of running footsteps and outraged shouts.

Nothing.

She let herself breathe normally. Time to go home, even with an imperfect sample. The way the atmosphere of anticipation built as she closed in on the Institute suggested that a sample taken from the building would be worth getting.

Before she could start moving, she heard a vehicle heading

her way. She froze, convinced it was coming for her, that someone had heard her and triggered an alarm. She stared at the headlights, unable to run.

The electric gates swung open, eerily quiet.

And the vehicle turned, its headlights swinging away from Agatha, and she saw that it was an ambulance, bringing another patient to the Stroud Institute.

The ambulance headed down the drive. After a slight pause, the gates began to close again. Before she had a chance to think her actions through and talk herself out of them, Agatha ducked out from behind the pillar and hurried between the gates.

They shut behind her with a metal click.

Now I have you, said the Institute, its words self-evident to her imagination.

No, she told it. You don't. I'm the one who's hunting you.

She half-convinced herself with her bravado.

The Institute loomed over her, glowering with the dim light that shone, colder than the moon, through a few windows. At the peak, the windows of Stroud's apartments blazed red, a cyclops's eye.

Agatha turned off the drive and into the trees, away from the eye's gaze. The lampposts along the drive gave her just enough illumination in the shadows to see her way. She went left, to the side of the building, and rushed in a crouch across the grass to the black stone mass.

No windows near here, and no door. She was hidden. She raised the hammer, winced in anticipation of the noise, and hit as quickly as she could.

Four taps, their echoes high and clear, and she knocked

a piece of stone from the body of the building. The heavy darkness over her seemed to quiver with a snarl. On instinct, she raised a hand to protect her face from the teeth or the jet of blood about to hit her.

Nothing touched her.

Silence clamped back down hard. Agatha felt the reach of the Institute across the grounds. The grass flexed under her steps like muscle tissue. The earth, hating her, paused on the edge of violent, carnivorous movement. She grabbed her sample and hurried back to the wall.

No way through the locked gates, and no way to climb the wall.

I have you, the Institute said again.

Not yet. You forgot the trees.

The oaks, thick and gnarled and ancient, lined the wall, and some of their branches went over it. It took Agatha a few increasingly frightened moments to find a tree she could climb, but there was one. She took hold of the lowest branch. The wood felt wrong, a heartbeat away from squirming. She fought through her disgust and held on. She climbed up, away from the tainted ground, knowing the tree could crush her with its limbs if she gave it a chance.

She climbed as if she were a child again, old moves coming back, fueled by adrenaline. A frightened squirrel, she hauled herself up to the branch that stretched over the wall, inched along it, and then dangled over the sidewalk. She let go, dropping a good five feet. She landed awkwardly. It hurt. She bit down on her yell, and it came out as a long, painful hiss.

She straightened, found her balance. Nothing broken, and she didn't have time for the pain of sprains.

She walked away from the Institute, its silent fury boring into her back.

She was shaking with cold and fatigue when she let herself back into the apartment. She couldn't sleep, though. The need to know kept her going a bit longer.

Agatha hurried to her office. She put her samples down on the laboratory table that sat against one wall and readied her microscope.

When she looked at them, her first thought was that she had pushed herself too far, and that exhaustion had wrecked her vision. She would have to try again tomorrow. The samples refused to come into focus. When she looked up, though, she could see clearly. There was nothing wrong with her vision. She peered through the microscope again and realized that the blur came from the sample. The stone was vibrating. Not enough to be detectible with the naked eye, or enough to be felt consciously by touch. It registered at the subconscious level, though. The stone felt unpleasant. Under high magnification, Agatha could see the thrum, and its irregular, complex rhythm.

The sample from the building seemed to be vibrating with a slightly greater intensity than the one from the gate.

A stronger link, she thought.

Link to what?

To the thing in Galloway. To the thing that would be coming.

She sighed, frustrated. She knew she was right, but her conclusions weren't based on science. She had evidence of something, but the specifics were still her intuition.

The specifics, but not the fact of the danger itself. She had felt it in Galloway. She had witnessed it on the *Leviathan*.

She knew it was coming. But she didn't know how she and Miranda, or anyone else, was meant to fight it.

We need to know more.

The terror, the time, and the expense of the trip, and had she gained anything?

Maybe. Confirmation of the threat, and that Donovan Stroud was involved.

That meant a clear direction of investigation. Except it was a direction closed to her. Only Miranda could follow it.

Could Agatha ask that of her? In all good conscience?

In all good conscience, could she not?

Fatigue finally caught up with her. She fell into bed, the unresolved question swirling in her mind. She fell asleep, and dreamed of serpents and the smell of the sea.

In the morning, while Wilbur, looking more rested than she felt, puttered about in the kitchen getting breakfast ready, she had another look at her samples.

She had no way to establish a quantitative measure of the vibrations in the stone. Even so, she could tell that the intensity of the blur had increased.

It's getting closer.

She went out again before breakfast, walked past the gates to the Stroud Institute, and tossed the samples inside. She didn't think she would learn any more from them, and she would not draw the horror to her home.

She listened to the warning of her dreams.

CHAPTER TWENTY-ONE

Miranda flew out of bed, across the room, and into Agatha's arms. She hugged the older woman fiercely, reassuring herself that she was real. Agatha hugged her back, just as hard. They stepped away and grinned at each other, giddy with mutual relief.

"I am so, so glad to see you," Miranda said. "I can't tell you how good it feels."

"You don't have to. That's how I'm feeling too."

Conscious that they were standing in the middle of the room, and that the other three were staring at them, Miranda led Agatha back to her end. They sat down on the edge of her bed and spoke in quieter tones, the ones people used when visiting, as if this would make them inaudible to the other occupants. It would, Miranda hoped, make listening in a bit more difficult and less interesting. Either way, torn between suspicion and the need to help, she had to be guarded in what she said.

"How was your trip?" she asked.

Agatha nodded to herself and gave an expressive sigh. "Exciting," she said.

"Good research for your book?" Miranda settled on their cover story for the moment.

"I think so. I feel like the book has some direction now, at least."

Nurse Revere appeared in the doorway, and Miranda fell quiet. Revere scanned the room, lips pursed in disapproval.

Agatha looked at her watch. "I'm sorry," she said. "Did I get the visiting hours wrong? Am I interrupting rest time?"

"Exercise," Revere said. "They should be exercising." Frieda, Lupita and Norma got out of bed. They shuffled past Revere and into the hall.

"Even during visiting hours?" Agatha asked, looking at Miranda instead of Revere.

"It's strongly encouraged," said Miranda. She stood up.

"You can talk and walk at the same time, can't you?" said Revere. She ignored Agatha and gave Miranda a scolding look.

"You're absolutely right," Miranda said. She put on her most obedient face, doing what she could to avoid being on Revere's list of problem cases. The instinct was a futile one, she knew. Donovan had her in his sights, so what difference did Revere's opinion of her make? Eyes were on her, whether they were Revere's or not. "Would it be all right if we went outside?" she asked. She hadn't ventured out of the Institute's doors since her arrival. The thought appealed to her now, especially since it would be easier to speak freely with Agatha on the grounds than in the halls. Other patients did walk outside. She saw them from her window.

"In the rain?" Revere asked sharply.

"Oh." Miranda looked back at the window and the drops running down the pane. "Never mind, then."

"That's all right," said Agatha, taking her arm. "Why don't we go to the library again?"

Revere pointed at Miranda. "Just be sure you don't go there to sit for ages. If I don't see you, I'll come looking."

"I'll be good," Miranda promised.

Revere sniffed, then swept out of the room.

Miranda and Agatha headed out into the corridor. Agatha looked dismayed when she saw the parade of shambling patients.

"What..." she began, then trailed off.

"Exactly," said Miranda. "There have been developments in your absence."

"They aren't encouraging ones."

"Why? You don't believe in exercise."

"This isn't exercise," said Agatha, her voice barely above a whisper.

"No," said Miranda. "It isn't."

Agatha took the first turn, following the signs to the library. Miranda slowed down. Agatha looked at her.

"You don't want to go to the library?"

Miranda waited until they overtook an old woman shuffling along with a cane. A few more steps, and they were in a bit of a gap between patients. "I had a bad experience there last time," Miranda said.

"Should we avoid it?"

She wasn't sure. Did it matter anymore? Was anywhere in the Institute safer than anywhere else? The library, at least, would give them a chance at some privacy. She wouldn't be there alone, and she knew to be guarded about what she looked at.

"Let's go," she said. "Be careful, though." She glanced around before speaking again. "The floor pattern is a labyrinth. Don't let it catch you up."

They arrived outside the library door a few minutes later. Miranda could feel the undertow of the pattern. It wasn't strong, no worse than the withdrawing of a wave at her ankles.

"Are you all right?" said Agatha.

"Can you feel it?"

"Yes. I can fight it too, though."

"Then so can I."

She opened the door. Going in was like stepping into a hard smile. *Been a while,* said the empty room. *Remember me?*

Miranda kept her gaze level. She walked over to the window and stood facing out.

The rain made patterns on the glass. Miranda looked past it, to the grounds below.

"I see what you mean," Agatha said at her side.

"You saw?"

"I did. Funny that we missed that before."

"We weren't looking before."

"Do you think we can speak freely here?"

Miranda shrugged. "Do we have a choice? No people here, at least. I don't know what else might be listening."

"Or if it can listen in other places, beyond these walls. I think it might."

"Then it's not going to like what I have to say," said Miranda. She told Agatha what had happened during her absence. Speaking quietly made it a little easier to stay calm. When she finished, the relief of having opened up to someone left her weak. She sat down, daring Revere to come in and object.

Agatha sat too. "Has there been any sign of Payton Wallace on the premises?" she asked.

"No," Miranda said, surprised. "Should he have been?"

Agatha sighed. "I'm pretty sure he's been Donovan's useful idiot. I had hoped I'd made him mine. I guess not." Then she talked about her trip.

Miranda's relief bled away.

Afterwards, they didn't speak for a few minutes. They held hands, processing the horror.

"So," Agatha finally said, "secret passages. How very gothic."

"Very," Miranda agreed.

Their forced levity rang cold in the hostile space of the library.

"You aren't planning on exploring them, are you?" Agatha asked.

"No! Not before we have a plan."

They looked at each other. They both knew she would have to go into that darkness sooner or later.

Miranda ran a hand down her face. "What *is* this place?"

"The abbey rebuilt," said Agatha, "and fused with the Stroud Spiral." She grimaced. "I shouldn't say *abbey*. I don't think the ruins were ever an abbey at all. Not a human one." She paused. "That's one answer. That's what this building is made of. But that isn't really what it *is*."

"Architecture is frozen music," Miranda quoted, thinking back to an earlier conversation, when it had still seemed possible that the Stroud Institute was a place of healing. "Architecture is embodied poetry."

"Architecture is ritual," Agatha finished.

"Not just the architecture," said Miranda. "The people in it. The walking."

"Yes," said Agatha. "The right kind of movement in the right kind of structure."

"A ritual to what end, then?"

"A summoning, I think." Agatha held up a hand and Miranda held back the question she had been about to ask. "To summon what?" Agatha went on. "We don't know. What will the being do? We don't know. Though we know it will be bad."

"Things are bad enough now. I don't want to imagine what they'll be like when whatever it is gets here."

"I think," Agatha said, "that it may already be present. Partially. We're looking at a gradual manifestation."

"Why do you say that?"

"The vibrations in the stone of the building. They're already happening, but growing stronger."

Miranda thought about her most recent vision, and how horribly tangible it had been. She still had the taste of the worms in her mouth. "All right," she said. "I can buy that. So what do we do about it?"

"You could see about leaving," Agatha said.

"To go where? Be safe how? Anyway, you know I can't leave. I can't run away. I won't."

"I know." Agatha squeezed her shoulder. "I had to suggest you get away. I couldn't live with myself if I didn't, even though I knew you'd stay to fight. You understand?"

"I do," said Miranda. "I do. Thank you. But since I'm not leaving, what do we do?"

"We have to learn more," said Agatha. "What I found out in Scotland has helped, but it isn't enough."

"Right, then." Miranda braced herself. "What's our path for finding out more? Is there another archive to comb through?"

"If there is, Donovan Stroud has it."

"I see." Miranda's mouth went dry. "We have to break into his quarters."

"You say *we*..." Agatha began.

"When I should be saying *I*."

"I can't ask this of you," said Agatha. "No one can or should."

"I know." Miranda's stomach fell away from her when she thought about what she would have to do. It dropped into darkness, leaving her hollow. "I said I would stay and fight, and this is how I can."

"I'm not even sure what you should be looking for." Agatha sounded both sorrowful and frustrated. "Papers or journals relating to Magnus Stroud would be a start, but there may be more, items I can't imagine."

"I've done research before where I didn't know what I was looking for until I saw it," Miranda said.

"This will be more dangerous than the British Museum's reading room."

"Don't I know it."

"So you're sure?" Agatha asked.

"Positive." Terrified, but positive.

"Then I have something for you." Agatha opened her bag and pulled out a thick volume. She handed it to Miranda.

"A Wordsworth collection," Miranda said. "This is thoughtful, but–"

"Open it."

She did. The center of the pages had been cut out. A set of lockpicks sat in the rectangular hole.

Miranda smiled. "You knew I'd say yes."

"I felt guilty bringing them, but I knew I had to. There's no way I could gain access to his apartment. It will be hard enough for you, but at least you're already on the inside."

"It might not be as difficult as you think."

"Oh?"

"Next Friday, there's a special session being conducted by Daria Miracle, one for the entire Institute. It's going to be held in the theater. A true occasion. Donovan is going to be in attendance." She gave a crooked smile. "It has been Announced."

"That sounds perfect," said Agatha. "Very convenient."

"Isn't it just. That worries me."

"You think he knows you'll try something?"

"What if he *wants* me to?"

Agatha didn't answer. Miranda kept her eyes on the world beyond the window, but what she saw was the labyrinth.

She had no choice, and a single path to walk.

All the way to what waited at the center.

CHAPTER TWENTY-TWO

The dreams and the visions pulled back again. Miranda's nights calmed. She slept well, and the instinctive anticipation of a blow melted away.

As her body relaxed, her dread grew. She had been right before to see a pattern, and that the waters of nightmare were just withdrawing ahead of a tsunami. She feared how terrible the next blow would be. It might deliver a nightmare from which she could not wake. Or one that would swallow all of Arkham.

Or worse.

She did nothing in the days before the grand event on Friday. She ate her meals, slept, and she walked, like all the other patients. She continued to feel better, too. No more fever, much less weakness. The cough left her alone sometimes for an hour or more, as long as she didn't take a deep breath. Her energy seemed almost normal.

She distrusted her recovery. She didn't believe in it because she could find no reason for it. Rest and then exercise were not cause enough. She found that she could believe in some force that gave her the strength to walk and walk and walk, because it needed her, and everyone else, to enact its ritual.

She walked, and she did as the nurses said. She read, and she took on her first volunteer work. The duties were light, limited to delivering a few trays on this floor. That gave her the chance to get to know other patients a little more, but she restricted her conversation to mundane subjects. That wasn't difficult. Her roommates had become less and less talkative, withdrawing into the inner vistas of their own dark paths and doubts. She accepted the reality that she could not count on any of them to be allies in the fight, because they could not fight. How could they, when she didn't know how to yet herself?

Maybe the summoning could not be fought. Maybe she would only make her suffering worse by trying to hold back the tsunami. Maybe she should just let the wave wash over her.

Maybe, maybe, maybe. At least the doubts were still her own. She did not have to face the collapse of faiths and certainties that she had never had.

Could any of them be saved? If the coming horror were defeated, what would happen to all patients who had followed the path so deep into the labyrinth?

She didn't know, and the question tormented her. She didn't want to believe that anything she did would be too late for them. She had to hope that they could be helped.

But the days went by, and they went further down the path. And more patients disappeared. The corridors were full of the walking obsessed, but not as full as they should have been.

•••

Payton Wallace put off visiting the Stroud Institute for as long as he could. The things Agatha Crane had said bothered him. They nagged at him during the day, gnawing at the strength of his smile, and at the pleasure he took in public appearances. At night, they niggled at his sleep, fraying the edges of his dreams. He kept touch on anything that hit the news about the sanatorium, and he spoke to Donovan Stroud a few times on the phone. Nothing turned up that seemed alarming. Of course, that was precisely what Agatha had told him not to trust.

He heard about the deaths, and they made him think he should worry. There were also reports of the people released, cured, and those made him feel better. Never enough, though, to relax completely.

Payton knew he should go to the sanatorium and see things for himself. Look around with new eyes. Put his acumen to work. The problem was, being seen there would connect him to the Institute, and he didn't want that, not if things went wrong.

On the other hand, what if things went wrong, and he hadn't made a show of investigating? Wouldn't that be worse?

He went back and forth on the question and finally decided to go. On a gray Wednesday, with the wind blowing hard, he called Donovan to say he was coming over, and drove to the Institute.

The wind sprayed water from the fountain over him as he got out of the car. He wiped his face and looked at the grounds of the Institute. All of this used to be his family's. But it wasn't any more, just as he had said to Agatha. Whatever happened on this land, it was not his responsibility.

Then why, when he looked at the lawns and the trees, did he feel a connection? It was almost as if the land owned him.

Nonsense. Where did that idiocy come from? It wasn't worthy of him. Payton was a practical man. He dealt in the realities of the political world. The reality he had to face here was the political fallout if he had helped push through some kind of disaster. If he got out in front of the problem, though, and warned of the disaster, then he might save his career.

He trotted up the stairs and reached for the doors, and they startled him by opening before his touch.

Donovan stepped outside. "Payton!" he said. "Always wonderful to have you here. I was in my office and saw you pull up, and I thought we might give ourselves the gift of fresh air for a bit. What do you say?"

"Sure," said Payton, wrong-footed.

"Excellent!" Donovan took his arm and guided him back down the stairs. "A stroll through the gardens will do us both a power of good." He turned right at the bottom of the stairs and started down a narrow path, marked out by gray flagstones, that meandered away from the drive.

They wandered around to the back of the Institute and then away from the building and into the trees, always following the stones. The path's direction looked random to Payton, a pointless meander in and out of the trees, yet as he walked, he felt himself drawn from one stone to the next as if a clear purpose guided his steps.

The ground kept drawing his eyes. He thought about the dead that had lain here, and perhaps still did. He thought about Donovan's reassurances on that front, and about the money that had made even the possibility of a problem go away. The old pest house was a forgotten piece of Arkham's past. Payton had been surprised Agatha had known about it.

"So," said Donovan. "To what do I owe the pleasure?"

"I thought I'd drop in, find out how things are going. It's been a while."

"Far too long! You know you're always welcome here, councilman. And things are going very well, very well indeed."

"I've been told there are some issues."

Donovan laughed. He clapped Payton on the back. "Show me the institution, of any kind, without issues, and I'll show you a miracle. Or a lie. There are always issues, and each one is an opportunity, leading to greater perfection."

"So there's nothing to worry about."

"I can't begin to imagine why you'd think there could be."

"You'd tell me if there was," Payton insisted.

"What possible business could this be of yours?"

Donovan's smile was so wide, his tone so cheerful, that Payton thought he had misheard. He had to remind himself that he was Councilman Payton Wallace, and that people didn't speak to him like that. "I staked my reputation on this place," he snapped. "And if I have to call in an inspection to preserve that reputation, I will."

"You should feel free to do so at any time," said Donovan. "But why would you? Tell me, are you in some way threatening me with something? I ask only for the purpose of clarification, you understand."

"No, I'm not trying to threaten you."

"Because you were very well compensated," Donovan continued. "So a threat would be very ill-mannered. Not to mention foolish. I doubt any sort of public outcry would do you any good."

"I wasn't–"

Donovan didn't let him speak. He carried on, relentless, smiling the whole time. "And you shouldn't ever imagine you can distance yourself from the Institute, councilman. Not with your connection to the land."

"It isn't mine."

"Isn't it? Perhaps the ownership runs the other way, then. You may have no legal ownership, but there is the fact of history, and you still saw to it that the land was untouched, as I asked. You exercised control. You are linked to the ground we walk on. Don't you feel it?"

Payton did. He felt heavier, as if each step reverberated to the center of the Earth.

"I would even say that you couldn't leave this path even if you wanted to."

The thought that Donovan was right terrified Payton. "That's nonsense," he said, his mouth dry, his voice weak. He didn't try to break from the direction of the stones.

Donovan laughed again. "Of course it is! All your worries are! Let me prove how well things are going. We're having a performance for all the patients on Friday. Why don't you come? It will put your mind at ease. You'll see that we are moving in exactly the right direction."

Friday evening arrived as both a threat and a relief. The thought of what she had to do frightened Miranda so much, she could barely swallow. But at least she would act.

After supper, the nurses swept through the wards,

shepherding the flock for Daria Miracle's performance. Miranda had hoped she could duck aside without being noticed, but no such luck. Revere marched behind her and her roommates, guiding them through the halls to the theater.

She wondered if Donovan had told Revere to make certain that Miranda attended. She found that possibility preferable to the one where Donovan wanted her to do what she was about to attempt.

The theater was in the central block of the Institute. It took up most of the floor one up from the lobby. Miranda and her roommates were in the last crush of arrivals, and she managed to take a seat in the back row, close to the door and away from the people who knew her.

The theater could hold hundreds. There was room for every patient, and all the staff, and there were still many empty seats. Miranda wondered what Donovan had in mind for this space. What events did he imagine it could host? What call would there be for twice the current number to be present?

Unpleasant possibilities hovered, half-formed, at the edge of her mind.

The ceiling, a shallow dome like the one of the entrance hall, called Miranda's eyes with such insistence that after a first, stunned glance, she knew she should not look at it and tore her eyes away. A massive fresco of a storm dominated the entire dome. The swirl and clash of dark clouds had such detail and a sense of depth that it seemed to move. It lured the eye and the mind to its center, where the darkness became deep and secretive.

Miranda looked around at her fellow patients. Many of them had their heads back, mouths open and slack, as they stared at the clouds, following the convolutions of the storm. Though seated, they were still traveling the labyrinth, their minds tracing the paths marked out for them by the clouds. The ritual had not paused.

The stage below was bare except for a single chair made from dark wood, polished with age and upholstered with material the faded red of old tapestry. A relic, Miranda guessed, brought over from Stroud Hall.

A movie screen dominated the wall behind the stage. Beneath the stage, a full orchestra tuned up.

At eight, the lights dimmed, and a spotlight shone on the chair and the center stage area. Donovan Stroud walked out from the left wing and into the spotlight.

He waved at the audience. "I'm Donovan Stroud," he said. "Some of you know me, and I know some of you. But we don't all know each other nearly as well as I would like. And though some of you have just arrived, and some of you have been here since we opened, I want to take this opportunity to welcome all of you. I mean that. I really do. This isn't just me spouting off the usual pat phrases. I'm speaking from the heart. Don't believe me? Then look!" He stretched out his arms, hands wide. "See! No notes! No cue cards!"

Applause. Laughter, followed by a lot of coughing.

Donovan grinned. He shook his head and shrugged in self-deprecation. "You're too kind," he said. "Too kind, my friends. And you *are* my friends. Even if we haven't met in person yet – and we will – you are my friends just by being here, and entrusting yourself to my care. The Stroud Institute is a dream, a potential, and you are going to turn that dream, that potential, into a reality. Have no doubts about that."

More clapping, and he applauded the audience. "Give yourselves credit. Please. You aren't my patients. You're my partners. We are going to achieve extraordinary things together. We already have, and just you wait!"

Rapturous applause. In the thunder, Miranda heard the energy of the desperate. The man before them spoke with energy, confidence, and an absence of doubt. They needed him. They needed the rescue he promised.

"I'm here to introduce a woman who doesn't need an introduction. All of you know her. All of you have been working with her. What I'm going to introduce, then, is what she will present to you tonight. Daria Miracle has spoken to all of you about the path, about walking through your troubles and your anxieties until you come out the other side. She has taken you by the hand and helped you find the way. Tonight, she is going to *show* you the way. Tonight, you will see the other side of Daria. You know her as counselor and philosopher. Now you will know the artist. Art is the voice of what cannot be said or conveyed through explanation. Art is transcendent. Let yourselves be transported. Let us *all* be transported. My friends, my partners, I give you Daria Miracle."

To more applause, the loudest and most desperate yet, Donovan bowed and sat down in the chair. The orchestra struck up. It played a sinuous, insidiously infectious melody. It coiled through Miranda's blood, urging her to rise, to follow, to descend. Daria came in from the right. She wore a black bodysuit wrapped in yards of flowing, diaphanous veils and scarves. She was the night and its clouds, come to dance with the wind.

She twirled once, then leapt into the spotlight. She landed in a crouch, arms wrapped around herself. Her head jerked up, her eyes wide. She stared into the spotlight. As if it were the sun, and she a dark flowering, she rose from the crouch, face ecstatic, arms stretching out to embrace the light. She arched her back, stood on pointe, and at the moment of her greatest extension, the spotlight went out.

The screen came to life. An experimental film unspooled. No, Miranda thought, correcting herself, this wasn't experimental. She would have called the film that in the innocent times before the Stroud Institute. There was nothing *experimental* about this. Donovan knew exactly what he had created. The ritual of the Stroud Institute continued, now in a different, more intense form.

Images cascaded across the screen, none visible for more than a few seconds, most barely a bright flicker before they vanished. Some frames were blank emptiness. Others appeared to melt and burn away, backdrops for Daria's gyrating, convulsing silhouette. Narrow paths and labyrinths appeared, vanished and returned. Patterns in stone, in hedges, in sand and in snow, hypnotic, insistent, calling, commanding.

Donovan wasn't even trying to hide the existence of the ritual any longer. He had dropped the mask.

Miranda felt time slipping away.

She wrenched her eyes from the screen. She stared at her feet, steadying her mind and trying to tune out the music. When she felt ready, she got to her feet. She edged past the few patients seated between her and the door. At the closed door, she hesitated. When she opened it, light from the hall would flood in. She would be seen.

She had no choice.

Her path, determined for her.

The screen flashed white, and she took the moment. She pushed out through the door and closed it again as quickly as she could. Then she hurried to the elevator, her rasping breath sounding deafening in the empty halls.

She could hope no one noticed her leave. The audience dazzled by the bright screen, Donovan facing the projector beam and seeing only a black mass of the audience.

That was reasonable, right? That wasn't just wishful thinking, right?

She wasn't doing exactly what Donovan had laid out for her, right?

It didn't matter. No choice, no choice. The only way forward. The only way she might be able to fight.

She took the elevator up to Donovan's apartment. She tried the door and was relieved to find it locked. Maybe he didn't want her in there after all. She fished the picks out of the pocket of her robe, knelt in front of the lock, and got to work.

She wished there had been a way to practice. Agatha had explained, in detail, how to use the tools, but the instructions, full as they were, had also sounded second-hand. Someone else had explained to Agatha how to pick locks, and she had passed the knowledge on to Miranda.

She was going to look very silly if this didn't work.

She felt in the lock, probing and trying to visualize the mechanism she was supposed to be moving. When the clicks came and she had the door open, she grunted with surprise. She looked at her watch. It had taken her less than five minutes.

"You have a future in this," she muttered.

Donovan had left a table light on – most likely to light his way when he returned, not for her benefit, she told herself. She took a quick look in the living room, but saw nothing she hadn't seen before.

She found his office at the end of the hall. She had to turn the light on here. She rushed to the window and closed the Venetian blinds, adding the hope that no one could see the light from outside to her lengthening list of wishes.

The room's roll top desk was open to her inspection. A quick look at the papers on its surface showed her administrative memos and receipts. She pulled open the drawers and found dozens of file folders. She would never have the time to go through them all. She took a step back from the desk, despair forming in the pit of her stomach.

She looked around, then moved to the display case in the opposite corner of the office. Its glass shelves held jewels on violet cushions and small sculptures that made Miranda hiss in distaste. They seemed to be mythological serpents of some kind. She had never seen anything like them before. They made her want to scratch inside her head. Their stone looked old. And wet.

A book sat on the bottom shelf, hard to see unless she crouched down. The dark leather cover was battered and cracked with age.

Too much to hope for that this was what she needed to find?

Another lock to struggle with. More to go wrong and more time to eat up, so the book had better be worth it.

The lock on the display case, smaller than the one on the apartment door, gave her more trouble. She swore at it. Stubborn, it taunted her. Finally, it relented, and she opened the case.

She picked up the book. It felt cold and damp. She opened the cover, and found the journal of Magnus Stroud.

Too easy. Too easy. It couldn't possibly be this simple, could it?

Yes, because it wasn't that simple. What was she going to do with the journal? She couldn't steal it. Not if she wanted to have some chance of pretending to herself that Donovan didn't know how much of a threat, if any, she and Agatha might be.

No. She had to read it here.

She had no idea how long Daria's performance would last, no idea when Donovan might come marching through the door.

No idea, and no choice. The realization made her hate Donovan all the more. She felt as if all the choices in her life had been illusions, every step a predetermined one down a single, twisting path, bringing her to this moment, when she finally saw that there had never been any branches off her destiny at all. The place had always been her destination. She had always been fated to move to the desk and sit, perched and tense, on the edge of Donovan's swivel chair. Always been fated to read this journal with her heart in her mouth, terrified of what she might hear in the apartment.

Terrified of what she might learn.

"Damn you," Miranda whispered, cursing all the souls and entities and currents of events that had brought her here.

CHAPTER TWENTY-THREE
Scotland, 1807

When the nanny was installed in the carriage, Magnus handed her his infant son, swaddled in blankets in spite of the August heat. Millicent Hardwick took Braden Stroud into her arms and held him protectively.

"I'll watch over him well, my lord," she promised.

"I know you will," said Magnus. His eyes never left the child. He could almost see down Braden's road of service to Crothoaka. *Your destiny is already written, my son.*

"Such a terrible shame," said Millicent. "Such a shame." She shook her head. "To have fallen so ill, so quickly, and for so long."

Magnus nodded, patient. He had all the time in the world. Millicent had served at the Yorkshire estate for years, looking after Magnus' young cousins. She had only just arrived, and he was sending her back immediately. She would not set foot in Stroud Hall, or see Braden's mother.

"If you don't mind my saying so, my lord, though I know it isn't my place, you're doing right by the wee thing. He'll be better off elsewhere until his mother isn't so poorly."

"I appreciate your saying so, Millicent. Those are my thoughts exactly. We will join you when we can."

He shut the carriage door and watched it drive off through the gates, dust rising in its wake.

Magnus started back to the Hall. The heat was suffocating. It had been a broiling August to date, excessively so, and there hadn't been a drop of rain in over a month. Magnus felt the heat go deep into his lungs when he breathed, as if the air were burning.

A perfect day for the culmination of his efforts.

Back at the Hall, he climbed the grand staircase to the second floor, and went down the west wing to the locked door at the far end. He leaned his forehead against the door. "It is done," he said to the being inside.

A faint stirring answered him. Magnus' hand brushed against the door. He almost knocked, but restrained himself. What lived in the room had forbidden him to enter, and he would not disobey.

He didn't know what to call the being on the other side of the door. He could not think of it as *Christina,* not since Braden was born and the transformation had begun.

Perhaps it had not really been Christina who had come back from her journey beneath the abbey. The real Christina, the poet whose work he admired, had pleaded with him to show her what lay below. He had found that he had had no choice but to let her go. He did not own the secret of the ruins. Crothoaka owned him, and Crothoaka wanted Christina to see, and know, and for her to do that alone.

Magnus stood sentinel in the ruins until she returned, and when she did, she was transformed. She spoke to him with a tone of command, and with eyes would brook no contradiction. “We must have a child,” she said. “A child of destiny.”

He had obeyed.

And so Braden had come into the world, to be raised in the knowledge of Crothoaka from the very beginning, to be taught the way of the labyrinth from his first day to last, and so be the first of the new line of Strouds.

Braden had only been a day old when Christina locked the door and forbade anyone from entering. The servants exchanged looks, but Magnus told them to do as she said, and they could hardly challenge him. Phillips asked just once whether the count wished him to send for the doctor. Magnus told him no, and Phillips let the matter drop.

“Farewell,” Christina said as she closed the door on Magnus. “Do not look to see me again.”

Magnus had obeyed, just as he had in everything else concerning Braden and, today, the Republic of the Arts.

The climax of his labors was at hand.

“I go to finish things,” Magnus said. “I will return tonight.”

More stirrings in the room. Eager ones.

Magnus left the Hall and walked through the heat to the Stroud Spiral. The sun speared his eyes. He held his hands up to his face. It seemed astonishing that they did not blister in the heat.

All perfect, all as it should be.

At the Spiral, he walked into the gap between the two most massive boulders, and he began.

Crothoaka guided his steps. He gave himself over to the impulse that came from outside his own being and told him when to turn left, when right, when to double back, when to circle which boulder. He never hesitated. He never had a choice to make. His feet walked the true path through the Spiral as surely as if it had been marked out in crimson light before him.

The afternoon fell away. Magnus had no sense of time. Nothing mattered, and nothing existed, except the need to trace the labyrinth, to perform the slow, utterly precise dance that was itself yet one more step of the larger slow, yet utterly precise dance he had been engaged in since the night below the ruins, and even before. Without knowing it, he had been dancing all his life for Crothoaka.

When he finished, he found himself outside the Spiral, leaning against the stone that, in defiance of the heat of the day, was cold.

The sun had set, leaving the land to an evening as oppress-ive as high noon.

Magnus jerked into motion again. He made his way out from the trees, onto the moor, and to Alfred's cottage. The painter opened at his knock. Alfred looked drained, starved. His skin hung in folds on his emaciated frame. He had lost much of his hair.

"My lord," said Alfred, his voice weak and hoarse. He stepped aside to let Magnus in.

The interior of the cottage had become a frozen vortex of art. Canvasses covered every square inch of every wall, every flat surface, and slid over each other in chaotic piles on the floor. There were still landscapes here, recognizably in the style of the Alfred Claymot who had arrived at the Republic of the Arts. Many more paintings, though, showed his new more obsessive and more sinuous brushwork. Perhaps they were landscapes. They were certainly nightmares.

"I wanted to tell you once more," Magnus said, "how pleased I am with the portrait you did for me." Alfred had completed it just before Braden's birth. It was, Magnus thought, a masterpiece. It looked, from anything more than a few feet away, like the work of the old Alfred. The new one, though, seethed beneath the surface appearance, visible only up close, and at the right angle. Or by touch. The portrait squirmed when touched.

"You honor me, my lord," said Alfred. "It does my soul good to know that I have done something that feels important." He coughed, and his entire frame shook.

"Your work is not done yet," Magnus said. "You may take my word for it."

"Thank you, my lord, thank you." Alfred struggled with a bow. He had to use the edge of a table to push himself upright again. "May I ask how you … ah … how… Christina is faring?"

Magnus smiled at Alfred's hesitation. He and Christina had not wed. The great work of the summoning had no room or time for such pointless customs. "She is deep into her journey," he said, finding it odd to refer to Christina in the present tense. "As are we all."

Alfred nodded. He coughed again, and clutched the table for support, knocking a canvas to the floor. "I am finding the way so hard, my lord. So very hard. And I cannot see the center of the labyrinth."

Magnus put his arm around Alfred's shoulders. "But you have reached it," he said.

"I have?"

Eyes shining, Alfred looked up at him, so he didn't see Magnus pull the dagger from his belt. Magnus rammed it up through Alfred's throat. Alfred jerked. His feet danced with the shock of death. Blood rushed warm down Magnus' hand. He withdrew the dagger and let Alfred's body fall. The artist's head bounced sharply off the corner of the table on the way down.

Magnus broke the leg of an easel, wrapped the top in paint-soaked rags, and lit them from one of the candles Alfred had been burning for light. It took no effort at all to set the cottage on fire. So dry, so hot, so filled with fumes, the room burst into flame at the merest suggestion from Magnus' torch.

He left the cottage at a run, dagger and torch in hand, and the fire followed in his wake. It spread out behind him, over the moor, and roared with crackling eagerness as it reached the trees.

Fueled by ritual and commanded by it, the fire traced the path of its own labyrinth. When it was done, it would consume the forest, but it had to follow the lines of the dance, and Magnus led it. He ran from cottage to cottage, tireless, ecstatic. He slashed throats and thrust the torch into faces. He killed every one of the artists whose patron he had been for a year. He destroyed the Republic of the Arts, and he rejoiced in the sacrifice. The Republic, he now understood, had only ever been created for this purpose, to be the offering to a greater dream.

The fire surrounded the Hall when he walked back up the drive to the front entrance. The earth moaned, its voice deep and pained. Magnus had seen the boulders of the Spiral burst into flame, one more wonder on a night thick with them.

The servants had gathered on the porch, terrified by the conflagration. Huddling together, they reminded Magnus of his arrival at Stroud Hall. They had been outside then too, to greet him.

He killed them. They were so stunned by his attack, so baffled by the sudden end of their world, that only the last few even tried to defend themselves. They went down easily.

Magnus entered the Hall and ran up to the room with the locked door. He reached for the key, but the door opened on its own. A young, dark-haired woman emerged. She was beautiful, her every movement a serpent's dance. Magnus stared at the being forged out of the flesh of Christina Blackstone. He bowed his head in worship.

"Truly," he said, "you are a miracle."

"Then Miracle shall be my name," said the woman.

"The ritual is complete," Magnus told her.

"Is it?" she asked, and though she smiled, her voice was stern.

"… no," Magnus admitted. If all had been accomplished, Crothoaka would be in the world. The god was not. "I don't understand."

"Come," said the Miracle. She hooked her arm through Magnus' and led him slowly back down to the ground floor, and to his study.

Waving, orange light bathed the room. The windows looked out onto an unbroken wall of flame.

The Miracle guided Magnus to his desk. She sat him down, put his journal before him, dipped his quill pen in ink, and put it in his hand.

"The work of all your life before tonight has been but a

prologue to the great ritual," she said. "Tonight is not the end, but the real beginning. The writing of the first chapter. And even that is not yet complete."

She opened his journal to the first blank page. "Write it down," she said. "Write everything down. This will be the work of generations of Strouds, and I will be there to guide them."

Magnus had begun writing as soon as the Miracle told him. He paused now, the nib hovering over the page, not quite touching. "Will it not fall to me to guide my son?"

"It will not."

He looked up at her. "Why not?"

She smiled again. "Because the sacrifice of this night must be complete."

"I understand."

And he did. Nothing more needed to be said. He saw what he had to do. He saw it in such precise detail that he wrote his coming actions down too as if they had already been done.

"There," he said, satisfied, and presented the journal for the Miracle's inspection.

"Good," she said. "The work is good."

"Thank you," said Magnus.

He left her in the study without looking back. He walked out of the Hall, out onto the drive. The barrier of flame rose higher than the trees, blinding, impassible, devouring, and yet advancing no closer to the Hall itself. The fire obeyed as he did.

He didn't hesitate. He walked off the drive and into the fire. He knew he would scream when the pain hit.

He did. For much longer than he had expected.

•••

The journal smelled of smoke, Miranda thought. It smelled of horror.

She knew more now, but still not enough, and still not how to fight. Maybe this would make sense to Agatha, though. She might draw some conclusions from what Magnus had done that might help them.

The journal didn't end with Magnus' atrocities. New hands took over, the lineage of the count chronicling the growth of the ritual year after year, decade after decade. Always more sacrifice, more murder, more cruelty, and more philosophical ravings.

Miranda started. Was that someone in the hall? In the living room? She listened, breath held.

The apartment clicked, the sound of a pipe in the walls, not the tread of footsteps.

She read again, and she came, at last, to the final hand. She read Donovan's entries. She read about how he moved the ruins and the Spiral to Arkham, and rebuilt them as the Institute. His words and his penmanship became frenzied as he drew near the completion of the ritual.

Hail Crothoaka, the Worm of the Labyrinth! Hail the conjurer of dark exegesis! Hail the sower of doubt! You have been with us always in the interstices of belief, and in the fractures of contradictions of faith. Come now and teach us the unity that comes through final collapse! Come, Great Labyrinth, and takes us all to the heart of your devouring!

That was all.

Miranda looked at her watch. She gasped. She had been here for well over an hour. She slipped the book back into the display cabinet and locked it again, Donovan's encomium ringing through her mind. She had memorized it without trying.

She tiptoed out of the office, down the hall, and to the apartment door. The emptiness of the rooms felt like the camouflage of a predator. She put her hand on the door handle and held one of the lockpicks like a dagger, ready to stab Donovan in the eye if she found him in the corridor.

She yanked the door open, and more emptiness confronted her.

Shut the door, lock it, and now hurry, hurry, take the stairs and not the elevator, and why do you have to breathe so hard, and why are your legs so weak, can't you go faster, go faster, go faster?

She made it to her floor, and to still more emptiness. No one was back from the performance.

That had to be it. She told herself she was not suddenly alone in the hospital. She told herself the hidden passages were not filled with things that had been patients and nurses, all watching her and hungering.

She hurried again, feeling so weak now, so tired, ready to drop, and the trip back to the theater was much too long. She would never get there in time, and she would have to explain to the people she would suddenly run into why she had left and where she had been.

But she saw no one, and as she approached the theatre, she heard the booming of music rising to a crescendo.

Instead of trying to slip back inside, she waited just to one side of the doors. When, a few minutes later, the performance did end, she let the first dozen or more audience members walk by, and then she joined the stream. No one seemed to notice. They were all too dazed.

Or too far down the labyrinth.

Back in her room, in her bed, the blanket drawn up to her chin, Miranda thought about how smoothly, really, everything had gone, and she wondered why Donovan wanted it so.

Part III

CHAPTER TWENTY-FOUR

Miranda slept.

Lupita lay awake, staring up. In the dim light from the hall, the ceiling was a doubtful mist of gray. Deeper and less solid than it should have been, it promised and threatened visions. Its murk might produce the shape of her fears. Would it not offer her hopes too?

But she would need hopes for her imagination to shape them, wouldn't she? They couldn't come from nowhere.

The ceiling's blur deepened with her tears. She wiped her eyes. Stop being like this. You weren't like this before getting sick. And definitely not before coming here.

She thought not, anyway. The memory of who she was like before became elusive. Hadn't there been a Lupita strong in conviction, and strong in faith? Had that been a real person, or just the construct of what she wished she were like?

She wanted answers. The ceiling offered nothing. In the night, the only answers were ones that hurt.

Daria offered things that seemed like answers. *Seemed.*

Lupita turned on her side. She looked toward Miranda's bed. She wanted to speak with Miranda very badly. Miranda was like the Lupita of memory or imagination. She had made it clear to Lupita that she was willing to talk and listen, but the new Lupita had been scared to accept the offer. Now, though, after the evening's performance, she needed to talk. Not to Frieda. The old Lupita would have laughed at the idea of confiding in that woman. Even the new Lupita saw the humor in that. And she didn't want to talk to Norma, either. She didn't trust Norma.

She trusted Miranda, because Miranda didn't appear to trust anything.

Lupita wanted to know what Miranda thought about Daria Miracle's performance. Lupita had been mesmerized every second of its duration. She had been unable to look away, even though a part of her had known she should. The ecstasy, and the sense of revelation, that she always experienced during the counseling sessions had been a hundred times more powerful. But when the performance ended, and she had shuffled with the other dazed spectators back into the halls, and the magic began to slide away, she began to feel unclean.

She felt even worse now. Everything was wrong. She didn't know where to turn. She kept trying to pray for guidance and failed. The words would not come, or if they did, they seemed alien to her, as if she were pretending to be a woman of faith, as if she did not deserve to call for help. She held tight to her crucifix, clinging to it as she would a life raft, but she knew it would not save her from drowning.

Doubt surrounded her. It mocked her.

Miranda seemed troubled too. Perhaps they could help each other. Perhaps together, they could keep their heads above water.

She had to speak to Miranda.

Lupita got up. She padded over to the other woman's bed. "Miranda," she whispered. "Are you awake?"

Of course she wasn't. She looked profoundly asleep, so far down into unconsciousness she might have been in a coma.

"Miranda," Lupita said again, a little louder. She shook her shoulder, and it was like trying to move a boulder. Could people grow heavier in sleep?

Miranda's stillness frightened Lupita, and she checked to make sure Miranda was still breathing.

"Miranda," she said again, despairing now. There would be no help for her tonight.

Frieda's sudden hiss almost startled Lupita into a scream. "*What are you doing?*"

Lupita turned around, shaking. "I'm sorry. I–"

"You'll wake everyone."

Lupita glanced at Norma. She slept on, her breathing slow and even, a placid smile on her face. Was she really asleep? Lupita didn't fully trust her appearance. Miranda, though, didn't stir.

"I'm sorry," Lupita said again to Frieda. "I just wanted to talk to Miranda."

"Why?" The question was sharp as a dart.

Lupita hesitated. Then, desperate to find a companion for her fears in anyone, anyone at all, even Frieda, she plunged in. "Don't you feel it?" she asked. "You know there's something wrong here."

"I don't know what you're talking about. Go back to bed."

"Please, Frieda. I've seen you looking worried."

"No, you haven't."

"*Please!* Please listen to me. Do you really believe all the things Daria has been telling us? Do you believe in the labyrinth?"

"I want to sleep. Stop being a ninny."

"But do you? Aren't you worried that–"

"I don't want to hear it."

"But–"

"Shut up, shut up, *shut up!*"

Lupita drew back from the venom in Frieda's voice and eyes. Norma slept on in bliss. Miranda remained submerged, as if being held down forcefully in sleep.

Lupita went back to bed. "I'm sorry," she began.

"*Quiet!*"

Lupita froze, motionless. She didn't dare move in case the rustle of a sheet enraged Frieda even more. After a few minutes, Lupita heard long, steady breaths coming from Frieda's bed. They sounded like a point being made.

Lupita closed her eyes, trying to silence her racing mind, trying to sleep.

She failed. She couldn't even keep her eyes shut, or find a comfortable position. Lupita turned onto her side, then her back, and then her side again, twisting and wrinkling the covers, making everything worse and more uncomfortable, her body an enemy, the bed an enemy, and the two at war with her and with each other.

With a sigh, she turned on her back yet again. The sheet tangled around her legs, tying them together. A lump of covers pressed hard against her right flank. She tried to smooth it out.

It moved. The ripple of a hundred tiny legs tickled her through her nightdress.

Her breath hissed out of her lungs in sudden terror. She beat against the sheets, fought to free her legs, kicked and struggled and finally fell out the bed, whining in horror.

She jumped up. The bump under the sheets still moved. She snatched the sheet away. The thing on the bed was almost a foot long. It had the segmented body and legs of a centipede, but was thick as a slug. Its black carapace glistened with slime.

Lupita backed away from the bed, hand at her mouth, scream caught in her throat. She couldn't get the shriek out. She breathed faster and faster, and the scream kept growing, becoming too great. It would break her jaws if it escaped.

Trapped voiceless by nightmare, she fled the room for the corridor. There was light here, at least, but weak. It made everything gray when she needed the blaze of sunlight.

Something skittered behind her.

She ran, desperate for help. The hall was empty, and everyone slept in the rooms she passed. No one saw her and asked what was wrong. If they had, perhaps that would have freed her to speak, and she could have said, and she could have begged anyone, everyone, to do something, anything.

Instead, she saw only nothing, and behind her, the skittering grew louder.

There was more than one, she realized. God in heaven, there was more than one, and they were hunting her.

She couldn't be alone. There had to be staff. If she found

no one, then she had to be dreaming, and none of this was real, and she could survive the terror of a nightmare, because it would end, and she would wake.

But she felt the jarring of the floor against her feet, and it hurt for her to breathe, and she had never felt anything, not really, in a nightmare before.

She turned a corner, the skittering closer, and saw the night nurse halfway down the hall. Lupita hurried to catch up with her. She would welcome being scolded. She would welcome embarrassment. She would welcome any unpleasantness as long as it banished the skittering.

"Please!" She had her voice again, but it came out as a wheeze, no louder than a whisper. The night nurse didn't hear her, and marched on.

"Wait!" Lupita begged. No response, but she had almost caught up. She grabbed the nurse's shoulder.

The nurse turned around. She had no face. A mass of worms, each as thick as a thumb, squirmed where there should have been a face.

Lupita found her scream. She stumbled back, arms flailing, as the night nurse reached for her. Wailing, she turned around and ran again. Daggers of broken glass scraped through her lungs, but she ran. She had no direction, no refuge, no thought, but she ran. Screaming, despairing, she ran.

She had no sense of her flight, only the need to escape the nurse, and the skittering that still followed. Lupita only realized where she was when a wooden barrier stopped her. Jerked to full awareness again, she found herself in the entrance hall of the Institute, and stood before the main doors.

She grabbed the handles and pushed, pulled. Locked, the

doors did not even rattle. She sobbed and pounded on them, hitting so hard the skin on her knuckles broke open. She looked over her shoulder, dreading the sight of her pursuers.

There was no one.

A cathedral's silence filled the hall.

Lupita's fists paused against the doors. She listened.

No more skittering. No footsteps of the approaching nurse.

Reflexively, she pushed the doors again, and they opened. She stepped out onto the porch. She took a deep breath of the night air. She was free. She could go.

And because nothing stopped her, she hesitated.

It had rained again. The ground was wet, the night cold. She didn't even have a dressing gown.

What was she doing? Only a fool would head out into the night like this. Did she want to make herself even more sick?

But the worms...

Not real. They couldn't be. She had had a nightmare. She must have fallen asleep after all. She had had a nightmare, a very bad one, yes, and she had leapt out of bed, maybe still half-asleep, and tried to escape the dream.

Wasn't that so?

Yes?

No?

She rocked from side to side. She couldn't decide. The reality of the nurse faded with the immediacy of the terror.

But what if she hadn't dreamed? She couldn't go back inside.

She hugged herself. It was too cold. Where did she think she would go? She had no money with her. Home was miles away. Any taxi that would even stop to pick her up would take her right back to the Institute.

Or to the hospital. She could say she had wandered away from there, and got lost. She could.

Every scheme seemed more senseless, more pointless. But going back was still too frightening to contemplate.

She had nothing but doubts.

Descending the steps, she started down the drive. With no goal, she moved because she couldn't stay still. She walked down the wet pavement, hoping for purpose, praying for salvation.

She only found more doubts. They wrapped around her chest, making it hard to breathe, and coiled around her legs, weighing her down. Lupita's feet dragged, as though struggling through ankle-deep mud.

And then she was. She looked down. The pavement of the drive flowed around her, viscous, sucking. The worms of doubt were real, thick as pythons, and they had her. They pulled her legs deeper into the asphalt mire. Lupita screamed, her voice lost and tiny in the vastness of the night. She tried to pull free. The coils squeezed tighter and hauled her down, past her knees, and then up to her thighs. She had no purchase for her feet. The impossible quicksand went down forever, and the depths, hungry, awaited her. She screamed again, and then a length of worm wrapped around her chest. Its embrace tightened. It forced the air from her lungs.

There would be no more screams now.

She flailed, sinking to her waist, and then her ribs. She pushed against the ground and her arms went down to her elbows. The sucking grasp refused to let them go.

Mouth open, tears streaming, hope fleeing, she struggled

on, but she could barely move now. The worms had her. The doubts had her. As they pulled her into the ground, and the muck pushed into her mouth and nose, they cursed her with understanding. They had won when she lost the last of her purpose and the last of her certainty. When she lingered on the porch, all direction and faith and belief gone, she had already begun to sink.

She went down into the darkness. Certainty had at last come for her, and it dragged her to the center of the labyrinth.

Frieda stopped pretending to be asleep when Lupita fled the room. She sat up, furious with Lupita for waking her, and even more furious with her for being gone and out of the range of her anger.

She hung on to the rage. As long as she felt it, she could keep the anxiety at bay.

She waited for Lupita to come back, rehearsing the scolding. The minutes went by, and then a half-hour, and Lupita did not return. Frieda wondered where she had gone, and when she did that, she lost hold of her anger. It slipped away, and the gnawing in her chest came back. She frowned hard. *Go away. Go away.* She didn't want the worries. They weren't her. She had felt them too much of late, and she didn't know what had happened to her old confidence that the world was meant to behave as she wished.

This was Lupita's fault. And Miranda's too. And while she was at it, where did Norma get the right to look so serene all the time?

She stirred the ashes of the anger with resentful thoughts. It refused to catch fire again.

She stared absently at Lupita's empty bed, stewing. She chewed her bottom lip.

Something moved under Lupita's sheet.

No. She was not having this. Frieda looked away. She got out of bed. She kept her eyes averted from Lupita's corner of the room as she pulled on her dressing gown and stepped into her slippers. She needed certainty to get rid of the rat in her chest, and to banish the terror that would come if she looked at the sheets and saw them move again.

The labyrinth was the way. So Daria promised. Walk the labyrinth. Reach the center.

The way to feel better. The way to *get* better. The way to be good. Frieda was anxious to be good in the eyes of the Stroud Institute. She needed to be one of the gifted, the special, the chosen. Whatever one of those was the right word, Frieda needed to be that perfect thing.

She started walking the halls, taking the familiar turns, as she had done so many times. She would walk the labyrinth, and that would make her feel better, and then she would sleep, and not think about things that worried her, or imagine things that frightened her, and Lupita could go to hell for starting all this nonsense in the middle of the night.

Frieda was alone for the first few minutes of her walk. She had fallen into the rhythm and was feeling she might walk all the way to dawn when she saw Nurse Holden walking toward her. Holden's rapid head twitch had grown worse, and Frieda couldn't look at the nurse's blurring face without feeling pain behind her eyes. Holden walked with steady, graceful, direct purpose, though. Frieda wondered briefly if she should be surprised Holden was here. Frieda hadn't thought she ever worked the night shift. The questions passed. They didn't matter. What mattered was showing Holden that Frieda was behaving, and doing her duty by walking, even when everyone else slept.

Holden held up a hand, and Frieda stopped before her.

"What are you walking?" Holden asked. Her voice had a new rasp.

"The labyrinth," said Frieda.

"Do you embrace the labyrinth?"

"I do," said Frieda, and she meant it. She realized that she had never been more certain of anything.

"Are you ready to greet the center?"

"I am."

Holden touched the wall. It parted. Frieda looked into the dark passage that had opened before her. It did not frighten her. She felt excited. She had come to where the path of her life had always been heading.

"Then come with me," said Holden.

They walked into the dark. Frieda knew the dark would soon move, and she welcomed it. She had moved beyond choice, and new worship bloomed in her heart.

In the morning, Miranda woke from a sleep so profound, for a moment she didn't know where she was. Then she took in the room.

And the empty beds.

And Norma's empty smile.

CHAPTER TWENTY-FIVE

"Good morning, sleepy head," Norma said.

How did she talk without losing that sickening wide smile? Shouldn't she be moving her lips?

"Morning," Miranda muttered.

Norma cocked her head. She blinked with a concern as plastic as her smile. "How are you feeling? You look done in."

Miranda felt worse than that. She felt as if a boulder rested on her chest, while her limbs had turned to lead. She couldn't imagine getting up. She didn't know what was happening to her. She also refused to confide in Norma.

Instead of answering, she said, "Where are the others?"

Norma ignored her question in turn. "Are you looking forward to walking? It's a lovely day."

As opposed to any other day inside the Institute? Miranda grunted.

"I'm sure you're as eager as I am to get going," Norma went on. "It's so invigorating."

"Is it?" Miranda couldn't help herself. She couldn't subject herself to Norma's artificial good cheer and not fight back.

"It really is," said Norma, the smile impervious and eternal. "If you're in the right spirit."

She knows, Miranda thought. She knows where the others are. Or she knows what happened to them. That's what's behind that smile.

She should have pitied Norma, who had been seduced by the power that whispered down the halls of the Institute. She did not believe for a moment that Norma had served Crothoaka before coming here. Norma had been changed, twisted into something other than her true self.

Not made to reveal her true self? Are you sure?

No. She wanted to think no one but Donovan and Daria had been corrupt from the start. She wanted to think that. And if she held true to that belief, she should pity Norma. She really, really, should. But right now, she hated and feared her.

"I'm not one for being in the spirit," Miranda said, encasing her words in ice.

Norma didn't answer. She just kept smiling.

Breakfast came, and there were no trays for Lupita and Frieda. Miranda didn't ask again where the other two were. She would only get lies or confusion in response. And she was so tired. She didn't have the strength for a pointless fight. She had to preserve her energy.

Get through today. Tomorrow, Agatha will be here. Tell her what you learned. She'll know what to do after that, right? Right.

Just because Miranda couldn't see how her knowledge of what had happened and the name of what was coming would help, that didn't mean Agatha would be stymied.

Agatha *had* to know what the next step would be. She had to.

Miranda conserved her strength. Eat, rest, walk, and do as you're told. Get through to tomorrow.

She found that she couldn't imagine the future beyond Sunday.

After breakfast, Nurse Revere appeared. "Time to walk," she said.

Norma leapt out of bed as if it were Christmas morning. Miranda could barely sit up. She had to use her hands to get her legs into position. She pushed off against the mattress to get herself on her feet. She wobbled back and forth, then fell back, knees buckling.

Revere rushed into the room. "What's the matter?" she asked.

On her hands and knees, Miranda said, "So tired… Can't stand." Her breath came in painful gasps. The boulder on her chest was flattening her lungs.

Revere lifted her, the nurse's wiry strength disturbing in its power. *How will I fight you when the time comes?* She settled Miranda back in the bed.

Miranda sighed, and the breath happened all wrong. It hurt her chest and made her cough. Revere stood motionless, looking down at her. Miranda couldn't focus on her.

She just wanted to sleep.

Revere was speaking. "… a doctor…"

Yes, yes, get a doctor. That was a fine idea. Someone ought to do that someday.

Miranda closed her eyes. She floated for a moment on top of the pain, and then she coughed and started to drown. She bobbed in and out of consciousness.

What's happening to me?

When the fever let her think, she understood. She had regressed. All the progress she had made towards recovery had vanished. She felt far sicker than when she had arrived at the Institute.

Down into the delirium of exhaustion and pain. Surfacing for moments. A doctor came. She didn't know who it was. Another of Donovan's useful tools. She had a vague awareness of being spoken to. She didn't answer. A stethoscope touched her chest. Someone gave her commands. Her body obeyed, though her brain barely registered the presence of others in the room. Voices spoke to each other, but not to her. At some point, the doctor left. She was alone again. The day slipped away. Everything slipped away.

She was slipping away.

I can't fight.

You *must*.

She forced herself to break through to the surface again, and to stay there. She would not let Donovan win like this. She wouldn't be a good little victim and fade into nothing, leaving the field clear for him and his nightmare ambitions.

She kept her breath as shallow as she could. Her head cleared. She looked around. From the light, she judged it was mid-afternoon.

Donovan sat in a chair beside her. There was no one else in the room.

"Hello there," he said.

Adrenaline spiked.

I *will* fight you.

"Hello," Miranda croaked.

"What a setback you've had," he said, still wearing the

mask of the concerned administrator. "You shouldn't scare us like that."

Miranda said nothing.

Donovan discarded the mask. His eyes glittered, hard. His face seemed to age, furrows deepening like knife slashes as he leaned forward, his expression determined. "Very well," he said. "Shall we speak of doubt?"

"I doubt there's anything to say."

His lips twitched briefly in a sour facsimile of amusement. "Wit," he said. "You must be feeling better."

"Doubtful."

The twitch again. "What is this? Mockery? That's beneath you, professor. You're disappointing me. I would have thought you might be curious about where absolute critical thinking can go."

Miranda shook her head slightly. Her skull felt heavy as a cannonball. "It goes against absolutes," she said.

Donovan's thin smile seemed genuine this time. "There you go," he said. "Proper engagement."

Miranda mustered the energy for an attack. "Yes," she said. "I engaged, and you diverted. Or didn't you understand what I said. There are no absolutes, and you should know that."

A shadow of uncertainty flickered over his face. It passed. He had shrugged off whatever she had said to disturb him. "You're wrong," he said. "I have the advantage over you in knowing that utterly and completely. But I would have thought you'd know better than to say that. After what you read."

There. So he had wanted her to find the journal. And she saw why now. He wanted her conversion.

Why, though? A point of pride? Why not just dispose of her otherwise, if she refused to march down the path laid out for her?

Well, he hadn't. Maybe she would find out why not. She *would* make him regret playing this game.

"I do know better," she said. "I know better than to bend the knee to your god, and to your foul philosophy."

Donovan stood up. "My my," he said. "I have to agree with the doctors. You do seem to have overdone things rather badly. I hate to see such a decline, and after all the way forward you had come." He made a show of sighing. "This goes against everything I want the treatment to be for our clients in this Institute, but your condition leaves me no choice. Following medical advice, I'm afraid you're going to have to cease all exercise. Nothing but bed rest for you."

Fine by me. She wanted no part in the walking ritual. She would rest, store up her strength, and then, when Agatha came by on Sunday…

"Bed rest," Donovan repeated, "and no more visitors. You're just not up to the excitement."

His grin was nothing like Norma's doll-like rictus. It dripped venom.

Gathering reality, Crothoaka flexed its coils. And Arkham shuddered.

Payton Wallace loved his office. It was, he sincerely believed, a statement about who occupied it. Payton had, since his first election, added to the prestige of the office with the careful choice of decor and accessories. "Clothes might not make the man," he liked to say, "but the office does." He was only half-joking.

The silver inkwell, more than a hundred years old, purchased at an estate sale three summers ago. The ornate mantle clock, its baroque bronze housing culminating in a figure of Venus seated on the top. The equally ornate frame he had found to complement his portrait on the wall. These things and more came together as one to announce the quality of the man who sat in this office. The people – the ones who crossed the threshold into his space, at any rate – deserved to know that they had elected someone of substance, someone who *mattered*.

Payton liked to take the lunch hour to spend some time alone and bask in the space of his accomplishment. He would sit at the desk and look at one object, and then another, and feel warm, and know that what he enjoyed and what Arkham needed were one and the same.

The comfort and warmth were what he needed now. He couldn't get Daria Miracle's performance out of his mind. It had dominated his thoughts since he had seen it, and he didn't know why. He kept trying to believe that the spectacle, so sublime, so captivating for the patients, showed him that all was well at the Institute. He tried very hard, but all he could think about was her movement, and how it seemed to push his soul down a coiling path he did not understand, but could not refuse.

Being in the office helped. Looking at the familiar and the beautiful helped.

Payton leaned forward to touch the clock. It sat across from him on the desk, at the edge, in the precise, measured-to-the-quarter-inch center, lengthwise. He ran his finger down the sinuous convolutions of the bronze.

It hurt. Pain, stabbing, sharp as a razor, sliced deep. He jerked his hand away and scattered drops of blood over the surface of the desk. He stared at the cut. It ran the entire length of his index finger. He made a fist, dripping more blood, and clutched his hand to his chest. He looked back at the clock.

Had someone broken something on it? One of the cleaning staff? If they had...

A shimmer passed over the clock, stopping his outrage cold. Thick, oily streamers dangled off Venus' upraised arm.

Payton jumped up and backed away from the desk. In the center of the office, he turned around slowly, his eyes caught by the sudden hostility of the room. It radiated from every object, and from the walls and ceiling and floor. He suddenly could not be sure that he had bought any of the things he saw. He would never have purchased that clock, not when it was so vile a thing. Then how did it get there?

How did anything get here?

The room did not want him. Its contents were foreign to him. A sheen of the strange covered them.

"What..." he said, but only in a whisper. He did not know whom he should call. He did not know if he should call anyone. What if they meant him harm? What if they had brought the clock?

What if they were responsible for that portrait? It looked like it was meant to be of him, but he distrusted it now. He did not know its intent.

He did not know anything. He was surrounded by

strangeness and uncertainty. Mewling, he curled in a ball on the carpet. He rocked back and forth, eyes darting around the office.

On the clock, Venus turned her head to look at him. She hissed. The ornamentation writhed, and then it began to crawl off the clock, across the desk, and down its sides, making for him. On the ceiling, shadows of serpents moved with heavy grace.

Councilman Payton Wallace began to scream. He was still screaming when the ambulance came, and the men with the stretcher bore him away. Though his voice eventually gave out, the screams in his head never stopped again.

Cleo Whitten opened the door of her Southside house. She planned to walk down to the drugstore a few blocks away and pick up some odds and ends. The novelty of being able to go for a stroll whenever she felt like it, and not feel out of breath, had not worn off. Since leaving the Stroud Institute, she had taken new pleasure in the mundane, taken-for-granted events of a day that became out of reach when she had fallen into the depths of her illness. She was well again. There had been times when she feared she never would be. Those memories were still sharp. She treasured the gift of living normally.

She also welcomed each day that came and put the Institute further into her past. She couldn't complain about her treatment there. And her stay had cured her. For most of her time there, she had felt safe, comfortable, and lucky to be receiving care of that level. She had felt less comfortable during the last part of her stay. The sessions with Daria had been the turning point. She had welcomed them, at first, but the more she thought about them, the more they troubled her. Daria's words, her grace and her lessons, had followed Cleo home from the Institute. They were beginning to fade, she thought, and with them the discomfort they created.

As the everyday returned, and the old habits returned, the old certainties did too.

But now, as she closed the door behind her and took one step down the wooden porch, she froze. She suddenly did not want to put her foot down on the sidewalk. The instinct stopped her so abruptly that she almost lost her balance and fell. She windmilled her arms, barely holding on to her purse, then steadied.

The ripple of a wave passed over her small yard. The grass rounded itself over the mound, and so did the concrete slabs of the sidewalk. Another ripple followed the first, then more in quick succession. Her yard undulated. The movement surrounded the house, and it extended out into the street. Cleo looked left and right, and saw the ripples move up the walls of her neighbors' houses.

With the ripples came a call. The image of the Institute filled Cleo's mind. The center of all things summoned her. She had to go back.

"No," she told herself, and wrapped her arms around one of the porch's posts. She shut her eyes so she would not see the hypnotic movement, but then the Institute became even sharper in her head, insistent, commanding.

"No," Cleo said again. "*No!*" She clung to the post, fighting against the psychic undertow that pulled her. If she let go, she would run to the Institute, and to the labyrinth.

Don't let go, don't let go, don't let go.

She would not walk that path. She would not go back.

She was trying to keep her footing in the torrent of a flood. But she held on.

At last, the current released her. She opened her eyes. The ripples had ceased. Her yard was still, the grass unbroken, the sidewalk no more cracked than it had been yesterday.

Cleo let go of the post with one arm, then the other. The urge to return to the Institute had passed. She had fought it off.

But she didn't know what she had fought.

And if it came again, stronger, she didn't think she would win.

She went back inside the house and locked the door.

In the streets and in the stores, in bedrooms and in cars, in Southside and in Rivertown, in Easttown and in Uptown, in all the corners of Arkham, the tightening of the coils made itself felt. The citizens felt the touch of the gathering god. Some barely noticed. It marked others forever.

An overture to the coming reign.

CHAPTER TWENTY-SIX

In French Hill, Wilbur called out to Agatha in a voice trying hard to be brave.

"Dear," he said, "is it possible that we have snakes in the building?"

Agatha looked up. She had been scouring her desk with cleaner. Some faint traces of the samples she had taken from the Institute must have remained. She had found what looked like slug trails on the surface in the morning. She had thrown herself into a full purge, while at the same time gathering all the protective amulets, of confirmed value or otherwise, that she could find. She grabbed two now. She had convinced Wilbur to continue wearing the medallion she had given him for the trip. Hearing the fear in his voice, she acted on instinct, taking the flat iron discs engraved with the elder sign.

She hurried to the living room. Outside, the afternoon had become overcast, and the light seemed much dimmer than it should be, the clouds drawing a lead lining between Arkham and the sun. Wilbur stood in the center of the room, eyeing the walls nervously.

"Snakes?" Agatha asked, following his gaze.

"I keep hearing sounds in the walls."

He held up a hand for silence, and they both listened. "There," he said after a minute, his face turning white.

Agatha heard it. She heard the awful, familiar scrape and slide from the *Leviathan*. She tried to follow the sound with her eyes. In the corner of the walls and ceiling, where the shadows had thickened, she caught the afterthought of movement.

It's here, she thought. Her chest tightened with despair.

Then she shook herself. Surrender would not help. And the sounds were not as loud as on the *Leviathan*. Here but not here, not fully, not yet, still some time. Not much, but some.

"Those aren't snakes," she said to Wilbur.

"Oh," he said, and visibly relaxed.

"It's something much worse," she said, hating that she had to scare him. But he should be frightened. Being scared could mean staying alive.

"Do I want to know…" Wilbur began.

"No, you don't," she told him. "Even if I could explain, and I'm not sure that I could."

Wilbur swallowed. "I suppose ignoring the sounds isn't an option?"

"It isn't."

"That's too bad."

He was doing his best to put on a brave show, and she loved him for it, but his voice cracked at the end, and his hands trembled.

Agatha knelt and grabbed one end of the Turkish carpet

that covered most of the living room floor. "Help me with this," she said.

They rolled the carpet, and she moved the coffee table out of the way. She had Wilbur stand in the middle of the bare floor, then raced back to her office to fetch chalk. She stopped in the kitchen on the way back for a pitcher of water and a glass. She gave them to Wilbur.

"What are these for?" he asked.

"For you if you get thirsty."

"If I get…?"

"You're going to stay where you are for some time," she explained. She left him for a minute, then came back with a bucket. "You might need this, too. You can't leave the circle. For *any* reason."

"Oh," Wilbur said in a very small voice.

She brought over one of the dining room chairs and a throw cushion from the couch. "For sitting, and for if you want to lie down," she said.

Wilbur sat. He didn't ask any more questions as she drew a protective circle around him. She marked it with elder signs and all the other symbols of protection she knew.

So much fumbling in the dark, she thought as she worked. So much she, and the other people who fought to hold back the dark in the world, did not know. Agatha believed that there had to be a way of understanding the threats, and the science behind the words and the incantations and the sounds and the symbols that seemed to help. There had to be rules that governed the universe. They just needed to be found.

She didn't know what the rules were today, with the light

bleeding away from the day, and sounds in the walls. Did the ones she had half-glimpsed in the past even apply? She just had to hope they did. And so, she drew the circle around Wilbur and hoped it would keep him safe. She needed him safe.

"Do not step outside the circle," Agatha said again.

"Okay."

"Don't do anything to break it."

"You already told me that."

"Promise me you won't."

Wilbur nodded. "I won't."

"Stay right where you are until I get back."

He paled again. "Where are you going?"

"To the Stroud Institute. That's the heart of what's happening. I have to do what I can to stop it."

"But what is *it*?"

"The thing I have to stop."

"You're not being funny."

"I'm not trying to be. I wish I had better answers. I just know that I have to try."

She hugged and kissed him, stepped out of the circle, and drew its final segments. Then she left the apartment.

The journey to the Institute showed her how much worse things had become. The air tasted wrong. It tasted of anxiety. She kept looking over her shoulder along the sidewalk, and the people she passed had a hunted look, their eyes darting about. She flagged a cab down after a block, and the cabbie seemed distracted. When she told him where she wanted to go, he looked puzzled for a moment, as if he didn't know the way, and when he did get going, she could see his uncertainty unnerved him. She didn't blame him. The closer she came to the Institute, the more uncertain she felt. Doubts crawled over every thought.

The cabbie drove hesitantly. He kept starting to brake, then muttering to himself. "Nothing there. Stupid."

He slowed down as they approached the gates of the Institute. "In there?" he asked.

Agatha knew how he felt. The building loomed. It governed the day with malice. At the same time, it pulled the eyes and the mind its way. The closer one came, the harder it would be to get away.

"Drop me off at the gates," she said. She could spare him the approach.

The cabbie nodded gratefully. He pulled away as soon as she got out, not giving her a chance to pay him.

It took an effort to pass through the gates. The grounds felt much more dangerous, much more infected, than on her last visit. She thought about how relieved she had been to get away.

And now I'm back.

She had no choice. She had to do what she could for Miranda, and with her. She had to warn her how badly things were going outside the walls of the Institute, how imminent the disaster must be. And she had to know what Miranda had found, if anything, in Donovan's apartment. Waiting to learn that, waiting to know that Miranda was all right, that all had gone well, had made the night and day an agony. At least she wasn't going to wait for Sunday's visiting hours. No point in keeping up appearances anymore. The crisis had come, and it was time to fight back, even in total ignorance. It was that or surrender. She would never do that.

Agatha jogged down the drive and up the stairs to the Institute's entrance. She tried the doors; they were locked. She pounded on them, and no one came.

She backed down the stairs and looked around. No sign of life on the grounds. No ambulances arriving, no groundskeeper working on the lawn. Only stillness, and the silence before the storm.

She looked up at the building. Could she work out which window was the one for Miranda's room? It looked out on this side. Yes, she thought so. She counted, picturing how many rooms she went by before she reached Miranda's room. The confusing geography of the interior didn't help, but from the outside, she could tell where she had to be to get the view from Miranda's bed.

There. That was the one. Two in from the end of the wing.

Agatha picked up a handful of stones from the edge of the drive. She threw them one after the other at the window. They bounced off with sharp ticks. After the fourth, the window opened. Miranda leaned out.

Agatha hissed. Even from this distance, she could see how haggard Miranda looked. She leaned on the windowsill as if it was all she could do to keep from falling. She lifted a hand for a moment and waved feebly.

"I can't get in," Agatha called. "The doors are locked."

Miranda nodded, as if this news did not surprise her.

"It's happening," Agatha said. "We're out of time. The ritual is almost complete."

Miranda straightened with visible effort, steeling herself. "Crothoaka," she said.

Agatha winced at the cost Miranda's lungs must have paid

for her to make herself heard. The word she spoke had no meaning, and it had too much. Agatha recognized it as a name, and understood that Miranda must have learned it from what she found last night. Agatha clenched her fists in frustration. Miranda knew more now, but there was no way for her to pass the information to Agatha, no way for them to fight together.

Miranda managed some more words. "What do I do?" she asked.

I wish I knew. "Fight," Agatha said, hating the burden she was placing on Miranda's shoulders, raging against her helplessness. "Fight in any way you can." She pulled a medallion out of her jacket pocket. It was an iron disc, etched in silver with an elder sign. "Keep this with you. It will protect you." *I hope.* She threw the medallion at the window. Her aim was true. Miranda reached out to catch it, missed, and it sailed past her into the room.

Miranda nodded. She closed the window.

Agatha stayed put. "I'll wait," she promised.

The medallion clattered to the floor behind Miranda. She shut the window, the cooling air raking her lungs, and turned around to retrieve it.

Norma had it. She held it up, examining it as if it were a dead toad. "What is this?" she said.

Miranda hadn't heard her return. She hadn't come back since the morning exercises had begun. Miranda had drifted in and out of wakefulness all day. When Agatha's stones had brought her back to full consciousness, she had noticed how still the hallway was outside her door. There were no walkers. No one around at all. But now here was Norma.

The other woman made a face at the medallion. "This is garbage," she said.

"Maybe," Miranda said. It hurt so much to talk. "But it's mine. Please." She held out a hand.

Norma closed a fist around the disk. "I don't think this is healthy for you," she said.

"Not… your business."

"I'm going to show this to Nurse Revere."

Miranda took a step forward. "Give it."

Norma turned to go.

Miranda lunged. It felt like she was trying to jump underwater. The weakness of illness and the sluggishness of nightmare fought her. She grabbed the back of Norma's robe as she fell, and they both went down. Norma snarled, teeth bared, and she clawed at Miranda's face. Miranda jerked her head back. Norma punched her, hard.

Miranda saw stars. She tried to hold on to Norma, her vision graying. Norma kneed her in the stomach, and Miranda slumped down, pain exploding in her head and wounded lungs. She was only vaguely aware of Norma pulling away.

Lying on the floor, her body a single bruised mass, she went down into unconsciousness again. The last image before the darkness was the medallion. She had only had one good look at it, when Norma gave it her hateful stare. The design leapt out at her, carved itself into her imagination, and kept her company when the lights went out.

She didn't know how much time had passed when she opened her eyes again and managed to use a bedframe to haul herself up from the floor. Hours, she guessed. The afternoon had been turning black, but now night had fallen. She dragged herself to her bed. How could she do anything? She didn't have the strength for anything except to collapse in bed.

You promised.

And there was no one else. Agatha couldn't get in. If Miranda didn't fight Donovan, then he would complete the summoning of Crothoaka.

He probably will anyway.

How did she think she would fight him? Norma had stolen the closest thing she had to a weapon.

The image of the elder sign burned in her mind's eye, as sharp as ever. She sat on the side of the bed and took up a pad and pen from her nightstand. She drew the elder sign, the blazing memory guiding her hand. She examined her work when she was done. Hardly silver on iron, but the symbol looked right. She traced its lines with her finger.

The worst of the exhaustion dropped away. She could move again. She stood up without having to lean on anything. She no longer felt the overpowering urge to sleep. Her lungs were still congested, her breathing ragged. Whatever force had alleviated her TB had given it all back. Her empirical physical health was not good. But the force, perhaps the same one that had been oppressing her all day, had lifted.

She got dressed. The process felt like donning armor. She would not confront Donovan clad as a patient. She shrugged into her coat and belted it tightly. Then she tore the sheet with the symbol off the pad, folded it, and put it in her pocket.

"Be thou my shield," she whispered to the elder sign.

Here we go.

She left the room. In the silent hall, she took a quick look in the nearby doorways. The rooms were not all empty. The beds were far from being full, but she saw at least two or three patients in each room. Wherever the others had gone, whoever had become like Norma, full converts, Miranda saw enough to allow her the hope that many of the people under the roof of the Stroud Institute were not her enemies.

She didn't know how she could help them, though. And they certainly couldn't help her. Without exception, they slept deeply. She tried calling out, and then clapped her hands, the sharp sound echoing weirdly in the silence. No one stirred. The power that had tried to pull her down had them in its coils.

"Stay safe," she said to them. "I'll do what I can."

She turned to the wall and felt carefully along it. She found the tactile pattern of the labyrinth, and then she found the circular depression that marked the trigger for the hidden passage. She steeled herself and opened the wall.

She had no flashlight or candle. Nothing to light the way. It looked like she wouldn't need one. The passageway was dark, but not black. A faint, green-tinged luminescence came from the walls. The path before her was clear.

The way of pilgrims, she thought. The labyrinth had welcomed all to its center. It wanted them there.

It wanted her there.

She accepted the invitation, and started down the path.

CHAPTER TWENTY-SEVEN

The passageway turned sharply, and then again, backtracking on itself before turning again and descending. After another short stretch, it curved, sloping upward. The curve went on so long that Miranda realized she had entered a spiral, one that somehow switched from going up to going down, and then up again.

The inner labyrinth made the rest of the Institute seem rational in its layout. Miranda had no idea where she was in the building. Within minutes, she gave up trying to locate herself. Soon, she found it hard to believe the world existed outside the labyrinth. She had always been in this passage. She always would be.

The walls changed the deeper she went. From the start, the air was damp, and the stones glistened with trickles of slime. Carved into rough, rectangular slabs, pitted and scarred, the stones brooded with their age and seemed to press closer to her, alert to the movement of prey. Gradually, the lines between the slabs became vague, as if the walls and ceiling and floor of the passage were made of a single mass.

The transformation pointed to revelation ahead. Miranda dreaded it. But she did not turn back. She doubted she would be allowed to, and she would not back down. She would see the path through to the end.

You say that like you have a choice.

The thought chilled. She resented it, all the more furiously because she couldn't deny it. She had a single path before her, with no branches, no junctions, no choices.

You are here, the labyrinth whispered, because that is your fate.

Her victory over fatigue was no victory at all. It was a capitulation to the inevitable.

Inevitable. Her life had turned into mere inevitability. She looked back at the moments that had brought her here, to walking endlessly through the damp, green twilight, and saw how all her options had been stripped away from the start. In Donovan's apartment, reading the journal, she had felt the same sense of iron destiny. The steps through the winding labyrinth from her home to this darkness were so obvious.

All the steps, all the little moments, some trivial and unremarked when they happened, others massive, but whose interconnections she had not seen at the time.

All the steps. Walking by the Institute every day, observing it gradually come into being. The thought of the place as her first choice for help when she fell sick. The days of care and nights of fear, the visions and the suspicions teaching her to be wary, to look for the danger.

She had resisted Daria's lessons. She did not want to walk the path Donovan had laid out for her. But then she read the journal he wanted her to read, and now she walked the labyrinth: could she say that she was here against his wishes?

No, she could not.

She thought about the mission she had given herself. She came to stop the project that Magnus Stroud had begun. She, a Romanticist, had come to destroy the work of a zealot of Romanticism. The symmetry of the conflict defied chance. If she tried to put down all the events that had produced this result to coincidence, her reason turned away, revolted.

Coincidence had not brought her here. Fate had. She accepted that.

Back and forth. Down straight halls, then curved ones. Up and down, twisting around angles so sharp, the passage should have crossed its own path.

The stones continued to change. The divisions between them had shed their disguise. They were wrinkles. As if the walls were flesh.

The passage twisting and twisting, like a thing alive.

The turns and the rises and the falls felt like the pattern of her life, seemingly random but destined.

She grew dizzy with the turns. She coughed, and she stumbled. She put out a hand to stop her fall. Her palm touched the wall; the stone was warm and wet, and it gave beneath her touch.

Like flesh.

Flesh that clung.

And she was in a lecture hall at Miskatonic, her lungs clear, her voice strong.

"My question for you," she said to the class, "is this: do Byron's heroes have free will? Think about it. Wouldn't that affect our judgment of them and their actions?"

"They do have free will," said one student. Miranda should know her name by now, this late into the term. She had trouble making out her features. Was the lighting dim? "Their tragedies are their fault."

"I see," said Miranda. She drummed her fingers against the lectern and nodded. "Their circumstances are the results of their actions, then."

"Yes," said another student, and Miranda couldn't quite place his name, either. She should be doing much better than this.

"And their actions are chosen, not preordained," said Miranda.

A half-dozen heads nodded. Most of the class regarded her neutrally. She couldn't tell if they were engaged by the debate or not. They sat very still.

"But is it possible," Miranda said, "that the choices themselves were determined by the formation of character? Were the Byronic heroes always going to sin because of all the life experiences that brought them to the moment of sin?"

She saw some frowns.

"You don't agree?" she said to the first student who had spoken. *What is her name?*

"I think that's a cop-out."

"How so?"

"Because that way, you could excuse anything."

"That's true," Miranda agreed. "Anything except the god who caused the circumstances to occur. And so the Byronic heroes rail against the gods and fates, but in the end do what has always been destined."

"*Exactly.*" The students spoke as one, the class pleased that she had learned her lesson.

Miranda frowned. The class had been going well, the students not just accepting what she said uncritically, but now she felt as if she had completely misread her own circumstances. Wasn't she the one lecturing?

Undulating movement passed over the class. The students' arms and limbs lengthened, turning into tentacles, their leathered skin a blotchy patchwork of red and white and dark green. The lecture hall trembled. The walls cracked, raining wood and plaster down. The ceiling broke open. It peeled away like burning paper, and Miranda looked up into a sky that had become a bulging, translucent gray membrane, ready to tear and unleash the writhing shapes and eyes behind it.

Miranda raised her hands to her own eyes, and she could see right through her flesh and bone, see and see and see, and…

She tripped and almost fell as the passageway sloped downward again, the gradient steeper than before.

She stopped, waiting for her breathing to calm and her head to stop spinning. She couldn't remember pulling her hand away from the wall. She didn't know how far she had come since she had touched it. There had been no slope, then, and she had been in a straight portion of the hall. The path here curved ahead and behind her. She had walked without seeing where she was going, while she had been caught in that…

…memory? Maybe. She couldn't be sure, except about the last part. What about the rest? She had given more lectures about Byron than she could count. She didn't remember the events of every class from term to term. There could have been such a debate. The memory now felt so clear, or at least what had been said. The faces of the students remained frustratingly vague.

Had the labyrinth plucked a forgotten moment from one of her classes and, in using it for its own ends, given the memory back to her? Or had everything been an invention? Her fists clenched in frustration, nails digging into her palms to remind her that real was real. She felt as she did when she woke from one of those dreams that claimed to be a recurring one, without any way of telling if she had really dreamed this before, or if the memory were itself a creation of the dream.

She mistrusted the reality of the lecture. It was too convenient. But when she denied it the stature of fact, all its elements receded from certainty too. She couldn't see the students' faces, so they weren't real – but when she tried to picture her students from this term, the ones she had taught not that long ago, their faces were misty too. How could she know if any memories were truly hers?

If she had always been in the labyrinth, then she had never taught. Her students, her office, her books, the essays she had to mark and the exams she had to invigilate, all of them delusions.

"No," she said aloud. She started walking again. "It is the…" She couldn't remember the date. She tried again. "I came to the Institute in March. I had a life before. I have not always been here."

But the memory of the sky, of the disintegration of the lecture hall, so real, so vivid, more precise than the ordinary, familiar recollection of the lecture.

"No," Miranda said again. "No, no, no." She put her hand in

her pocket and clutched the paper with the elder sign. Such flimsy material, so weak, yet the comfort it gave her was real. A folded corner poked her palm. She felt the texture of the paper against her fingers. The strength of the symbol reached to her soul.

It didn't matter if the lecture had ever happened or not. The horror at its end had not happened. Not yet.

"Not ever," Miranda promised herself.

Air, warm and clammy, pushed against her. In the unknown, unseen center of the labyrinth, something hissed. The flesh of the walls moved. They shifted, a muscle stretching, coming to know itself.

She clutched the elder sign harder as she understood what Donovan had written.

Hail Crothoaka, the Worm of the Labyrinth!

Donovan's words, and words were important. Precision mattered. *Of* the labyrinth, not *in* it. The worm and the labyrinth were one. The twisting passages inside the Institute were becoming the summoned god. She was within the manifesting Crothoaka, swallowed already, and when the summoning ended, the Worm would burst out of its stone cocoon.

Miranda fought back a wave of panic and the need to turn around, to run and run and run, to be out in the clean air and not be in the monster, go now now *now*, before it's too late.

She forced herself to keep going, and even held back the grunt of terror that tried to force its way out from her chest.

"I will fight. I will fight. I will fight." The sound of her voice helped, another reminder of existence beyond the confines of her head.

The path kept going down, and kept turning. The way

became narrower, then wider, and then narrower once more. As the expansion began yet again, Miranda realized that the walls were moving. They were contracting and expanding with a slow, measured rhythm, and the sluggish breeze blew and stopped, blew and stopped, and she should recognize breathing when she encountered it. She had grown so conscious of her own lately.

She kept to the middle of the path, trying to draw her shoulders in. The walls came in close, and she didn't want to touch them again.

She refused them. They insisted. The walls curved inward, stretching, an echo of the membrane of the sky; before she could deny that memory again, they squeezed her from both sides.

And she was ten years old, in her parents' house, bored of her books one Sunday afternoon and looking for something else to read, something *grown-up*; she had been told that she could try anything that interested her from the *grown-up* bookshelves.

That Sunday, a warm fall day, she found *Frankenstein*. She started reading it. She didn't understand it all. She persisted, though, getting through more each day. When she ran into passages that she felt sure were crucial but couldn't puzzle out, she spoke to her mother.

A few days into her project, in the evening, a wet one now, with the leaves turning into brown mulch in the gutters outside, she asked her mother why Victor Frankenstein, when a child, seemed angry with his father about some alchemy books he had found.

They were sitting beside each other on the couch. Anne

Ventham put a bookmark in the volume she had been reading and looked at the page Miranda was showing her.

"He's trying to blame his father for what happens later," Anne explained. "He says that if his father had explained things a different way, then Frankenstein would have agreed with him that the books were nonsense. Then, he would not have become obsessed with them and their ideas, and he would not have made all the other choices that finally lead to creating a monster. Do you understand?"

"His whole life is his father's fault?" said Miranda.

"That's more or less what Frankenstein is saying. That doesn't mean he's right." After a thoughtful pause, her mother continued. "I think he's just making excuses and trying to shift the blame. But I think it *is* true that reading those books did influence who he grew up to be in a very, very important way."

"Can that happen? Can just reading a book change you?"

"Or maybe decide who you are. Yes, honey."

Miranda didn't know if she found the idea exciting or frightening. Either possibility seemed like a good reason to hug her mother, so she did, and her mother hugged her back, and hugged her, and hugged her, arms reaching around and around and around, slithering and squeezing, rough with scales, crushing now, and Miranda couldn't breathe, and her mother hissed, and her long, twitching tongue tangled in Miranda's hair.

Miranda gasped, her chest filled with broken glass, and she rushed forward, down the sinuous path, away from the memory and its horror. The memory had to be false, another construct of the labyrinth, except that it was all so vivid, and she remembered everything else about that fall and her first encounter with *Frankenstein*. It was true, true, true, that the right book at the right time could shape you, could set out the path of your life. Because she had read *Frankenstein*, she had become a Romanticist, and so she was here, in the labyrinth, the right book dooming her to this horror, the right book appearing not by chance but by fate, her path decided from childhood, and earlier, from birth, and earlier, always already decided, her descent into the labyrinth always already mapped out.

And if she said no, if she denied this truth, then what – were all her memories wrong? Were they all illusions, thin dreams of free will and mirages of life? All wrong, all lies, all fed to her by the labyrinth at its pleasure, in its perversity, because she had always been here, only been here, the labyrinth the only reality, the only truth?

"No," she said again, then louder, to prove that she could. "No!"

The floor of the corridor had leveled off, and the walls had become sinuous, curving left and right and left and right, as it breathed in and out and in and out.

"No," Miranda said again, not as loud, but with determination. She twisted sideways to avoid the touch of the walls. She would refuse the binary choice of horror the labyrinth offered her. She would not accept its truth. She would disprove it through victory, by freeing the patients of the Institute from the labyrinth's grasp.

She heard human voices chanting. She listened with care, and rubbed the paper of the elder sign for some reassurance of reality before she could be sure that the voices weren't in her head. They grew louder. Each curve of the corridor brought her closer to them.

She couldn't make out the words. Meaning crouched just out of reach. She strained to hear better, to make out the call, because it was a call, yes, she made out that much, and the satisfaction pushed her to move faster, to get closer, and learn the rest. Only then did she realize that she was answering the call.

Miranda forced herself to slow down, and put her fingers to her lips. They were moving, trying to shape the syllables, as if she were five again, and sounding out the words on a page. She pressed her lips together, held her mouth closed. Crothoaka would get no summons from her.

She slowed down some more, making her steps deliberate, advancing with caution, keeping clear of the walls.

Here we go. Almost there. This is when you fight, really fight. The journey here had been a prologue.

Another bend, and the corridor ended. Beyond an archway lay the center of the labyrinth. It was a huge chamber, much larger than the Institute's entrance lobby, much too big a space to be contained within the walls of the building. Perhaps Miranda had descended far below the foundations of the Institute. The chamber could be a cave. It had rows of twenty-foot stalactites and stalagmites running down its left and right sides, except they weren't mineral formations, because they were too smooth, too perfectly shaped like fangs, and they weren't sculptures either, gleaming with venom and the imminence of motion.

The mound in the middle of the room, around which all the people had gathered, was an altar, with a rounded top, and a front that sloped, undulating, nearly to the archway. Yes, an altar.

But also a tongue.

Green, pulsating mist oozed around the chamber, jerking and turning to the rhythms of the chant. Donovan stood directly opposite Miranda, on the other side of the altar, arms outstretched, fingers crooked into claws, his head tilted back in ecstasy as he led the song. Maybe fifty patients and staff were gathered in a semi-circle around the altar. The light and their worship had transformed their dressing gowns and uniforms. To Miranda's eyes, they looked like ceremonial robes to her now.

Daria danced. She moved among the worshippers, around Donovan and the altar, and back to the patients, weaving a path, and marking it too, because her arms stretched long, serpentine and boneless. Her hand on one shoulder and the limb weaving around the shoulders of a dozen other celebrants before the caressing hand followed, leaving a gleaming, viscous trail behind on faces and necks.

Miranda stayed just inside the archway. They hadn't seen her yet. She had this moment to act. She didn't know what to do.

Then Nurse Holden shot around the side of the arch from where she had been hidden against the near wall. Her head twitched up and down and side to side, the movement so harsh and rapid it should have broken her neck, but her smile was wide, so wide, and as she struck rattlesnake-fast and grabbed Miranda's arms, her gargling voice repeated the first words she had said to her when Miranda had arrived at the Institute, a thousand centuries ago.

"What do you think you're doing?"

CHAPTER TWENTY-EIGHT

Holden dragged Miranda into the chamber. Her hands were rough, covered in minute insect legs that scrabbled against Miranda's skin. Her grip was unbreakable. Miranda tried to pull away, but Holden didn't seem to notice. The ring of worshippers parted, and Holden pulled Miranda toward the altar.

The chanting changed. The people turned from the altar to face Miranda, and they shouted what sounded like hails, but using a word that Miranda had never heard, that she could never pronounce without her tongue being transformed. The word slithered into her ears. It wrapped around her mind and tried to burrow in deep. In that repeated syllable she felt the taint of triumph, of welcome, of delight and of hunger.

She saw many faces that she recognized in the congregation, all changed as the culmination of the great ritual approached. Norma's smile had grown until her lips reached all the way around to her ears. Her teeth had grown too, longer and wider and brighter. She chanted, and she laughed at Miranda, her teeth clacking together with castanet mockery.

Frieda's eyes had crept out of their sockets and clung to the lower cheeks, just above her chin. They stared at Miranda with cold fury. Pale, grub-like things filled Frieda's eye sockets, twitching with tension.

Nurse Revere's face flowed with movement. She looked like herself for a moment, and then her head became a writhing explosion of great worms. They flailed out from her skull, reaching for Miranda as she passed, then curled back in on themselves, the markings on their bodies reforming the illusion of a human face for a moment, and then repeating the cycle.

A choir of horrors, a congregation of monsters. Any thought of appealing for help, of trying to break through the Institute's conversion, died. Miranda would find no help here.

Holden presented Miranda to Daria. The Miracle's arms twisted like rope around Miranda's, brought her to the altar, and forced her to lie down on its rounded surface. It moved under Miranda's back, a muscle tasting her presence.

"You are loved," Daria said. Her voice changed, sliding across registers to one painfully familiar.

No no no, Miranda thought. *I will not allow it.* Her mother had died three years before. She would not let this creature taint her memories.

But Daria kept speaking in the voice Miranda knew, and the taint spread. "You have always been loved, because of who you are, and who you would become, and of this moment, when you would do what you were born to do. How proud I was, when you asked me about Frankenstein." The serpent arms tightened in a parody of reassurance. "How I loved to hold you close."

No no no no. Miranda fought against the insinuations. But the re-experienced memory, turned monstrous, held on to her with a grip as unbreakable as Daria's. She could not split the real from the false. The joyful and the evil were alike in vividness and detail. They were one.

Daria held her down, and Donovan smiled at her. He wore a gray, hooded robe. Symbols sewn in black thread adorned it. Miranda recognized none of them, but she saw the labyrinth's pattern in them. They were all formed from a single, unbroken line, and a thin trace connected them all. Donovan was the only one of the faithful who had not been transformed. His face was as it always was, and he looked at Miranda with the same open friendliness as ever.

"This is the greatest moment of your life," he said. "You don't believe me right now, but you will."

This was the fight, Miranda thought. Somehow, this was when she had to strike back. She had no strength against Daria. She had no hope against the congregation. But Donovan needed something from her. If she could deny it to him… If she could use it against him…

But what did he want? Her conversion? What did one more or less believer matter?

"You're very sure of yourself," she said, stabbing in the dark. "So sure that all the physical changes are for other people."

No crack in Donovan's joy. If anything, he seemed pleased by her defiance. "It isn't for me to decide the fate of my body. That will come soon, I'm sure." He produced a dagger from somewhere in the folds of his robe. "Everything will be soon. The waiting is done."

He ran a finger down the length of the blade. The knife had

been forged of a metal blacker than obsidian. It had a rough texture like iron, yet shone in the green light like glass. The twists in the blade gave it the impression of being in motion.

"How many people have you murdered with that?" Miranda asked, revolted.

"Sacrificed, you mean," said Donovan. "And the answer is none. Nor will I today. You will complete the summons by sacrificing yourself to the Worm of the Labyrinth."

"If you want me dead, I am not going to do your work for you."

"But you will!" Donovan assured her, eyes shining with zealotry.

"How can you be so certain?" Miranda saw the hint of a way to fight back against Donovan. Doubt and certainty lay at the core of Crothoaka's spell. Donovan was, truly, Magnus' heir. Both men were idealists, driven to take their tenets to the ultimate conclusion. Men who rejected the orthodoxies of their times, but then kneeled before another dogma.

"I am certain because of who you are," Donovan said. "You are here for one purpose alone, and not the one you think. You were chosen long ago, you know. You were chosen long before you came to the Institute."

Miranda struggled against Daria's grip. She didn't want to hear. She began to lose hold of the embryonic tactic against Donovan.

"You must have known this," said the priest of Crothoaka.

She thought of the vision the night before she came to the Institute. She thought about the intimations of destiny that had assaulted her mind during her journey through the labyrinth.

Lies. All lies. She mustn't grant them the status of truth.

The thoughts would not shake loose. Insect legs in her brain, scratching, scratching.

"You can't think your tuberculosis was the result of a chance infection," Donovan scolded. "There is nothing random in the steps that brought you to the Institute. It took no effort at all to put you in the presence of contagion. We had time, after all. Months of construction before we would be ready to receive you."

"Why?" she asked before she could stop herself. She knew she shouldn't ask, but she had to know.

"Because you are the perfect final sacrifice. You complete the art of the ritual."

"Because I'm a Romanticist?" Even in her terror, she almost laughed at the absurdity of the idea. Then she remembered how she had seen the dark perfection in the nature of the conflict, and absurdity melted away before destiny.

"Not just that," said Donovan. "Not even principally that. Your scholarship is not the totality of your identity. It isn't your primary marker. You are the great doubter, Professor Ventham. You distrust all orthodoxies – social, political, and religious. You doubt all authority. You question everything. That is why you are here. Yours is the perfect conversion."

"Then you'll be disappointed."

"I won't." Always that confident smile. "Confronted by the god of doubt, and the certainty of its existence, you *will* convert."

"No," said Miranda.

Donovan didn't answer. He didn't seem to hear her. She tried to shout louder and found that she couldn't speak. The refusal stayed in her head, weak and alone. The chanting had changed again, become much louder, become an incantation and a call, directed at her and her alone. Rhythmic, hypnotic, it swamped her hearing, and then all of her perception. Her vision tunneled. Donovan receded from view as she fell down the well of consciousness.

Her awareness floated in deep nothing. Something in the void stirred. She mustn't look. But she had no body here, no eyes to avert, only her soul caught by its awareness of the serpent divine.

She witnessed the uncoiling of Crothoaka. Sublime, vast beyond her conception, the god appeared to her first as a storm of tentacles, a grasping, flailing maelstrom. Then, as the god filled her perception to the shattering point, she saw that the tentacles were the folds of a single, linear being, the labyrinth incarnate.

The vision changed, then. With the insect legs scrabbling deeper into her mind, her awareness multiplied. She became legion, seeing everywhere in Arkham first, and then more and more and more. She witnessed the reign of Crothoaka begin. She saw the spread of the plague of doubt. It vectored through the population on the wings of thought, in the disintegration of all assurances, and it came for the people in physical form, in devouring coils of insect and worm, in the disintegration of physical identity, in the end of every kind of self. And behind the doubt came the wave of the new certainty, the only one, the certainty of cataclysm that was Crothoaka, and all was devoured by the labyrinth.

Miranda saw it all. She saw the inevitability of it all, and she was the tiniest, most miserable of creatures doomed to be consumed, and what was there to do but submit before the truth? As the crawling things in her head dug deeper and deeper, she asked herself: would she dare to stand before a god? How could her feeble doubts compare before the Lord of Doubt? Crothoaka lived and waited in the fissures and contradictions and lacunae of every structure of belief, ready to bring them all crashing down.

In the end, Crothoaka was beyond all doubt. In the end, she had to surrender.

The pummeling cascade of visions of nightmare ended. Miranda returned to her body. It weighed her down with weakness. There was barely any need for Daria to hold her. The Miracle made a sound between a hiss and purr. Her limbs shifted around Miranda's arms, a spiral hug in preparation of release, because the time had come for her to take the knife and do what fate demanded.

Submit.

No.

Her defiance, so small, just a spark, but silver and precise. She could speak again, and she muttered. Donovan looked startled. He had expected to hear something else from her lips, and its absence threw him.

"What did you say?" he demanded.

"Paradox," Miranda said, a little louder, the spark gathering strength, lengthening, a silver thread now, a thesis in formation. She called on the image of the elder sign. She traced its shape. She made it into an argument. "Why do you accept it?"

Donovan didn't answer.

Miranda pressed her advantage. "Crothoaka is ultimate doubt, and therefore absolute certainty. You don't believe in critical thought. You don't suspend belief. You just sought a new dogma."

Donovan stared at her. His face twisted in confusion and anger. "You reject your fate, then," he said.

"Not my fate."

"You would have experienced the new perfection of sacrifice."

"I will not give you the perfection you need."

He shook his head, even more angry. "Not that I need. That I want. Your death is still the full accomplishment of the summoning."

"Is it?"

"*Yes!*" His voice broke with the shriek.

She wilted and went limp.

"Crothoaka!" Donovan shouted. "Your reign has come!" Instead of ecstasy, desperation filled his voice.

Desperation born of doubt.

He raised the knife with both hands. He brought it back over his head. Miranda saw the arc, and the pause before its descent as if she had all the time in the world, as if she had always known this moment, as if she had seen it so many times in forgotten dreams that her role in the event had become instinctive.

With a surge of energy her body must have been saving since she arrived at the Institute, Miranda snapped out of her possum act. She slipped out of the grip of the startled Daria. She grabbed Donovan's wrists as he brought the dagger down, used his momentum against him and turned the angle of the blow. She pushed with all her strength, and plunged the dagger into the stomach of the doubting priest.

Donovan gasped. His eyes widened in shock. His face went gray.

The chanting stopped. A second of perfect silence fell over the chamber.

Then Donovan fell. And Daria began to scream. And a hiss built up, a hiss greater and older than the voice of mountains, and the hiss became a roar of anger, a roar to shatter thunder.

The chamber began to shake.

CHAPTER TWENTY-NINE

Agatha felt the roar as much as she heard it. Tremors rolled through the grounds of the Stroud Institute, knocking her off her feet. She struggled to her knees, looked up at the building, and braced herself for the monstrous emergence.

It did not come. Cracks appeared in the foundation; they raced up the walls. Windows frosted, then shattered. Glass and fragments of stone rained down. Agatha shielded her face, managed to get to her feet, and staggered over the bucking earth, out of the range of the glass.

With a deafening crash, the entrance doors blew inside, as if a giant's mace had smashed them in. The stained glass of Donovan's apartment flew into bits, but most of it went in, not out. The roof over his quarters buckled.

The facade began to distort around the cracks, forming concavities.

There would be no emergences, Agatha realized. The Stroud Institute was in the earthly throes of an implosion.

She's done it.

Screams came from the rooms with broken windows.

Agatha raced to the entrance, the momentary exultation at Miranda's victory gone in an instant. The building had turned back into a hospital full of patients, and it was about to come down around their ears.

And Miranda was in there, somewhere.

The floor of the lobby trembled, its surface breaking up like an eggshell, tiny pieces of marble bouncing up and down, like pellets on a drum. Agatha ran to the fire alarm on the wall behind the reception desk. The shrill clang of bells erupted in the halls, cutting through the deeper sound of the agonized roar, and the ever increasing groan of the Institute's walls.

The shaking was worse than outside, but Agatha found her balance. She started up the stairs, coughing in the clouds of dust that wafted down. She crossed paths with the first of the patients before she reached the first floor.

"What's happening?" one woman asked, her eyes wide with terror.

"A collapse," said Agatha. She kept climbing, and called back, "Get out as fast as you can. Stay on the grounds and wait for help, but keep well back from the building."

She went up, and the traffic of fleeing patients increased. She urged them on, but they didn't need her encouragement. The rattling and shaking of the stairwell gave them all the incentive they needed.

Agatha hit the top ward of the west wing, breathing hard, and got out of the way of the patients lining up for the stairwell. No one, she saw, seemed willing to risk the elevator. Most of the patients were able to walk, and they carried the ones who couldn't.

All the windows on this floor had disintegrated, their

shards littering the floor. As Agatha ran past a deserted room, she heard, drawing closer, the *clang clang clang* of the fire engine bells.

She made for Miranda's room, and the position in the halls where she had described finding the passage.

Be open, Agatha thought. Please be open.

The gap in the walls was there, its sides ragged, cracks spreading out along the walls, the labyrinth pattern clearly visible now as it began to disintegrate. Beyond the threshold, the passage sloped down sharply.

Agatha hesitated. Miranda had said it started off straight and level. Her first impression had been that it was specific to this floor. Agatha wondered if she had found the wrong entrance.

No, it had to be this one. The location was right.

Everything collapsing, she thought. Everything changing – just like the odds of finding Miranda, and of either of them getting out alive.

No choice. She didn't care about the odds. She cared about the right thing to do.

She rushed down between the writhing walls.

Miranda felt the inversion of the summoning as clearly as the tolling of a cathedral bell. She saw the logic of the catastrophe as if she had commanded it herself. Magnus had walked into the flames of his estate strong in the full certainty of his cause. Donovan died in the agony of doubt.

The ritual died too in the moment of its completion, riven by its own contradictions. The serpent of doubt turned on itself and devoured its own tail.

Miranda felt a certain pride to perceive the nature of her victory even as she accepted that she was about to die.

The fangs of the cavern crumbled and withdrew into the stone. The chamber itself began to contract. The walls pressed in toward each other, and did not withdraw. The ceiling bulged down, splitting open and dripping pink ichor.

Miranda slid off the altar. She stood, stunned and off-balance, expecting to fall, surprised when she managed to take a step, and then another.

Daria wailed, her voice rising and falling through multiple octaves of ululation and base snarl. Her limbs whipped around, slashing the air, and then her body lost coherence. Her final, grotesque dance began, her flesh ballooning and contracting, stretching and flowing, becoming a perpetual inhuman transformation.

The congregation joined her in the dance. No chanting from the throats now, only screams, and the screams came from mouths that opened in arms and chests and foreheads. Then they were simply indiscernible shapes as the skeletons broke down. Caught in the logic implosion of their god, the things that had been people flowed together, and toward the flesh vortex of the Miracle.

Miranda weaved between them. The last face she saw before there were no faces was Holden's, and she thought she saw sorrow mixed in with the agony.

At the archway, Miranda looked back; all the flesh was still screaming.

She turned away. A vicious tremor shook the chamber, smashing her against the side of the archway. She sagged in pain.

She could give up. She had done what she had come to do. Why pretend she could work her way back through infinite length of the labyrinth?

Because she had won. She had fought with nothing, and she had won. She wouldn't stop fighting now.

She headed into the tunnel. Spasms shook the walls. Their breathing came in tubercular gasps. The tremors rocked Miranda back and forth, and she had to work hard to keep her balance and not touch the flesh of the dissolving god.

The tunnel began to climb. A massive tremor hit, and with it a violent, hissing shriek and a blaze of silver, the lightning strike of pain. When Miranda's dazzled eyes cleared, she faced a junction for the first time. The walls were splintering open, the path turning into a web of fragments. The labyrinth had become a maze.

Miranda hesitated over the choices. Then she forged ahead. This passage was narrower than the others, but it went straight, and it went up. Space had become meaningless on her journey to the center of the labyrinth, but she clung to the intuition that the great chamber was beneath the Institute. So she had to climb up, up out of the darkness, up towards the light – if there still was light to find, light that did not squirm with green agony.

The flesh of the walls tore into flaps. They whipped across the passage, snapping like torn sails. Miranda tried to run past the rags. They touched her but just for fractions of a second. They had lost the power to hold her. During the brief contact, she encountered shards of memories and possibilities, but they did not swallow her consciousness. She still saw the hall and its billowing curtains of skin. The memories burned all the same, bright and jagged as trauma. None were true, or all of them, or some. Miranda cried out against them, against the violence being done to her history. Would she ever know what was real in her past again?

She forced herself to move faster, to turn the pain in her lungs and the pain in her mind to anger, and the anger to energy, the energy she needed if she hoped to have a future.

The slope steepened, becoming a mountain path for her to climb, and she didn't have the strength for speed now. All she had was the will to force herself to take one more step, and then one more, and no, I can't, it's too steep, too far, no, I can't, I'm too weak, but yes, a step, now another, now another, keep going, don't fall, don't fall, don't…

Finally, the pain and the exhaustion and the disease won. She tried for that one extra step, that last one that could be turned into maybe one more, but she couldn't move, and she was blacking out. She tried to shout – for help, for defiance – but she had nothing left. She fell.

Arms caught her.

Agatha caught her.

Miranda blinked. Her breath stopped for a moment in the fear that this was a delusion, a final wish instead of a memory. But Agatha held her, and joy gave Miranda the power to stand again.

"How…?" she began, in a voice like a crow's.

"You're just a couple of floors down from the entrance," Agatha said, shouting to be heard over the roars and screams of the labyrinth. She put Miranda's arm over her shoulders and started them both up the slope. She laughed with relief. "Not far at all. And not far to go."

Not far, but far enough. Hope of escape turned the final minute of the climb into an eternity. Ichor flowed in torrents from the ruptured walls, making footing treacherous.

I'm getting out, Miranda thought. Damn you, I'm getting out.

Another huge tremor slashed through the passageway as she and Agatha lurched out of the ruins of the labyrinth. The passages screamed and devoured themselves. The walls crashed together in a futile attempt to take Miranda down with them.

She was back in the ward she had come to know so well. It was dying too. The ceiling pressed down, and the floor had split into slabs that leaned in every direction. Dust choked the hall. The building shook as if a titan were pounding it flat.

Alarm bells rang and rang, and they were the sound of the real world, a mechanical cry, and Miranda embraced the din of normal. She focused on it, instead of the rumble of the building that sounded too much like the rage of the thing within it.

Agatha hauled them to the staircase.

"The other patients?" Miranda asked.

"Outside," said Agatha. "The fire department is here, too."

Good, good. Miranda took comfort in the emptiness of the halls.

Let us be the last ones here.

The stairwell swayed. Heavy chunks of masonry smashed down after the women. Agatha pushed Miranda against the wall and the railing to avoid being hit. And when they finally reached the lobby, fires had broken out. Dragged by Agatha, Miranda stumbled across the floor through the final convulsions of the building. Flames exploded out of a gap in a wall, licking the air just over Miranda's head. She heard a deep, crackling groan, and looked up to see a slab of stone ten feet wide break free of the ceiling and fall their way. Her determination not to die inside the monster gifted her with one more burst of adrenaline, and she sprinted, actually *sprinted,* side by side with Agatha.

Through the doorway and down the buckling stairs of the porch, and she took her first breath of outside air in a century, and she learned how sublime a single breath could be.

And now her weariness would not be denied. The debt of strength her body owed came due, and she couldn't go any further on her own. She leaned on Agatha, and they moved down the drive to where the patients clustered around the fire engines and the ambulances.

They turned around to watch the end.

The great thunder of the implosion came from the depths, and it seized the Institute. The roof went first. It fell in, and then the walls rushed at each other. The building went down like a closing fist, and Miranda heard the firemen shouting in as much surprise and shock as the patients. They had never seen a structure devour itself. The tremor of the final collapse split the grounds open. A wall of dust swept out from the grounds, choking and blinding.

Miranda coughed and kept coughing, sure she would finally expel her lungs from her body. When the dust cleared, and she could finally draw breath again, murmurs of wonder ran through the crowd.

The Stroud Institute had vanished. It had compacted itself down into a crater.

"I don't get it," one of the firemen kept repeating. "There should be more. Shouldn't there be more? I don't get it."

The wreckage was too small, too concentrated.

"Where's the stone?" Miranda whispered to Agatha. Twisted metal protruded from the heap. Smashed beds and doors and medical equipment lay entangled with one another. Glass lay everywhere. There was stone, but it was marble, and there were pieces of concrete. She saw almost no trace of the rock that had come from Scotland.

"Gone," said Agatha. She hugged Miranda. "Killed and gone."

EPILOGUE

The snow fell in thick flakes, as it should in mid-December, when Miranda came out of the main entrance of St Mary's Hospital. Agatha and Wilbur were waiting for her. Wilbur had the passenger door of his Model T open, and he rushed forward to take Miranda's bag. Agatha embraced her and asked, "Ready to go home?"

Home, where Miranda had not been for the best part of a year. Oh yes, she was more than ready. But she was also not in a hurry. She wanted to savor the day.

Wilbur stashed the bag and then hovered. "We should get you out of the cold," he said.

Miranda laughed. "I'm all right," she said. "I'm better, really. The cold won't hurt me. In fact, if I could just have a minute..." She tilted her head back and let the flakes fall on her face. She stuck out her tongue and laughed again at the gentle fairy-touch of the snow. She breathed deeply, enjoying the sharp, clean cold, the cold that would no longer make her cough.

"I'm so tempted to walk back," Miranda said.

"It's miles back to French Hill," Wilbur objected.

"What if we split the difference?" said Agatha. "You said yesterday that you wanted to pick up a few things at your office. Wilbur can drop us off at Miskatonic, and we'll walk the rest of the way."

Miranda nodded. "That would be nice." It had been too long since she had really, properly stretched her legs. The exercises she'd been allowed to do in the hospital grounds for the past several weeks had felt too limited. They were the promise of a walk, not the real thing.

They piled into the car and Wilbur drove off.

"You're restless," Agatha commented.

"Can you blame me?"

"No."

At St Mary's the rest cure for tuberculosis had been strictly enforced. During the first part of her stay, she hadn't even been allowed to read for more than a few minutes a day. Days and weeks and months of nothing in the days, of boredom such as she had never imagined possible. Having her lung collapsed through a pneumothorax procedure had been welcome as an event that broke up the monotony at least as much as the help it might or might not bring to her condition. There had been times when she found herself thinking fondly of the early days at the Stroud Institute, when she had still thought of it as a place of healing.

Cleo had come to visit her, too. Miranda treasured the friendship as one of the truly good things to have come out of the darkness of the Institute. Miranda had to reassure Cleo that she shouldn't feel guilty about being one of the Institute's success stories. Cleo didn't know what had happened in the end, but she had told Miranda about the movement in her yard.

"Do you think the place left a mark on me?" she asked.

"No," said Miranda. "You're better. You're well, and that's all that matters. The Institute is gone. It can never hurt anyone, and you're not the only one it actually helped."

Miranda did think about that, another of the paradoxes that circled Donovan Stroud. He and his ancestors were idealists in every sense. The Institute might have been a facade and a means to provide the bodies necessary to complete the ritual, but Donovan couldn't do anything in half measures. He made the facade so convincing, it was real.

Wilbur left Miranda and Agatha at Miskatonic University and took the bag home. Miranda kept the empty briefcase she had asked Agatha to grab for her at her apartment. She and Agatha strolled across the campus to the Humanities building. The Quad was deserted, classes and exams over for the term. The snow fell, shrouding the roofs and ground with calm.

Miranda had wondered what setting foot in her office for the first time in so long would feel like. She was prepared for the space to feel strange, someone else's place of work. Instead, she stepped into the warm embrace of the familiar. The stacks of books had waited patiently for her, and were glad to see her. The desk invited her to sit, and she looked out at her view of the Quad with a real sense of homecoming.

"Do you know," she said to Agatha as she put the books she needed in the briefcase, "I'm actually looking forward to the start of the winter term."

"Would you like me to check if you still feel the same way once you're marking papers again?"

"You can, but I know I will. It's going to feel good to be back."

They headed home in the gathering white of the afternoon. By unspoken agreement, they did not alter their route from the usual. Agatha did touch her shoulder as they drew near the gates of the Stroud Institute.

"Are you going to be all right with this?" she asked.

"Yes. I want to see it."

They stopped at the gates. The pillars had fallen with the rest of the Institute, and concrete ones had been raised in their place. The gates never opened now. They sealed off the gangrenous limb from the rest of Arkham.

Snow covered the ruins, softening their shape. Miranda looked through the bars at a vista of drab emptiness.

"It was looking pretty overgrown before the snow came," said Agatha. "City council is just letting it go. Use the wall and gate to keep the kids from hurting themselves in the ruins, but that's about it."

"Is anything going to be built here?"

"Not that I've heard."

"Just as well," said Miranda. "I wouldn't trust that ground."

"Nor would I. Better to just let it be another Arkham eyesore."

They walked on.

"That wasn't too hard?" said Agatha.

"No. I'm glad my first look at it was in the snow. Makes it look so changed, different. It's just a place now."

"That's good."

Miranda felt a slight clench in her chest when she unlocked her apartment. She was more nervous about what her home would feel like than her office. She hadn't had the night visions in the office. She was glad to have Agatha's company.

Once inside, she relaxed. This *was* home. The space belonged to her, and she to it. She walked through the living room, running her hands on the back of the sofa. She smiled at the prints on her wall. She'd missed them.

"Good to be back?" said Agatha.

Miranda smiled. She gave a happy sigh, and all the tension flowed out of her limbs and shoulders. "So good," she said. "Glass of wine?"

"Please."

When they were both on the couch, glasses of pinot in hand, Miranda said, "I worried home might feel tainted. Things started here. But it just feels right. No more visions."

Agatha said nothing.

Miranda looked at her. "What?" she asked.

"Not necessarily anything."

"But not necessarily nothing, then. Come on, out with it."

"I can't promise that you won't ever have visions again."

Miranda took a healthy sip of her wine. "I am so grateful you waited until I was out of the hospital to say something like that."

"You were supposed to rest. I wanted you to."

"Thank you." She steeled herself. "All right. Tell me what you mean about the visions."

"Just what I said. No promises. They might never recur. But Donovan targeted you for a reason, and you also saw things that helped us understand what was going on. You might have some powers of sight, and that's something you'll have to accept."

"Okay," Miranda said slowly. "But it's over, right? Everything we fought. It's over."

"Yes ..."

Miranda began to wish she'd poured herself a much bigger glass. "That sounds like a qualification."

"Donovan is dead," said Agatha. "What he tried to do is finished. You destroyed the ritual, and sent Crothoaka back across the veil. Yes, all of that is over."

Miranda rolled her eyes. "All of *that,* she says. Are you trying to worry me?"

"No. Not at all. I guess you could say I'm trying to issue an invitation."

"Oh?" Miranda felt curiosity now. It took the edge off the dread.

"I don't think it's an accident that Donovan came to Arkham to complete the ritual," Agatha said. "And just maybe it isn't an accident that you were here. The right person in the right place at the right time."

"Didn't feel right to me," said Miranda.

"It was, though. You stopped him, and the horror he tried to unleash." Agatha gave her a solemn look. "Other things have happened in Arkham," she said. "Other bad things."

"I can well believe it.

"And there will be more. I don't know why they happen here, but they do."

Miranda nodded, realizing that she didn't feel surprised. The atmosphere of the town, one she had only half-noticed but had also been unable to completely ignore, began to make sense as Agatha spoke.

"I try to understand what's happening, and I try to help

stop the bad stuff. I'm also not the only one. You've been through a lot, and you'll get absolutely no grief from me if you just want to put it all behind you."

"No," said Miranda. "I can't do that. I won't pretend it didn't happen, and that nothing has changed."

"Then would you help us with our work? There is so much to be done."

"It's going to be scary, isn't it?"

"Yes." Agatha grinned. "But not boring."

Miranda grinned back. "You should have led with that."

Tom Spalding walked along the cliffs beyond Durstal. He stopped about a mile from the edge of the Stroud Estate. He watched the angry December waves slam into the base of the cliffs. A freezing drizzle had started. The wind blew needles of water against him, which ran down his hair. He wiped the water from his face. It would be getting dark soon. He should head back to the inn, where light and warmth waited.

He should. He had come here hoping for some clarity. He would turn around in a minute.

The land here is blighted. Agatha Crane's words. *Run, Tom. Run.*

He hadn't run. Durstal was home. Run to where? Anywhere, he supposed. But he had roots here, deep ones. And if he left, what about all his friends? What about the rest of Durstal? Did Agatha expect him to organize an exodus?

That wasn't fair. She hadn't asked him to do anything. She had warned him. Anything else was his responsibility.

He had done nothing after Agatha and Wilbur left. He had gone on as he always had, as everyone in Durstal did. Chin up, make the best of things, and be wary if things look wrong. Don't disbelieve the stories you hear, and don't go looking for trouble.

Durstal was home.

The storm that had come in the spring, not much more than a week after Agatha had left, had frightened him badly. It had torn roofs off and felled trees, and there had been sounds in the wind that no one talked about afterwards. He had spent the night with his hands over his ears. He knew he had not been the only one.

Since then, he hadn't slept well. Months of broken nights, and worse now that the winter storms had come and kept coming. He was so tired. And he couldn't stop thinking about the estate.

He watched the waves. He listened to their crash and boom. Gradually, he realized just how deep the boom seemed to go. Or perhaps, from how deep it came. Rhythmic, huge.

Furious. Like a voice.

He found his clarity.

Run, Tom. Run.

ACKNOWLEDGMENTS

I do so love writing horror fiction, and so my first thank you is to you, the reader, for having accompanied me on this journey.

When it comes to the research for this novel, I owe a particular debt to Betty MacDonald's *The Plague and I,* her sparkling, witty memoir of her experience in a tuberculosis sanatorium. I have taken all kinds of liberties with the details of treatment, the better to serve the dark purpose of the Stroud Institute, but to put it most succinctly, any accuracies are entirely thanks to this book, and the errors are all mine. My debt to the book goes beyond its value as research, too. It was hearing about *The Plague and I* on the wonderful podcast Backlisted that provided the initial inspiration for *In the Coils of the Labyrinth*. For more specific inspiration as to the Stroud Institute itself, I must credit Dario Argento's films *Suspiria* and *Inferno* (especially the latter).

Huge thanks to Marc Gascoigne, Lottie Llewelyn-Wells, Nick Tyler, Anjuli Smith, Paul Simpson and everyone at Aconyte Books for all the support. Special thanks to Charlotte

Bond for her superb editing, which I know will serve me well in many books to come.

Thank you to John Coulthart for his amazing cover, which provided me with further inspiration as I wrote.

Thank you to Katrina Ostrander, Claire Rushbrook, and everyone at Fantasy Flight Games for their guidance, and for entrusting me with this little corner of the Arkham Horror universe.

Thank you also to my fellow writers Michael Kaan, Stephen D Sullivan and Derek M Koch. Our online sprints and mutual support were wonderful motivators.

And, as always, my heartfelt, loving thanks to my wife, Margaux Watt, and to my stepchildren, Kelan and Veronica, for everything and more.

ABOUT THE AUTHOR

DAVID ANNANDALE is a lecturer at a Canadian university on subjects ranging from English literature to horror films and video games. He is the author of the *Marvel Untold* Doctor Doom trilogy, and many titles in the *New York Times*-bestselling *Horus Heresy* and *Warhammer 40,000* universe, and a co-host of the Hugo Award-nominated podcast Skiffy and Fanty.

davidannandale.com
twitter.com/david_annandale

ARKHAM HORROR
The Red Coterie has been unveiled…
ARKHAM HORROR
Conspiracy!
Arcane mystery!
Secret societies!
SECRETS in SCARLET
EDITED BY CHARLOTTE LLEWELYN-WELLS
A secret organization ruthlessly seeks
power over supernatural terrors
in this globe-trotting anthology of
arcane mystery & adventure.